Advance Praise for
Somebody Told Me

"*Somebody Told Me* is the heart-wrenching and hopeful look at
faith, gender, and sexuality I've been waiting for. It walks a careful
balance of funny and thought-provoking, a testament to Siegert's
skill. I wouldn't hesitate to recommend this to any reader wanting
a compelling and captivating read, or any teenager dealing with
rejection, upheaval, and finding their voice in the world."

—Kate Brauning, author of *How We Fall*

"Siegert pulls no punches, tackling issues such as abuse of power,
and acceptance, head-on in this important page-turning novel."

—Helene Dunbar, author of *We Are Lost and Found*

"Mia Siegert is an explosive talent in YA literature, with a writing
style both raw and unflinching. Siegert's bold voice is impossible
to forget."

—Laurie Elizabeth Flynn, author of *Firsts*,
Last Girl Lied To, and *All Eyes On Her*

"Mia Siegert has crafted another magnificent tale of heartache and
growth—a story unafraid to confront sensitive issues of gender,
sexuality, and religion with compassion and courage. I highly
recommend this book to anyone and everyone."

—Chris Kluwe, former NFL player and author of *Otaku*

"Poignant, honest, controversial yet not any less important and
timely—*Somebody Told Me* will stay with you long after you finish
the final page and fuel a conversation that needs to be had."

—Alice Reeds, author of *Echoes*

SOMEBODY TOLD ME

MIA SIEGERT

Carolrhoda LAB
MINNEAPOLIS

Carolrhoda Lab®
An imprint of Lerner Publishing Group, Inc.
241 First Avenue North
Minneapolis, MN 55401 USA

For reading levels and more information, look up this title at
www.lernerbooks.com.

Image credits: Thinkstock/Getty Images (rosary); Jason Kolenda/Shutterstock.
com (vent); LUMIKK555/Shutterstock.com (stucco); BanksPhotos/Getty Images
(silhouette).

Main body text set in Janson Text LT Std.
Typeface provided by Linotype AG.

Library of Congress Cataloging-in-Publication Data

Names: Siegert, Mia, 1985– author.
Title: Somebody told me / by Mia Siegert.
Description: Minneapolis : Carolrhoda Lab, [2020] | Summary: After an assault at
    an anime convention, bigender seventeen-year-old Aleks/Alexis moves in with
    their uncle, a Catholic priest, and decides to help strangers anonymously after
    overhearing parishioners' confessions.
Identifiers: LCCN 2019008525| ISBN 9781541578197 (th : alk. paper) | ISBN
    9781541582255 (EB pdf.)
Subjects: | CYAC: Gender identity—Fiction. | Sexual abuse—Fiction. | Priests—
    Fiction. | Forgiveness—Fiction. | Self-esteem—Fiction. | Family life—Fiction.
Classification: LCC PZ7.1.S536 So 2020 | DDC [Fic]—dc23

LC record available at https://lccn.loc.gov/2019008525

Manufactured in the United States of America
1-46896-47800-11/15/2019

For my friends and family

1 ALEKS

The last place I ever thought I'd live was next to a Catholic church.

I stared at the street view on my phone screen. The building I would live in looked pretty normal. You know, two stories, flat roof and brick siding and a fire escape. And the church itself was pretty humble-looking too. Not some huge cathedral with gothic architecture and creepy statues of Jesus getting crucified. At least on the outside.

"The rectory's actually very comfortable, according to your aunt," Mom said, knuckles clenched so tightly around the steering wheel that they were blanched. "Very homey, aside from the church office. It's basically an apartment. The couple of other priests attached to Saint Martha's live in a separate space, so you'll have a fair amount of privacy."

"Yup," I said, putting my phone away. We'd been over this before.

Mom's eyes remained locked on the road ahead of her. Not one glance behind. "And the cemetery is right across the street. Your uncle said you're welcome to treat it like your backyard and use it anytime. Well, almost anytime. No barbeques during a funeral."

I snorted. "He actually said that?"

"Mm-hmm. He was dead serious, too."

Damn. What sort of heathen did he take me for? Granted, I hadn't even seen the guy in years. Not since he went from being an Episcopal priest to a Catholic one. According to my internet research, there are only about two hundred people in the country who've gone this route—marry, convert, become a priest—so it was no surprise that Uncle Bryan took his new calling seriously. But you'd think that if he got to keep his wife, he would've been allowed to keep a sense of humor too. "What does he think I'd do if someone died? Tie a badminton net up on the statues? Play horseshoes with the American flags?"

Mom chimed in: "Croquet through the headstones, stomping over letters and stuffed animals for the deceased."

"Damn, Mom. And I thought *I* was brutal." I waited for her smile. It never came. She gazed ahead, unblinking. She'd never admit she was hurting, that my decision tore her to bits, but she radiated so much pain I could feel it in my chest.

I sank in my seat. Well, no need to keep riffing about the cemetery. Wasn't like I was planning to set foot in there anyway. Not because I was afraid or thought cemeteries were eerie, even though they kind of were. They just made me sad. Maybe a little angry. I wasn't really sure why. Last year, maybe I'd have taken advantage of it with my cosplay group just to get an edgy photo for tons of likes. Something provocative by the inevitable statue of Mary. I'd done that sort of stupid shit a lot, especially with him.

Don't go there, Aleks, I reminded myself. That part of my life was over. No more trolling, no more CAPSLOCK LOLZ, and definitely no more being an asshole just for a bunch of likes. I was going to pretend that segment of time didn't exist. I'd always been good at pretending.

Although I should have, I hadn't deleted my social media accounts. Believe it or not, Mom was the one who convinced me not to do it. She thought that one day I'd get nostalgic and not have anything to look back on. I'd taken her word for it because she'd been in tears as she said it. Figured that came from personal experience, maybe with my aunt. So I just disabled notifications and comments and logged out of everything. I didn't want to deal with the messages from my friends. Former friends, I mean. Why was past-tense so hard to say? To think?

I didn't want to deal with the other bullshit either. You know, the "faux trans" or "ugly girl" crap that made me nauseous. I'd dealt with that for years, people refusing to believe my identity was legit, people insisting that I was calling myself bigender for attention. I was done with going to conventions where at least three girls would approach me, asking me if I was a boy or girl and, if I said boy, ask "Are you sure?" about seven times before adding, "because you're really hot." And I didn't know if that was because they were lesbians or because they wanted to make sure I was an effeminate guy because that meant they were still straight. And my friends would laugh, especially him, saying, "Yeah, you're such a hot guy" while the voice inside said something else:

> *Imposter.*
> 　　　　*Where's your dick at? Huh?*
> *Packed away?*
> 　　　　*Who does that?*
> *Fake.*
> 　　*Liar.*
> 　　　　*Loser.*

That voice still made me shudder. It crept in like a waiting storm, then suddenly it was there, breaking down my mental walls like a hurricane, destroying everything in its path. It was there way before I got in trouble. And afterward, it never went away. Sometimes the voice sounded just like one of my exes. Ring, ring, ring. Buzzing in my ears. No matter how many times I tried to tune it out, it wouldn't leave me. No. It became louder. Faster. Pulsed like my heartbeat. Like its own breathing, living thing.

Imposter.

Liar.

Fake.

Louder, louder, LOUDER.

The noise was almost unbearable by the time we pulled up in front of a sign that read SAINT MARTHA ROMAN CATHOLIC CHURCH. Loud enough for me to scrape my nails against my scalp, sliding down to rub my fingers against the back of my neck, getting the tension out. *Shut up, shut up, shut up, shut—*

"You doing okay, Aleks?" Mom asked, her voice shaking.

Trying to sound convincing, I said, "Yep. I'm good." After all, this was my idea.

"Because if you're having second thoughts, we can call this off. I could ask for an emergency leave from work—"

"Mom, we've been over this."

"But—"

"Seriously, don't." And then to prove my point, "If you do, I'm going to feel guilty as hell. So don't. Please."

She fell silent.

The second I'd told my parents I wasn't safe, Mom had started looking for transfers. There weren't any openings. I couldn't let her quit, not when she'd spent so long building her career, trying to get her twenty years to collect pension. And Dad was stationed in Iraq. It wasn't like I could say "come home" when he was on active duty.

There were only two options I could think of.

One: Do nothing.

Two: Move in with Aunt Anne Marie and Uncle Bryan while Mom waited for a transfer to go through or until I went to college, whichever came first. I had two more months of summer break before I had to decide where I'd spend my senior year of high school, so it was the perfect time to move.

"You know what kind of people they are, right?" Mom had asked me once she'd regained the ability to speak.

"Yeah, I know," I'd said, although I was mostly guessing based on offhand comments she and my dad had made. My parents had strong opinions on Catholicism, so strong I used to fear that if I ever met a Catholic, they'd curse me simply for existing. But then I got older. I learned that extremists and shitty people exist everywhere. Sure, some Catholics might be scary, but a person could say that about members of literally any group. I was trying to be a less shitty person myself these days, so I didn't want to make assumptions about my aunt and uncle. Especially because *I* wasn't like anyone else I knew, even in the cosplay communities I'd belonged to.

The last time I'd seen my aunt and uncle, I was little. So little, I didn't remember how old I'd been. I didn't know if they had converted to Catholicism yet or if Uncle Bryan was still an Episcopal priest. I did remember being entranced by Aunt Anne Marie's sewing machine and liking Uncle Bryan's laugh.

But I also remember an argument through the walls and the door slamming. Mom's sobs: *What happened to her?*

What happened, I guess, was that she was a good Episcopalian girl who grew up to marry an Episcopal priest, and then gradually both she and her husband got into Catholicism. Fun fact, courtesy of my internet research: Protestant clergy are sometimes allowed to switch teams and become Catholic priests, and if they're already married, they're allowed to stay married. I still didn't get it though. Like, did celibacy laws still apply? In which case, what was the point?

My aunt was a puzzle even without all that. My grandparents on Mom's side were pretty liberal, always vocal about equality, just cool in general. They died a couple of years ago, but back when I was twelve, after Mom told them about me coming out as bigender, they called to tell us all about joining their local PFLAG group. But Aunt Anne Marie wasn't like them. I had so many friends who'd broken away from their conservative families as they discovered more inclusive values. I didn't think I'd met a single person who came from a family as chill as Mom's and left for Faux News. It was different. Weird.

Living with them still had to be better than what I was running from. Coming here was the safest option, because it was the last place anyone would ever think to look for me.

Mom parked the truck and turned the ignition off. "We're here."

The rectory—the priests' residence—looked just like it had online. Right up against it was another building that I knew was the church. It actually looked like an extension of the same building, except the windows on the church part were more arched and the double doors at the front looked more imposing.

We climbed out of the truck. I approached the building

and traced my fingers along the cracks in the brick facade. Up close, it looked nicer than in the pictures. They must have done some renovations recently.

There was some chattering and commotion as people came out the front doors of the church, a few yards away. *Don't make eye contact, don't make eye contact*—but they went the other direction, oblivious. I exhaled, relieved. For now, I was still invisible. Just the way I wanted.

The front door of the rectory opened. Immediately, I withdrew from the wall, moving to stand next to Mom. An older woman clattered down the steps with an uneven stride, like she was in pain but trying not to limp. Surely that couldn't be . . .

Mom cleared her throat. "Hey, Annie."

The old woman corrected her: "Anne Marie. Please."

I barely kept from gawking as Aunt Anne Marie approached. This didn't make sense. Aunt Anne Marie wasn't *that* much older than Mom. Like a few years. This wrinkly-faced woman looked like she should have been my grandma instead of my aunt.

She embraced Mom stiffly and briefly, like she was being polite even though she couldn't stand to be near her. Judging from Mom's expression, the feeling was mutual. Next, she moved to me hugging me for just a second, if even. Like she wasn't sure it would be welcome. "It's—it's good to see you, Alexis."

A rock formed in the pit of my stomach.

Before I could open my mouth, Mom said, "It's Aleks today. He and him."

"It's fine," I told Mom quickly. I'd already decided I wouldn't publicly present as male here. I didn't know if that counted as going back in the closet or whether it was self-preservation.

Mom frowned. "Pronouns are important."

"I know, but not today. Okay?" I touched her arm. "It's fine. I promise."

Mom frowned but dropped it. Good. Last thing I wanted was super high tension around me before I even moved in. Besides, this was *their* home. I was a temporary guest. Coming here was *my* idea. I knew what I was getting into. Sort of.

Aunt Anne Marie didn't respond to my mother. She looked at me, smiling. It seemed genuine but also strained, like it'd been so long since she smiled it ached. She looked so old. So tired. So thin. Had Uncle Bryan aged that quickly too? "I was worried you'd look more . . ." She trailed off, leaving me to fill in the gap:

Butch? Queer? Covered in glitter with rainbows shooting out of my butt?

Aunt Anne Marie tried again. "I was worried you'd stand out. If you stay like this, you'll fit right in."

I exhaled with relief. Good. Fitting right in was exactly what I needed, even if boy-me was going to hate it in about 0.0008 seconds, and probably girl-me too. It didn't matter how much this place sucked because it would be safe. If I hid inside my skin, I wouldn't be in direct danger. No one would notice the ugly girl. She was innocuous and easy to ignore, which was perfect, even though sometimes, just sometimes, I wished she wasn't so ugly.

Here's the sad part: I never thought she was ugly until people told me again and again that she was. All those school formals, me standing awkwardly by the wall as everyone was asked to dance except me. That kid who threw a tape dispenser at me in class, telling me to put it on my upper lip to rip the mustache off. The classmates who called me an ugly slut for wearing layers of tank tops in winter when, really, I just got overheated and sweated through my clothes. I guess the masochist in me preferred the bullying to the silence I now was seeking. Any attention was better than no attention, or so I'd thought. I knew better now.

How would people here react if they saw two different people with the same face? If I left the house as a girl one day and a boy the very next? Would they think I had a twin? Think it was a costume? Condemn me to hell? Hold signs outside the rectory and shout slurs at me?

I could picture all that so clearly. Images of horrible things happening to me, worst-case disasters, gleefully narrated by "the voice." No matter how many times I told it to shut up, it was always there. Left ear, right ear, crashing like a turbulent sea.

"This is just temporary," Mom said to Aunt Anne Marie. Then, almost as an afterthought, "Thank you for doing this."

Aunt Anne Marie looked at me instead of my mother. "We're family." Like she was erasing Mom from existence. The tension was so thick, it was almost visible. Was there ever a time when she and Mom were close? Like when they were children? Had they confided in each other, whispering secrets in the dark? It was hard to imagine. The few times I'd asked Mom about Aunt Anne Marie, she'd said, "I don't want to talk about her." I never pressed. My parents had taught me that if someone doesn't want to talk about something, you should leave them alone. Don't prod snakes.

"There are going to be a few ground rules," Aunt Anne Marie said.

"Ground rules?" Mom asked. "You didn't say anything about ground rules on the phone."

Aunt Anne Marie turned on my mother. "I haven't seen you in years. Not a word of communication. When you called me out of the blue, I gladly stepped in. Money doesn't grow on trees—"

"Fine!" Mom reached in her purse for her wallet. "If you want money—"

"I don't want your money. I want to get to know my niece. Is that a crime?"

I flinched. From that perspective, she sort of had a point, even though she'd called me "niece" after Mom had requested male pronouns today on my behalf. Although it was hard to swallow, I could forgive it for now. Tons of people made mistakes, misgendering people out of ignorance rather than cruelty. I'd known to expect it here.

I'd never heard the term bigender until I was twelve. Honestly, I can't remember if I'd *ever* heard it. One day I woke up and, out of nowhere, said, "I'm bigender." Everything immediately felt right, like I'd had a massive epiphany. Simultaneously, it made me really . . . lonely. I couldn't even find much use of the term online. Of course, the internet is full of people who identify outside of the male or female boxes. Genderqueer and genderfluid have floated around in the mainstream for a little while, but those terms never fit me. There's a lot of crossover in those brackets, a lot of beautiful transition and blending, but for as different as I was, everything was black and white. There was no gray space. I'd wake up in the morning and know whether I was a girl or a boy. Rarely, in the middle of the day, I'd change. When that happened, it wasn't a gradual shift. More like a light switch. Off on, on off. And almost always, that sudden shift felt *bad*.

But now wasn't the time to think about that. Now was the time to play "blend in" and avoid rocking the boat so that I'd stay safe. My aunt and uncle, despite their religious views, were safe. *Thou shalt not kill.* Maybe I could suggest an addendum: *Thou shalt not be a douchebag to thy nephew.*

"What are the ground rules?" I asked.

Aunt Anne Marie looked delighted that I was talking to her. "We eat dinner together at six unless your uncle is helping a troubled parishioner."

I wondered if "troubled" meant a depressed person or a sinner. Or were depressed people automatically considered sinners?

"If he's late, we wait for him . . ."

Ooh, toxic patriarchy! Oh boy, oh boy, oh boy!

". . . unless he tells us ahead of time that we should eat without him, which is the case today. He's helping out with the summer day camp over at the school." She nodded toward a building across the way: Saint Martha Elementary. "We'll eat without him. He's a very busy man."

I'm sure he is.

"Also," Aunt Anne Marie said, "do you have a nice dress?"

Define *nice dress.* "Um . . . yeah? I think," I said cautiously as the voice in my head screamed, *It's a trap.* "If not, I could sew one, I guess. Why?"

"You'll need one for Sundays, when we go to church."

Mom's eyes widened. "You can't make Aleks—"

"Mass is nonnegotiable," my aunt said. "If Alexis is going to stay here, it's what we do. Can you imagine a priest's niece not attending?"

Mom grumbled beneath her breath, "Unfortunately I can imagine a lot of things."

"Do you want us to help or not?"

Mom glanced at me, like somehow she was failing even though she was trying her absolute hardest.

I touched her arm. "It's just a dress."

"It's more than just a dress."

She was right, but that wasn't a problem for today. "Mom, really. It's okay. I can deal."

At least for the next few months.

Mom hesitated but then sighed. "No making Aleks say grace before meals or any of that."

"That'd be *her* choice."

I flinched. Was the emphasis on "her" intentional, or was I extra sensitive today?

When Mom called my aunt and uncle to bring up the idea of me staying there temporarily, one of the first things she said was, "Alexis is bigender. That means some of the time, they identify as female and Alexis, and some of the time they identify as male and Aleks. They're also queer. If either of you make them uncomfortable or spout homophobic, nonbinary-phobic nonsense, I'll rip out your throat."

Mom could be a little theatrical sometimes. And by sometimes, I mean all the time. I had to inherit it from someone. I'm sure my aunt and uncle weren't impressed, but I thought it was pretty damn funny. And it certainly couldn't have sent a clearer message.

Let me give my aunt the benefit of the doubt just for today. Maybe for the next week, since there would have to be an adjustment. A learning curve.

What if it's longer than a week? I tried to ignore the nagging worry. *What if she uses only female pronouns forever?*

Fake trans.

Loser.

Liar.

Aunt Anne Marie continued, "I wouldn't be surprised if *Alexis* finds that this is the right path for her."

Sure. I might also find that I enjoyed bashing my head against concrete.

Aunt Anne Marie looked at her watch. "As I said, your uncle will be working late tonight." Was he really working late or was he deliberately avoiding Mom?

. . . or me.

"Let's get your things to your room, get you settled, and have a little dinner. Okay?" She forced another big smile. "I'm so happy I'll finally get to know you."

"Sounds good," I said, forcing some pep into my voice.

As we walked to the back of the truck, Mom latched to my side. Quietly, she said, "If you need an escape . . ."

"I'll let you know immediately. I promise."

"No heroics—"

I embraced my mother, cutting her off. I turned my face against her neck, trying to remember the smell of her perfume and the way her huge hoop earrings jingled. "Thank you," I whispered. "For letting me do this."

"I'd do anything to protect you."

"I know."

"Is there anything else I should be doing?"

"No, Mom. It's not you." *It's them*, I thought. *It's their fault. His* fault.

"Aleks?" Mom asked, worried.

"I'm fine," I said instinctively. Then, with the bravest face I could muster, I grabbed the first box.

2 ALEXIS

Saying goodbye was a million times harder than I thought it'd be. Partly because in the middle of unpacking, I had an unexpected gender-switch, which basically felt like the worst mood swing ever.

I took my sweet time unloading all my stuff so Mom could stay just a few more minutes. Mom had insisted I have my sewing machine, my cosplay, and all my containers of fabric. *All* of them. I knew she suspected I'd miss my old hobby. Even if I did miss it, I wasn't planning on using my sewing machine again. Just the idea of it made my stomach churn. Sure, if I needed a dress for church, that was one thing. But costumes? That was part of the life I was leaving behind.

My aunt and uncle's living space in the rectory really was like an apartment. The spare room had a futon that we folded up and tucked against one wall to fit the bed my mom had insisted on bringing. There was a decent-sized closet, enough space for me to store everything. Once all my boxes were all stacked inside, it was almost six and Mom agreed to stay for dinner. Anything to get a little more time with me.

To call the meal awkward was an understatement. The food was good, but you can only compliment someone's cooking for about ten seconds and then you're out of things to say. After a few minutes of silent eating, Aunt Anne Marie picked the worst possible topic for small talk. "So Alexis, are you thinking about college?"

"Um . . ."

"Arts school," Mom jumped in. "We think there's a good chance for scholarships."

Crap. In reality, I had no clue what I was going to do about college and had almost forgotten about it altogether. I'd planned to go for costume design, and I had a good shot at a few scholarships because of my costume work. Two schools were actively scouting me out, following my social media accounts, dropping hints that my work was good enough for the stage and screen.

But I wasn't doing that anymore. Costumes. That was part of my old life. I needed to let go.

"Congratulations," said Aunt Anne Marie.

"Yeah, well," I mumbled, "applications aren't due till the fall, so . . ." I trailed off with a shrug.

We muddled through the rest of the meal, and then it was time for Mom to go.

Honestly I wasn't sure why I felt this unprepared. It wasn't like I hadn't said goodbye before. At the end of conventions, my friends and I used to huddle together, arms intertwined as we said, "I love you," and kissed each other adieu. I'll miss you. See you at the next one. See you hours later online, posting pictures of our weekend shenanigans, commenting and laughing. Falling into a post-convention funk because a weekend of pretend and living off Pocky, bananas, and soda and having eight of us crammed in a hotel room one of our parents checked us into was over and we were back to real life. Homework. School.

Gym class. Tests. But soon enough there'd be another con, a reunion for our group.

This sort of goodbye with Mom was different, maybe because part of me wondered if this was it. If I wouldn't ever go home.

✝✝✝

Although I wanted to, I didn't call Mom right after she left. I knew if I did, she'd turn around and refuse to leave without me. I wished I could call Dad, but with him in Iraq that was also impossible.

I could deal with this on my own. I wouldn't wear boy clothes on boy-days. I definitely wouldn't go online unless I wanted to Skype with Mom or Dad. That way I wouldn't be tempted to log into my social media accounts. Quiet as a caterpillar, keeping to my temporary room, that was the right path for me. That was safe. Perhaps I'd take some long walks listening to audiobooks or podcasts or some alternative rock. My aunt and uncle wouldn't hurt me because I wouldn't give them anything to hurt me over. They'd only recognize Alexis—girl-me, right now—or they'd see nothing, and I'd just fade into the yellow wallpaper.

They couldn't see Aleks. I had to harness Aleks in. Boy-me would alienate my aunt and uncle within minutes even if it wasn't deliberate.

They won't see me, I reminded myself. *I will be invisible*. Considering how I looked now, my aunt and uncle could rest easy. that I wouldn't be bringing home boys or girls or getting into trouble, like the Good Lord wanted. Ugh.

You deserve to be hurt.
But here's the thing.
People don't respect you enough to hurt you.
You're so worthless, no one would bother.

No. The voice might have been right that people didn't respect me, that I was worthless, but it was also wrong. I *was* hurt, and I *didn't* deserve it.

I hadn't told my parents what happened—how could I?—but it was almost like Mom knew from the way I spoke, from the way I refused to make eye contact. Almost like Dad could see it through a grainy Skype video. If I told them about the last straw, I'd have to tell them about all the other last straws. You know, the kind where you say, "This is it," and then a few days later say, "It's okay" because someone apologized and you felt guilty as hell because how dare you hold a grudge, and it was your fault for being such a cute boy anyway and you were cool with this as Aleks so why can't you be cool with it now too?

No. I couldn't burden my parents with all that. I had to do this. The shame of not leaving would've been unbearable, more so than the embarrassment of running away.

It could have been worse.
You don't have the right to be upset.
Imposter.
Liar.
Fake.

A reminder every. single. day.

You're a liar.

                                   An attention whore.

           You're indecisive.

There's no gray space for you here.

                     No gray space anywhere.

You don't belong.

               Fake.

I gritted my teeth and continued to fill my new closet, hanging clothes neatly and in order. Femme stuff on the left, masc on the right, quickly shuffle the costumes in without looking at them. If I didn't see them, they didn't exist. Especially *that* one . . .

A shoe divider rested in the center. At the bottom of it were heavy Tall Men Shoes, with the hidden height extenders constructed in the sneaker itself. At the top were my strappy heels. Not that I wore them often despite how cute and shockingly comfortable they were. Not to school, because then I'd need to change for gym. And in the summer, the heat would make my feet swell so they'd blister and hurt. Like that one time I wore heels on a date because we wouldn't be walking far, except then we got distracted by a park, and a fountain, and a statue, and when I finally took off my shoes, I'd found pieces of skin stuck to them.

          Foolish purchase.

                 Useless.

        Pretty, but useless.

Just like you.

                  Only subtract the pretty.

Waste of money.

My eyes drifted to the plastic makeup organizer I'd carefully filled with fun things I'd bought on clearance. I didn't really know how to use a lot of it. No one had taught me. Online tutorials could only do so much when one was too impatient to practice. At least I had them for a day when I'd get the guts to use them. Like my basket of hair supplies, mostly untouched, after the time I spent two hours on my hair to give it that messy-but-I'm-a-badass look and my ex-boyfriend said, "Your hair's awful. You really need to brush it." He gave a little smirk, a shrug, and a "sorry but it's not the 80s" when I told him it was intentional. He was a jerk anyway. The type of guy who'd tell all of his friends when I was on my period like it was their business. Or his. Or anyone's but mine.

My sides ached. I rubbed the skin on the inside of my hipbone. It was almost that time. I'd bleed soon. And I hoped to hell I'd be Alexis when *that* happened. Any time that happened when I was Aleks, I'd have uncontrollable rages, fits of self-loathing, despair because I couldn't just take the damn testosterone and be done with that shit. If I was Alexis, it was something that happened and one day would stop, the end.

I stood on a chair to put my wig heads on the top shelf of the closet, ones with short wigs that I used to wear on boy-days. That just left a few boxes that held my cosplay and my sewing machine. They also contained my chest binders, compression shorts, and packer. I wasn't any less boy, but I put them with the cosplay stuff because I wasn't going to put them on again. I'd planned to leave them at home, but Mom made me take them. *Be yourself,* she told me. Myself was the last thing I needed to be.

"Alexis, I'm heading to bed," Aunt Anne Marie called from behind the closed door.

"Goodnight," I said right back.

"God bless."

I flinched. "Um. Same?"

There was a pause. Was I supposed to open the door? The ground rules didn't cover things like the proper way to say goodnight in this household. "Your uncle's working late," Aunt Anne Marie said. "He'll be tired when he comes in. You'll get to meet him tomorrow."

Now I was positive Uncle Bryan was avoiding me. "Um, okay."

"Goodnight." The patter of her footsteps faded away. That was my cue to quiet down for the night. My parents had never given me a curfew, although I tried to be considerate. They worked hard and I felt guilty about the times I must have kept them up with the whir of my sewing machine, the rattle against the table as the needle pierced through layers of fabric.

I had to be even more courteous here. My aunt and uncle were almost strangers. I mean, really, I hadn't *seen* my uncle yet. You'd think he would've made an effort to welcome me into their home. What if he didn't want me there? Aunt Anne Marie was so on edge . . . maybe that was why. Maybe she'd gone against his wishes by agreeing to take me in.

I glanced at my phone for the time. I wasn't tired, not really, and I didn't want to risk going online either. If I did, I'd slip. Plan on watching Netflix then get on social media instead. I'd have to face them. Countless questions—*Did you move?*—halfhearted, fake apologies—*Sorry, so sorry*—that I didn't want to accept.

Here's what was really devastating: For a long time I'd thought my cosplay friends were the most accepting people I'd ever met. Not that everyone at conventions was like that.

Several times someone had randomly called me a commie, thanks to the features I inherited from my dad's Russian Jewish family: medium olive-toned skin, black eyes, black hair. But I'd always gravitated toward a diverse group of people. Different colors, faiths, orientations. People who were already marginalized, who never gave anyone grief about where they belonged on the LGBTQ+ spectrum.

Except when they did.

Like when we were trying to get organized for photoshoots. Somebody, usually one of the white cis girls, would start casting us into roles. The token straight guy, the Korean beauty, the 'oh-no-she-didn't' black woman, the-insert-incredibly-offensive-stereotype-here. And if you strayed from your assigned role or, God forbid, embraced intersectionality, people would push back. Come on. Be a team player. This is fantasy, it's for fun, don't take yourself so seriously. And are you sure you're not really just a trans boy?

Without a second thought, I'd crawl back, ready to begin the cycle again, ready to be hurt again.

Maybe that wasn't so bad. Was it better to have some social life with terrible people than be completely isolated?

You're doing it again.

You can't have it both ways.

You deserved to be hurt.

You ran. They stayed.

You deserve to be alone.

"Stop," I said out loud, like one behavioral psychologist I saw in middle school had suggested. It didn't really work for me though. Sometimes it made the noise worse. I'd slide my fingers through my hair, grip the back of my skull, and rock forward and backward for hours, trying not to shriek. I stopped seeing that therapist, but that habit was now rooted in my mind. Another thing I needed to stress over.

I hit the lights, trying to not think about the packed boxes of cosplay in my closet, my binder, my compression shorts, my packer. The stuff that made everyone swoon once I was dressed. Girl-me wasn't hot. Not like boy-me. Girl-me was invisible, which I used to hate and now craved. Invisible meant no one would see me. No one would hurt me because I wasn't pretty enough to hurt.

I had just settled in bed, not sure if I loved or hated the little nook that the frame was squeezed into, when I first heard it:

"Father, forgive me, for I have sinned."

The hell? The voice in my head had *never* sounded like that before. It always was standoffish and cynical and just plain mean.

I got out of bed and looked around. Nothing. But the voice continued, "It has been seven days since my last confession."

I knelt on the floor, peering under my bed. A vent was set into the wall, near the floor.

Great. Of course my new room had to be next to the confessional in the adjacent church building. I didn't want to hear what these strangers had to say, and I *really* didn't want anyone to hear what *I* said or did in my room. It'd go both ways.

And now, I could distinctly recognize my uncle's voice as he asked, "What did you do?" although I hadn't heard it in years.

I was about to get up and find some fabric to cover the vent, to muffle the noise, when the voice said, "I committed a theft."

I froze.

"Have you done this before?"

"No. This was the first time. I didn't want to. I—I didn't know what else to do."

Holy shit. I considered yelling "Thief!" at the vent but knew I never would. If I were Aleks right now I'd have the balls to do something like that. Not while I was Alexis.

"Tell me what happened," my uncle said gently.

"I didn't know what to do. I went over the cap on our EBT. A spaghetti dinner at the church once a month isn't going to cut it. My kids need to eat."

My sides ached.

"Why didn't you ask for help?"

"I can't do that," the woman said, her voice wavering and rising in pitch. She was crying. "Everyone around here knows I had a career, knows my husband made a good living before he had to go on disability. They saw how I used to spend money. You know, I've still got my old Lexus. It's not worth anything now but people assume. They think I'm gaming the system. Did you know grocery stores have signs everywhere saying I couldn't even get something hot? Won't let me buy organic. I'm given dirty looks any time I pick up anything that isn't a bag of chips."

"You had a tough choice to make," my uncle said. "Unfortunately you picked the wrong one."

Wait. Slow down. Was he berating her for trying to survive? Sure, stealing wasn't the ideal solution, but she was backed into a corner.

"I don't know what to do, Father."

I must have misheard . . .

"Why not get a job?"

"I don't even know where to start," she said. "I haven't

worked since the kids were born and everything's online and I don't know what half of the jobs are anymore."

"You can't *not* try. That'd be unfair to your kids. Maybe you could work at a grocery store or a coffee shop."

"That wouldn't be enough to risk the Medicaid loss. I did the math. We would lose my husband's medication. My kids wouldn't be able to see a doctor. It's so messed up. You can be too rich for Medicaid but too poor for a tax credit for health insurance."

"You're positive that would put you in that bracket?" my uncle asked. I couldn't tell from his tone whether he was shocked or skeptical.

"I checked minimum wage. I even rounded up. I'd need something like my old job to make sure we'd be in the clear."

My uncle was quiet for a while. "It's not easy. God is clearly giving you a few trials, tests of faith. You should have come to us for help, but I understand that your intent was selfless. This sin can be absolved."

"Let me atone, Father."

As my uncle led her through a series of prayers, my heart practically shattered. I didn't know this person, but I wanted to give them a hug. Before I could process what I was doing, I was out of my room and heading down the hall to the front door of the rectory.

The sidewalk outside the building was a little busy, something I'd need to get used to, but I wasn't paying attention to the people walking by. I waited, eyes trained on the front doors of the church. Sooner or later, the woman would have to come out.

Finally, after about five minutes, the door budged. I ducked behind a garbage canister and peered around it. A woman hurried down the street.

Instinct kicked in before I could think about it. I kept my head low, weaving between pedestrians as I followed her. I didn't want to get too close. A few times at conventions, I'd heard footsteps behind me. I'd spun around, fists up, ready to strike. Usually nothing happened. I was lucky, mostly. Except . . .

No. Not going there. *Ever.*

I was following this woman down the street. She didn't look back once, like she wasn't afraid. Trusting in her confession to keep her safe even though she was going through hell.

Stop following her. Creeper.

She walked to a parked car and beeped it open. I pulled out my phone and quickly snapped a photo of her license plate before she drove away.

Delete it.
　　　　Delete it now.
　　I'm serious, freak. Delete it. FUCKING DELETE IT.
What are you doing?
　　　　　　　　Stop it!
　　　DELETE IT!

I shoved my hands in my deep pockets and turned back toward the church, my new home. There was something I needed to do.

3 ALEXIS

When I first got into cosplay, I was really obsessed with this
anime series, *Synthetica*, a heaven-hell apocalyptic story that
should have been cliché but somehow wasn't. I identified really
strongly with Jay, the protagonist. He could be a bit of a rag-
doll sort of character, so passive I sometimes wanted to scream
at him. He wasn't particularly special—aside from the bionic
wings implanted by scientists. And yet he persevered, trying
to save the world from destruction even though he wasn't the
prophesized savior, because screw prophecies.

Luckily he had the help of two scientists, Ian Godby and
Aaron Swatson, plus Raziel, the archangel of secrets, who
guided Jay through the mess. When I first started watching,
I'd been blown away by how grotesque the angels were, until a
little online digging revealed that they were based on real traditional depictions of archangels. Turns out that according to a
lot of lore, angels actually looked like Lovecraftian nightmares
instead of pretty, innocent babies.

For the past three years my cosplay had revolved almost solely
around that series, but lately I hadn't wanted to think about Jay.

Now, at my computer, with my headphones on, I dared to
play the soundtrack for the first time in almost two months. As

I listened to it, I felt some of my old confidence returning. The beauty of *Synthetica* was that you didn't have to be handpicked to be a savior. You could be ugly and weak and totally wrong for the job, and still pull it off.

I typed the woman's license plate information into my search bar. It was super easy to identify her. Scarily so. Just a few keys, search, and there she was: Wanda Elmwood. Opening up a new tab, I typed her name into a social media app. There were a few people with the same name, but one avatar matched her face and the location matched our town.

Her profile and most of her page were public, like she assumed that no one would look her up. That her life wasn't special enough. I saw pictures of her kids. Her husband. Everyone was smiling. If I hadn't heard Wanda's confession and had just happened to see her on the street, I'd think she was wealthy. I'd probably be one of those people assuming she was gaming the system because she didn't "look poor." Like poor had a look. What was it supposed to look like anyway? Torn clothes? Tired people covered in dirt?

Check your privilege, said the voice in my head.

It was right.

But it kept going, sentences colliding with each other. So much commotion, I didn't know what the hell was actually going on. Droning in my ears constantly. *Make it stop, make it stop.* I needed to think like a heroine. No. Like a guardian angel.

Wanda Elmwood said she'd sinned. But anyone in that situation would. I'd steal. Mom'd steal. Dad was in the freaking army and even he'd steal if it was to make sure we didn't starve.

She'd asked for help. If my uncle wouldn't offer it—if God wouldn't offer it—maybe I could. Like Raziel guiding Jay, I could guide Wanda.

I opened up another tab in my browser and pulled up the online white pages and job seeker sites. It didn't always work. Some people scrub their internet presence clean. But others use their birthday as a password.

I stared at the screen. "Unbelievable."

Within seconds, I didn't just have her address and phone number but the information for a million of her relatives. Data that was probably mined and sold from subscriptions and who knew what else. I was pretty careful and I still got on a lot of lists after I started going to conventions and signing up for giveaways. For every time I hit "unsubscribe," I'd be put on another list.

And it wasn't just mailing list junk mail. Sophomore year, my ex thought I was cheating. To try to catch me, she went to a website where a person could anonymously send an email to anyone saying, *One of your recent partners just tested positive for an STD. Please get checked at your nearest physician and contact every person you've been intimate with.* I didn't even suspect her. So oblivious that I complained on the phone to her about getting on a spam list, then fell silent when she confessed. Said it was a joke. Even though I was naive, I knew she wasn't joking. She always did stuff like that. Like, how dare I decide to wear a skirt with fishnets to the mall? Clearly I was just trying to get men to stare at me. When I said that I wanted to wear fishnets and a skirt for *me*, her fist met my mouth.

You deserved it, the voice in my head berated me.

No. Fuck that. I didn't deserve to be hurt.

Yes, you did.
You were too stupid to realize it was abuse.
You were too stupid to walk away earlier.
Cheater.

That part wasn't true. I dumped people. I didn't cheat.

You would have cheated.
You deserved it.
You deserved it.
Slut.

Stop it. Stop it. Stop it. I didn't have time for this spiraling right now.

I kept looking through the results from my search. A resume popped up, one that she must've uploaded to a website recently. That'd make it easier—

Yikes.

A whole page of garbage written in Comic Sans stared at me. From what I could gather, she'd been an administrative assistant for various small businesses back when "proficient in Word 2007" was still a meaningful job skill.

You have no right to comment.
Fake trans.
Attention whore.

I squeezed my eyes shut. It was hard to ignore the voice when it kept getting louder, more chaotic, more painful. I couldn't let it distract me now, not when I had an agenda. In school, often I fizzled out after the voice kept saying, **Why bother? You're just going to get Bs anyway.** I'd thought it was right. What was the point in breaking my brain studying if I couldn't get an A? The voice wanted me to get sidetracked, which meant I was getting to the root of something either really good or really bad.

I copied Wanda's info down in a notebook. Writing things

out by hand often helped me focus. The connection of hand to pen unlocked a door to new worlds. I wasn't just thinking outside the box, I was thinking outside the universe.

An idea came to mind. One that frightened me. Possibly illegal. But it might work. It might help her.

You're too much of a coward to do this.

I gritted my teeth. The voice couldn't win now. This wasn't about me giving up and accepting a B or C instead of an A. This was about Wanda Elmwood and making sure her children were safe, not starving. And it was a hell of a lot easier to tell the voice to shut up when it was for someone else.

With quaking hands, I started creating a new resume for her, filling in an online template with the information I'd found. To fill in the most recent gap in her employment history, I wrote, *Stay-at-home mom*. It was unprofessional, I knew it was, but I was pretty sure that job recruiters would understand a break in employment if she was a mom. Based on her background, I clicked on every admin job opening I could find. My parents told me never to have shame, to do whatever it took to survive. Maybe it wouldn't be a perfect job, but surely I could find her something . . . right?

As I filled in each field, my heart started pounding. Doubt crept in. What if I somehow made this woman's life even worse by doing this? No. She was desperate. She needed money. She needed a way to feed her kids without having to resort to stealing. If that wasn't rock bottom, I didn't know what was.

I hit a mid-range salary default, then changed another setting so her resume would be circulated through more job recruiters.

Now or never. I uploaded the resume.

Everything became quiet until I inhaled sharply, still shaky. I needed to keep busy. This could have been a terrible mistake.

I closed the window, almost knocking my seat over when a tab with my personal email popped up. I was signed out. Hovering the cursor over the log-in made my chest ache. I knew what was waiting there.

Danger.

I shut my computer down, vowing I wouldn't turn it back on for the night.

FROM: Robin, Lee
TO: Yagoda, A.
SUBJECT: Hey

Hey Alexis,

It's me, Lee. I tried emailing you from my other account, but it bounced back. So I tried this one. Did you block me? I guess I'll find out soon. I don't blame you if you did, but I hope you change your mind.

I just wanted to say I miss you. I went to a con this weekend and your friends said they had no clue where you were.

I'm worried. We're all worried. We'll make it up to you. Cosplay any characters you want. Didn't you say you missed our Synthetica group? I promise I won't bitch about you being Jay . . . as long as I can be your Godby or Swatson! LOL. ;)

Seriously, send me something short so I know you're okay.

Love,

Lee

—

I looked and saw a sea
  roofed over with rainbows,
In the midst of each
  two lovers met and departed;
Then the sky was full of faces
  with gold glories behind them.
                    —Ezra Pound

4 ALEXIS

Ever since I was little, I always had trouble sleeping. Even when I was too young to understand it, there was constant noise in my head. Thoughts about anything, everything, all the time. Unanswerable questions, like what sort of life is out in space? Are there parallel universes? Time paradoxes? Would we be swallowed up by the sun? Would we remember? Because I swore things like this had happened before. Crying in Times Square when I was five because a balloon flew away after I was told to hang on tightly. I lost so many things, wasted so much money, wasted so much space. I was the worst. I was too old. I wanted to be little again, to redo every mistake I made. There was shame. So much shame.

But last night, miraculously, I'd slept. No NyQuil. No Xanax. No small bit of bourbon I'd mix into a glass of hot cocoa, a trick my parents taught me with the absolute promise that I wouldn't abuse it no matter what. Last night I crawled in bed, prepared for the voice to start telling me how much of a waste of space I was. But instead, I only heard one thing:

You did good.

I waited for the insult, the inevitable follow-up. But nothing came. Just those three words:

You did good.

And everything became quiet,

                    quiet,

                                    quiet . . .

Sheer bliss.

I don't remember falling asleep. I don't remember dreaming about anything either. Since I was little, nightmares had haunted me. A fire down the road. Me with my red plastic pail standing in a yard, wanting to bring water to help the firefighters while knowing I was completely helpless. An incident at a concert, people I cared about getting killed, me getting killed while an NRA lobbyist offered up thoughts and prayers. In my subconscious mind I got hurt, humiliated, by everyone, anyone. Mentally. Physically. Sometimes I didn't know if punishment got me off or horrified me or both.

So a peaceful night meant everything. Silence was the biggest gift I could receive, followed closely by sleep I hadn't known I needed.

When I finally got up and checked the sleep monitor app on my phone, it showed that my sleep was restful. It also showed I was under for thirteen hours. What the hell? I'd hardly ever even made eight hours, except when I was super sick. This must have made up for years of exhaustion. Endless fatigue.

I actually took the time to look in the mirror. The bags under my eyes were a little less dark. I was in a good enough mood to go to the sink, scrub up my face with a slew of beauty products, do my hair, and put on a little makeup. Something fun, just for me. You should do it too. You're worth it.

I waited for the voice to berate me, to tell me how ugly I was. It stayed blissfully silent. I turned my head from side to side, studying my reflection in the mirror. I felt . . . pretty.

I pulled on skinny jean capris and a nice sleeveless top. The clothes were snugger than they used to be. I sucked in a breath. Curves. They were just curves. I wasn't Aleks, and I wasn't going to dress like Aleks when I next became him. I didn't need to work out to the point of exhaustion, counting all my calories just to make sure that there was no evidence of softness. After deliberating, I yanked out the strappy heels at the top of my shoe divider. Why not?

I headed to the kitchen, a little wobbly since I hadn't worn heels in a while. Aunt Anne Marie had left a note on the fridge: *Getting groceries.* There was a ten-dollar bill with it, clearly meant for me.

Not a sound. I was alone. It was kind of weird that I still hadn't seen my uncle face-to-face, that the closest I'd come so far was hearing his voice through the vents as he absolved people of their sins. I pocketed the cash and looked in the fridge just in case. It was half-filled with condiments, but nothing really to go with them. There was one string cheese in there that I ate, but it wasn't enough. I was seriously starving.

I left the rectory and padded down the steps to the street, slowing by the front of the church. A couple of long tables were set up in the grass, with some people I assumed were parishioners clustered around one side of them. Behind the tables stood five nuns in blue robes and white veils—huh, I'd always assumed nuns only wore black habits. There was a guy with them too. A priest, judging by the white collar at the neck of his black shirt.

I squinted in the bright sun. The priest *definitely* wasn't my uncle. He didn't look too much older than me. Kind of weird. Where exactly was Uncle Bryan? If it wasn't for the confessions I'd overheard, I'd half-wonder if he actually existed.

Something sweet with hints of cinnamon filled my nostrils. A bake sale. My stomach growled. I shoved my hand in my pocket, fingers curling around the ten-dollar bill.

I stalled. I couldn't be stupid or naive. These were the type of people who might say things like "We love everyone because Jesus told us to! Oh, except the gays. And the Muslims. And Jews (even though Jesus was Jewish, but that was *different*). And immigrants (Jesus was American, didn't you know?). And Planned Parenthood. And fornicators. And tattoos, unless they're quoting Leviticus of course. And pepperoni pizza on Fridays. And—"

"Hey."

I looked up. A nun came out from behind one of the tables. In the midday sun, I could see her clearly. She looked my age even though she must be in her twenties if she was a nun. Right? I vaguely remembered some documentary saying that a person can technically join a convent at seventeen but that most orders require aspiring nuns to go to college first.

She had dark eyes and brown skin, contrasting with the bright blue of her habit, and she was a lot prettier than I'd assumed a nun would be—

Internally I recoiled. Was I really checking out a nun? That had to go against so many codes of ethics, especially hers. My cheeks must have flushed a dark scarlet because I could feel the burn on my skin and oh God she was looking at me, stop looking at me, stop looking at me, stop—

"You just moved in with Father Moore." The nun said it like a statement, not a question. How was a person supposed to respond to that? For once, I waited for the voice to coax me. But it remained silent. Maybe it was gone for good.

Fuck. Could I take it back? I'd pick the voice any day over the panic.

The nun seemed to sense my discomfort. "That probably came out not the way I intended. Your uncle mentioned his niece would be coming, and I saw you unpacking yesterday. I wanted to extend a greeting."

Great. Just what I needed: for her to be really, really nice.

"Uh, yeah." I fumbled. "I'm living with him and my aunt Anne Marie for a while. I, uh, I haven't seen him yet. He was working late, I guess. And out this morning. He's, uh, he's not here?"

The nun pursed her lips. Her expression was unreadable. "He's very busy."

"Yeah. I, uh, I noticed." Great. I was fumbling all over my words. Boy-me would never do this. "You uh . . . been here awhile?"

Wow. Great going, Alexis. That's totally not skeevy at all.

"Yeah. I guess it's been awhile," she said, seeming kind of amused. She held out her hand. "I'm Sister Bernadette."

I hesitated and then shook it. "Alexis." Her hand was weathered, scarred at the knuckles. "You uh, you having luck with the bake sale?" I asked politely.

"Can't complain."

"Could be better?"

She grinned. "If you phrase it like that, *anything* can be better instead of just being fine."

Touché.

"I thought nuns weren't allowed to have sweets. Like the whole mandatory living through poverty thing?"

"Who says I'm eating them?"

Checkmate. I couldn't help but smile back at her.

"Hey." The young priest tapped Sister Bernadette on the shoulder. I didn't know a priest could be so young. Did they have access to some sort of elixir? "I've got to get to class. You have this under control?"

Class? Priests went to class? Was he a teacher or a student?

"I already told you, you didn't need to come," Sister Bernadette said.

"I wanted to help."

Translation: *I wanted to hang out.*

That seemed . . . weird. Did priests hang out with nuns and parishioners just because? Like regular people?

"Go," Sister Bernadette insisted, swatting him off. Maybe she was uncomfortable with his familiarity. The young priest nodded as he hustled away from the table, slinging a backpack over his shoulder. He looked both ways before crossing the street and getting in an old Honda Civic.

Great, his presence had broken the flow of conversation. I looked back at Sister Bernadette, unsure of what to say. "So . . ." I gestured to the table. "What's the money going to?"

"Charity," Sister Bernadette said. "We're partnered with a few of the local organizations."

Under my breath, I muttered, "I'm guessing Planned Parenthood isn't on your donation list."

Sister Bernadette gave me a once-over. "You're pro-choice, I'm guessing?"

And hella queer and agnostic, I wanted to say, twirling around on my toes with fake fairy wings as I threw a handful of rainbow glitter up in the air. But I wasn't Aleks right now.

And the whole point of being here was to stay on the downlow. Instead, I clenched my fists defensively. "Well, I'm definitely not anti-choice."

Sister Bernadette glanced back at the tables with the nuns, who were laughing about something. Then, so softly I could have mistaken it for the wind, she said, "You're not the only one who believes in choices."

"Huh?"

"You heard me."

No. No way. She wasn't implying what I thought she was, right?

"Tell you a secret," Sister Bernadette continued. "My favorite subject in school was science. Especially human biology. Bodies are fascinating."

She broke eye contact again and took a few steps back. I couldn't believe it. A pro-choice nun? Didn't that completely go against Catholic doctrine?

But I'd been so wrong about Wanda Elmwood, thinking she was a crook when she was desperate to take care of her children instead. *Don't stereotype*, I reminded myself. I couldn't assume what Sister Bernadette's beliefs were.

But if she believed in the right to choose, how could she have been allowed to become a nun? Was it a lie that she'd discuss in her own confessions? A secret just for herself?

I pulled out the wrinkled ten from my pocket. "So . . . what do you recommend?" That was as much of an olive branch as she was going to get from me.

She looked at the bill, eyes widening a little with surprise, then at the table. "Pastries are a dollar."

I ran calculations through my head. Generally I tried to save up as much as I could. Even when I cosplayed, I put more than 50 percent of my money into savings just in case. I wasn't sure what the just in case was, but I was always serious about it.

With hesitation, I handed over the bill. "Just . . . whatever looks best to you, I guess."

Sister Bernadette took it. "How much change do you want back?"

Eight dollars.
You gotta keep saving. Just in case.

Ah. The voice again. It was almost comforting to know it wasn't lost, although I certainly wouldn't miss it at night. Maybe to spite it, I said, "Keep it. If you're really . . . if this goes to . . ." Great. Now I'd lost the ability to speak.

She smiled warmly and put the bill in their small cash bin. Next she got a paper box. I watched her go along the tables, picking through danishes and rolls. I also watched her put in way more than ten, more like seventeen, until the box barely closed at the lid. She returned and handed it over to me.

"Thank you so much for your contribution."

"Thank you for breakfast. And uh, lunch. For the next few days." Great. I was babbling like a fool and Sister Bernadette was smirking.

"I hope to see you soon, Alexis."

Her smile was so disarming, it made me sweat. She looked as if she saw girl-me. As if girl-me wasn't invisible. I wasn't a pretty girl, but I could fool people sometimes with the makeup, the decent hair, the tight jeans, the heels.

My palms started to sweat. Being visible, like boy-me, was bad. It wasn't safe. Even if so far the only person who'd noticed me was a nun.

I turned and hustled back to the rectory. I had to think of something else, *anything* else. The food really did smell fantastic, and by now I was starving. My stomach growled, aching hard, but I made myself wait just a bit longer. I poured makeup remover over a washcloth and aggressively scrubbed at my face. I got everything off except a little smear of black eyeliner, almost like it was intentional. It'd have to do—for now.

Stop thinking about the nun.
You're so going to hell for this one.
Slut.
Cheater.
Whore.
Ugly girl.
Ugly girl.
Ugly girl.

I almost smiled. Of course the voice would be back to berate me.

But as I brought the box to my room and sat on the bed with it, the voice didn't make another sound. Like it wanted me to do the right thing. Everything was blissfully quiet except for me munching on a pastry—and soon, murmurs I could recognize by tone as my still-unseen uncle's voice. Strange that he wasn't helping with the bake sale, hadn't poked his head out to say hello . . .

I grabbed my notebook and pen, nestled in bed, and started listening to the next confession.

5 ALEXIS

Forgive me, Father, for I have sinned.
    Bless me, Father, for I have sinned.
    Help me, Father, for I have sinned.
    Save me, Father, for all of my sins.

The precise words may have varied, but the penitence of each churchgoer was consistent. Many were tearful, and pretty much everyone sounded full of remorse. No one seemed bored, or like they were there only because they had to come. There was something oddly comforting about that, something kind of touching about how sincere these confessions were.

And yet the sins themselves generally turned out to be low-stakes and mundane. Profanity. An inappropriate look. Lost tempers. Just ordinary slip-ups. Listening to them for hours was exhausting. It was depressing hearing how broken up people were about transgressions that weren't remotely important. Carrying guilt and shame for literally nothing.

"I caused bodily harm to someone," a woman in the confessional below said. There was more than just remorse in her tone, but I couldn't tell what it was. I was so drained, I wasn't sure I wanted to know.

"Who and why? How so?" my uncle asked in alarm.

"My brother."

I sat upright on my bed, poised with my pen and notebook. This was serious.

"What happened?"

"He's hard to manage," the woman said. "He gets violent tantrums. My whole family is bruised from head to toe."

"Have you talked to him about it?"

"We can't. He's nonverbal. We've tried things. Sign language. Classes. But—earlier today, he lost it. I don't know what I did, if I did anything, if it was sensory overload. I don't know. He went ballistic and started destroying the house. Then he came at me. So I took a broom and hit him."

I sucked in a breath.

"I hit him. Just once, but it's inexcusable," she said softly, like if she raised her voice she wouldn't get all the words out. "I'm at the end of my rope, Father. Help me. Please."

"I don't know if I can," my uncle said, unable to hide the revulsion in his voice. The woman began to cry. My fists tightened. What the hell was my uncle doing? "This is a serious offense. Criminal."

"I know it's serious. That's why I'm here. I'm begging you for help."

"You caused harm to a vulnerable person in your care and you're asking for forgiveness? I've only seen you at Mass a few times this year."

"I'm not asking forgiveness. I don't deserve it," the woman sobbed. "I'm asking for help for him."

"You need to get a grip," my uncle said.

She needs help, not a grip!

A long pause. Something seemed to change in the air. Like he'd counted to ten to calm himself down. "Please. Deep breaths."

After another brief pause, he continued, "Pray more. Come to Mass every day. Show God you're remorseful for hurting him."

No way. Was he really using her suffering to promote church attendance?

By now, the woman was sobbing. "How can I come to Mass more often? I have no one to watch my brother."

"Your parents?"

"They're in California."

"Husband?"

"Are you serious? He's the mayor *and* he has to keep the bodega running—how is he going to have enough time to do it?"

I did an internet search on my phone. Max Mackell was the mayor. A few more swipes with my finger brought up his wife, Elizabeth. She was older than she sounded at seventy. Despite Googling, I couldn't find the name of her brother.

This couldn't just be a dead end. There was an old woman who was out of her depth caring for her brother. Hitting anyone was wrong, under pretty much any circumstances, and yet, I couldn't help but sympathize with this woman. Maybe it was because she didn't ask for forgiveness. She came to my uncle for help, and his response was to reprimand her for not going to church more often.

I sat on the bed, absolutely stumped, well past my uncle leading her through a series of Hail Marys. Doing nothing wasn't the answer, but I didn't know what I could do. Except . . .

You do know what you could do, the voice said.

My chest began to pound as I pulled up the website for the local police station.

What if I was making the biggest mistake of my life? This woman was asking for help, not a citation.

But if she'd hit her brother once, it was fair to worry that she'd hit him again, especially if she felt this desperate. And even if I didn't want to make things worse for her, I knew I needed to do something to get it to stop.

I clicked on their anonymous tip page and started typing.

It's come to my attention that a man with a severe cognitive disability is currently in danger at the residence of Elizabeth and Max Mackell.

I paused and read over the note, flinching hard. Noooooope. This wasn't right. This made them out to be monsters. And I wasn't even sure I was using the correct term to describe Elizabeth's brother. My fingers tapped away at my computer, deleting what I had written to start over:

I need help for Elizabeth Mackell's brother. He's nonverbal and has gotten violent with Elizabeth and Max. Recently, in self-defense, one of them hit the man in question. Please help them. They're good people who are in over their heads. Without help from the government or a nonprofit or some-one, everyone in that home could be at risk.

I reread it a few times, biting my lip hard as I went over each word. Although it was an anonymous tip, I added a name at the bottom: *Raziel*. A little afterthought, tagging myself to show I was serious. And it seemed appropriate. Raziel was meant to be the archangel of secrets, with six wings and thousands of eyes. Watching people, or watching God? I wondered.

Before I could consider deleting the name, I hit send.

And that was the moment I realized I was no longer Alexis.

6 ALEKS

At six o'clock, I dragged myself into the kitchen for dinner. Thanks to the unexpected gender-swap, I felt like I'd been hit with a semi. It was really rare for me to switch so frequently. Stress must have somehow contributed to it, because I couldn't think of any other reason. By the time I got down, staggering like I was drunk, I almost tripped in the doorway.

Holy shit. It was him. Uncle Bryan.

He looked at me and rose from where he sat at the table. He was wearing black slacks and a black button-up shirt with his priest's collar. I figured this was probably as casual as a priest could get.

It was like my uncle had aged twice as fast as he should have, just like Aunt Anne Marie. His hair was completely gray, and he had more wrinkles than I'd expect for a guy in his early fifties. There was something creepy about it. Maybe I was looking at him extra hard because of the confession I'd just overheard. How dare he? How *dare* he?

Or maybe because it was me, now, Aleks. And no matter how hard I tried, I couldn't quite get "asshole" out of my system when I was boy-me.

"I'm sorry I wasn't able to see you sooner, Alexis," Uncle

46

Bryan said, embracing me in his long arms. "You look well." His tone was warm, but something beneath it was as cold as ice.

"It's good to see you, Uncle Bryan." Glad you could fit me in between your other duties, like berating that desperate woman in the name of God and all that is holy, can I get a Hallelujah? "Thanks again to you and Aunt Anne Marie for letting me stay."

The corner of his mouth twitched. "You're our niece. Of course we would."

Suspicions confirmed: even if he said otherwise, he did *not* want me here. It was Aunt Anne Marie who'd insisted.

I scratched the back of my neck. *Niece*. Getting misgendered when I was deliberately hiding as girl-me was a small grievance, although I suspected that if I asked them to use male pronouns or wore my boy-clothes today, they'd still call me Alexis. Aunt Anne Marie did when I first got here.

Aunt Anne Marie gestured for us to sit at the table. I was about to pick up my fork when she cleared her throat. "We say grace."

Oh. Right. So much for it being my choice. "Oh. Uh. Sorry."

"It's not your fault, Alexis." Again, I flinched. They didn't know. I mean, they knew I was bigender, but they didn't know I was Aleks. That wasn't on them. I wondered whether I should correct them or let it slide. "I know that's not how your mother does things. Our parents weren't exactly great role models."

My throat tightened. Did he just throw shade at my mother to my face? *And* my grandparents? "Mom's *great*."

"I'm not saying she isn't," Aunt Anne Marie said. Uncle Bryan raised his brow. A blatant lie on her end. "I grew up there. I know her well."

Yeah. Okay. I was pretty sure I knew my mother way better than her estranged sister.

"Let's discuss this after grace," Uncle Bryan suggested before bowing his head. He touched his forehead, like Aunt Anne Marie. I tried to copy their movements. "In the name of the Father"—he touched his heart—"the Son," then his left and right shoulder, "and the Holy Spirit, Amen."

For a second, I wondered if I'd said my thought out loud.

"Bless us, oh Lord, thy gifts which we are about to receive through thy bounty, through Christ, our Lord. Praise to you for bringing Alexis to us, and grant that we may guide her to the fullness of your light."

My mouth became dry as he and Aunt Anne Marie signed the cross. Involuntarily, my lips mumbled an "amen," but I couldn't keep from staring. Guide me to the *light*? What the actual fuck? Like I was in the dark because I was different? This wasn't part of the deal that Mom insisted on.

My mind moved to Sister Bernadette. Would she have said a prayer like this one? Had she only been kind today to entice me to convert?

Everything was confusing me. I was getting paranoid for the wrong reasons, detached from the things that were actually happening. These fears weren't rooted in reality.

Okay. Rewind. Focus. Try again.

What's your truth?
Is it the same as everyone else's truth?
What's really real? Don't you know?
Idiot.

Deep breaths. Focus. Go over the facts. Keep it simple.

I'd just moved in: that was fact.

I hadn't seen my uncle in years: also fact.

He was now a priest: fact.

Priests said prayers: fact.

Right. Okay.

Difference between fact and fiction distinguished.

Of course it offended me that Uncle Bryan had seemed to imply I was in a bad space. But he clearly meant well. This was what I would choose to believe: he meant well but was awkward and offensive by accident. If he'd known I would be offended, he wouldn't have said that. Or he would've phrased it a different way. He might not have wanted me here, but since I was here, he seemed to be trying to be helpful and caring.

And I guess he wasn't all wrong about me being in a bad space. Being bigender wasn't the problem. My parents weren't either. Fault lay with the people who'd hurt me. Yes, they were a bad space. The worst.

My aunt and uncle were family. Family who seemed to want to get to know me despite years of silence.

"So," my uncle tried. "Some of the sisters said you stopped by the bake sale?"

"Ah. Yeah. I talked with Sister Bernadette a bit. She was nice."

He nodded with surprise and approval. Like perhaps this was a promising sign. "I'm glad to hear that. I'm sorry I wasn't able to see you earlier. I teach a summer class, so things have been hectic."

My aunt cleared her throat. She looked at me and braved a smile. "So your mom said that you sew?"

"I used to," I said, only then aware of the sting of the past tense. *Used to.* A huge part of my life was dead. Erased. Without that, what did I have? Before getting into cosplay, I didn't have friends. I made excuses for my isolation: people my age just didn't like the stuff I did; I was an old soul in a young body; what I liked put me on a higher level of consciousness than many; I was better and really I didn't need those people anyway.

But I craved it. Craved contact. When I got into anime and cosplay toward the end of middle school, I was brought into a community. And maybe my new friends didn't care about the other things I liked, maybe they weren't into the arts the same way I was, but there was an undeniable bond. I was part of something. I was the beautiful boy.

No more.

Without those memories, I had nothing. I was nothing. But if I kept those memories . . .

For a second, I could see him in my mind. One second too many. I'd rather be nothing than that used, tricked-out joke.

"I made a lot of cosplay." They gazed at me, confused. "They're, uh, they're costumes, for Japanese animation mostly. Sometimes I use the term interchangeably with comics and other stuff. I would dress up and everything at conventions. It's really fun. I mean was really fun."

Aunt Anne Marie's lips pursed. "You shouldn't be partaking in dressing up. It's demonic."

My uncle raised an eyebrow. "No it's not."

She looked startled. "But—"

"We've always appreciated the arts in Catholicism. We dress up for events, holy days." Huh. Maybe Uncle Bryan wasn't an intolerant monster after all, despite his harsh words in the confessional.

"But—"

"Demonic costumes? We're not Jehovah's Witnesses."

My aunt wilted under his words. I wondered if she even had a reason for being anti-costume, or if she was just suspicious of anything different. She cleared her throat. "Do you sew anything that isn't . . . that?"

I wasn't sure what to say. "You mean not-costumes?" I shrugged. "Not really."

Uncle Bryan glanced at his watch. Before Aunt Anne Marie could say another word to me, he said, "I have to get back to church."

"So soon?" Aunt Anne Marie asked, rising to her feet.

Uncle Bryan kissed her forehead. "A lot of people are struggling with their sins. Someone needs to help save them." He then walked around the table to embrace me. "I'm truly happy you're here, Alexis."

His embrace was a little different than before, like he wasn't sure what to make of me. "You should talk to your Aunt Anne Marie about sewing. She's very good."

"Really?" Vaguely, I remembered the whir of her sewing machine, my fascination with watching her. I swear, she was making me a Halloween costume. So what happened between then and now? And why would she think costumes were demonic if even my uncle was cool with them?

Aunt Anne Marie shrugged, but I could see a flicker of pleasure on her face. "I try to stay humble. People spend so much money on clothing, it's easier to make one's own."

"I'd love to learn a few things from you, if you didn't mind."

For a second, I thought my aunt would burst into tears. Instead she got up to clear the table.

By the time I got back to my room, a confession was already in progress. Grabbing my notebook, I hopped onto my bed, ready to begin the process again.

†††

Oh. My. God.

Could there be anyone more pathetic on the planet?

Maybe I was still in a bad mood from Elizabeth's confession earlier. But it was definitely becoming clear that most confessions weren't big deals. Things I couldn't help with, like someone wracked with guilt for eating that extra slice of pie (what did people have against pie?) or someone who "couldn't help but cheat" (and okay, maybe their significant other received an anonymous email because seriously, screw that guy).

But this dude was the worst. Like the type of person who'd tell everyone "I'm such a nice guy" while crying into his coffee about being single. He was weeping the second he stepped into the confessional. He could barely get out the words, "Bless me, Father, for I have sinned. It has been one day since my last confession."

One *day*?

I rolled my eyes. This was going to be bad. And boring. Blubbering messes wouldn't be able to do something awful like rob a store because they'd get caught in two seconds.

"What troubles you?" my uncle asked. He sounded possibly a little annoyed. I didn't blame him. It was tempting to scream into the vent, "Get over it, loser!"

No. That was something the old me would have said. I was going to be nicer. More like girl-me. And if the guy was at confession, it meant he was trying to get better, unlike all the jerks I used to be friends with. Especially . . .

No. Don't go there. Do *not* go there.

Pen poised, ready to take notes, I waited.

"I don't know what to do," the guy began. "It's my girlfriend. She cheated on me because I would not engage in pleasures of the flesh without marrying first."

Seriously?

Dude was confessing because his *girlfriend* cheated? Not him. His girlfriend! Gag me.

My uncle sighed in the way that suggested he was barely containing a groan. "We've talked about this before. You abstained from sin. If she continues sinning, that is her fault. Not yours. *Hers*."

"I got her to break it off with him. But then I went on her computer. She's still emailing that man saying how much she loves him. And she told him she's only with me for my money. But I'm in debt! I keep trying to pay everything off, and she keeps spending what I have."

I suddenly felt a lot less snippy than I had five minutes ago. A couple of my exes had cheated on girl-me, dumped girl-me for someone better. Not that they were really long relationships, maybe two or three weeks, mostly online after fan service at a con. Maybe some people wouldn't think those relationships counted, but I did. I think I started when I was fourteen or fifteen, the hand-holding sort of stuff. I was a lot of people's first kiss. Everyone acted like it was such a big deal. Earlier this year someone made a joke that I was breaking college one-night stand records at just seventeen. Everyone laughed. Well, everyone except me.

You know what's weird? Boy-me never was dumped. Not once. Of course, whatever gender I was, I was still the same person. But while girl-me tended to see the best in people, boy-me got bored quickly. As Aleks I was more about hook-ups, sexual exploration. And I know for a fact that I broke hearts.

Hearing this guy fall apart reaffirmed how horrible rejection felt on both sides. Boy-me would cringe when people crushed on me. It didn't help that a bunch of my friends were really into yaoi, the m/m kind of anime, sometimes used as a convenient general term for boy/boy love. *I'm not a character,* I wanted to scream more than once. Boy-me envied girl-me for having the freedom to love, to crush.

"Envy is a difficult thing to admit," Uncle Bryan was saying in the confessional. "You should not have gone on her computer. Fortunately, this is easily absolved, but that still leaves you with a larger choice to make. You need to break up with her. There are many good women out there who respect the will of God."

"Is that the only way to be absolved?"

"Eliminating the problem gets rid of the source of the sin, so yeah. I think so."

"I'm just so lonely. I just wish—I wish I had someone . . ."

Yeah. And I wish I had something to punch after listening to this moron. He must have incredibly really low esteem to stay with a known cheater.

Ugh. Losing patience right after remembering my own heartache and loneliness was super shitty. So many times, especially before I got connected to the anime world, I'd been the loser wishing I had someone. And so many times, I'd been willing to give people second chances they didn't deserve. I'd learned the hard way that it wasn't worth it.

"Anthony, you need to break up with her and get her name off your bank account. Close it."

"But how am I supposed to come up with twenty-five thousand dollars?"

"That's a separate issue. Right now you need to focus on cutting this negative influence out of your life . . ." My uncle's words faded into the background like white noise. Twenty-five thousand dollars in debt? That would be hard to pay off. I could understand why he felt trapped, hopeless.

I scribbled down the name *Anthony*, then quietly tiptoed across my floor. As soon as I got outside, I headed back to my hiding place behind the trash can.

A minute or two later the church doors swung out, and I watched a man stumble down the steps. Was he drunk? It was hard to tell whether the wooziness was from fatigue or alcohol. I wasn't sure if he was the man in the confessional until I saw his face. It was beet-red from crying. Most definitely Anthony.

Don't do it. Don't be a creeper, the voice in my head said. I ignored it.

I followed Anthony at a distance. He didn't get into a car; instead he dragged his feet down several blocks to an apartment building. He fished out his keys and grabbed the mail from the 2B slot. I scribbled down the address and waited as he disappeared. I didn't know what I could do with this information, though.

Don't waste your time on this loser.

I squeezed my eyes shut to drown out the sound. Buzzing in my ears. Louder, louder, louder.

You're powerless. You can't help this guy.
He's a loser.
Just like you.
You can't be helped.
You can't be saved.
No one wants you.

I shuffled back to the rectory, head low, hands shoved deep in my sleeveless hoodie's pockets. By now, the church people had packed up the bake sale. A flash of black caught my eye. A few priests stood together in a circle, including my uncle, conversing softly. One of the priests laughed, hard. Even from afar I recognized him. He was the priest who'd been at the bake sale, and he seemed significantly younger than the rest. I took a few steps closer before I stopped, turned around, and walked up the rectory steps. What would be the point of approaching them?

Once I was in my bedroom, I locked the door and stripped in front of the mirror. I inspected every inch of my body with loathing, rubbing my thumb over a faint blood stain on my inner thigh. Great. Of course I'd get my period *right now* when I was already in a bad mood *and* Aleks. Couldn't ovulation sync up with girl-me?

I looked in the mirror. Poked my bloated lower abdomen. Flinched. Felt the ghosts of dozens of hands. And for a moment, I could hear everyone chant, "You have to! You have to!" loud enough it shook my body's core. I didn't see the beautiful boy I was supposed to be. I didn't see an ugly girl either. I saw a victim, and that scared me way more than just being ugly.

I redressed quickly, scooting to the bathroom to use a tampon and wash out the blood from my underwear. Beneath the hot water, I scrubbed the fabric together, sudsing up, gritting my teeth against the pain. I was dangerously close to remembering. Not that I'd forgotten, but I didn't want it at the forefront of my mind. That was my old life. This was my new one. And if I remembered one thing, that meant I'd soon remember the rest.

I flopped on the bed and glanced at the notebook. Anthony's desperation looked back at me. Twenty-five thousand dollars of debt. I couldn't imagine. How did anyone climb out of such a huge hole? It'd take winning the lottery, years of work in a good industry, not splurging on anything ever. Living on dried ramen and potatoes, and by then, with all the interest accumulating every day, you still might not be able to pay it off. Like one woman I'd read about who had twelve thousand bucks' worth of debt from college and now, thirty years later, had paid more than *two hundred* thousand dollars with no end in sight.

To get that far in debt because of his girlfriend's spending habits, though? That seemed even worse. Maybe it was an unbelievably stupid mistake to give her access to his accounts, but that didn't excuse what she did. Of course, laying the blame on her didn't take care of the problem either.

My eyes drifted to my closet, the boxes at the top. I swallowed. There were a lot of ways to make money, one way in particular that had earned me a pretty decent nest egg. Before I could talk myself out of it, I grabbed a step stool from the hall closet and brought it into my bedroom. Cautiously, I pulled the box down to the floor.

This wasn't for me, I reminded myself. It was for Anthony.

I pulled off my sewing machine's dustcover and unwrapped its cables, then spread them out on the desk, moving my laptop to the side. Next I got out a small folder of sewing patterns and fabric I'd collected over the years. The whirring of the sewing machine and tap-tap-tap of the needle moving through fabric was familiar, although my hands trembled a little with each seam and dart.

You really think you can help? the voice in my head nagged. *You can't do it.*

But couldn't I sit back, doing nothing. I had to face my fears and try. And if there was one thing I could do without too much thought, it was this.

It took a few hours for me to create a few cosplay pieces, a little longer to take photos with my phone. I sat by my computer, gazing at my online shop, which was listed as CLOSED. I'd shut it down a few weeks ago, but I still had a bunch of unsold items. Cosplay pieces that I'd packed away in one of the boxes now sitting in my closet. Stuff that my fellow anime geeks would've paid good money for. Stuff my friends—former friends—would've fawned over.

For a moment I felt the temptation to check my social media profiles, see what was going on, see how many people missed me.

I needed to get away from the computer. I didn't want to slip.

But I had to try to help this guy. This wasn't for me. It was for a stranger in need. And I was going to raise one thousand dollars to give to him, as a motivator to dump his girlfriend and fight his debt.

With a deep breath, I pressed OPEN and began to upload pictures and descriptions of the new items. Almost instantly, before I could even finish my listings, I received a shop notification: *item sold.* I looked at the time of the listing and sale: under five minutes. A lucky, fast sale—

Except my notifications lit up again, and again. I printed shipping labels and order confirmations as I sorted items on the floor. I'd need boxes. Fast. Damn it.

You're too slow.

I snapped my fingers. Liquor store.

With all of the shipments of alcohol, they'd have tons of boxes in their recycling out back. Since I wasn't going in with a fake ID to try and buy something, they wouldn't care if I took any. I could buy a few rolls of wrapping paper from the dollar store as well as permanent markers and shipping tape. If I covered the alcoholic logos on the boxes entirely my packages wouldn't get denied. I could do all of that tomorrow, easily.

I could do this. I could help someone get his life back on track.

For the first time since *it* happened, I believed things were going to be okay.

7 ALEKS

That night I set an alarm on my phone to make sure I didn't sleep in too late. Miraculously, the voice was mostly quiet, just like the room. It was almost too good to be true. I didn't trust it. Every few hours I'd wake up and pinch myself to see if this was real, although once my alarm clock went off I pulled my pillow over my head. Five more minutes.

No. There wasn't enough time for five more minutes. I needed to get to work. With the previous day's sales, I was confident that I could hit my goal of one thousand dollars, so I hustled off to run my errands.

By the time I returned with tons of boxes and packing supplies and logged into my site, my heart almost stopped. My shop's inventory was cleared out. Completely.

I looked at the total profits, then read them again. Unbelievable. In the course of one night and one morning, I'd sold just over two thousand dollars' worth of merchandise. I grabbed a notebook and scribbled down the numbers to double-check. Even though the system was laid out clearly, I always liked keeping track of everything by hand. It helped me recognize the realness of it all and gave me a sense of pride. I'd started paying taxes when I was sixteen because I sold over five thousand dollars' worth of costumes last year. At the beginning of this year, I'd hit the three-thousand mark, which had boosted my confidence that I could get into a good arts college and major in costume design.

Except I didn't think I wanted to go to school for costume design anymore. These costumes I was making and selling now—these were to help that guy, Anthony.

The numbers added up. This was legit. Somehow I'd made twice the amount I'd been aiming for in under twenty-four hours.

How was that possible?

I wasn't a BNF (Big Name Fan) anymore. Surely my fellow cosplayers hadn't been checking my site every day to see if it was back up and running, waiting to snatch up my stuff . . . had they? These orders weren't in my head. The receipts were proof enough.

There was a knock at my door. My aunt peered in. "Is everything all right?" Immediately her eyes snagged on the boxes and the mess of costumes across the floor. She looked horrified. "What are you doing?"

"Making and selling things."

"Those costume things?"

"Um . . ."

"You know I'm not a fan," Aunt Anne Marie said.

"Why?"

"Because they're demonic."

"Uncle Bryan said they're not."

"I . . . don't agree. Halloween, people worshipping the devil . . ."

"But this isn't for Halloween," I said. "They're for conventions."

"Still, it's bad."

"But *why?*"

Aunt Anne Marie frowned, folding her arms over her chest. No good answer would come from this, if any at all. "I just don't like it. You're creating things for gain. Out of greed."

Yeah, and you're really reaching with that one.

"It's not for profit." Not this time, at least. I hesitated. I couldn't just outright say I was listening in on confessions. I knew better. So instead, I said, "Somebody told me about someone who's in a lot of trouble, and I want to help."

My aunt paused. "Trouble?"

"Yeah," I said. "Someone who's in debt. It's not their fault. I thought I could put a dent in it."

My aunt's expression changed. She walked in the room, looking at the packed boxes. "Are you keeping any of the proceeds for yourself?"

I hesitated before saying, "Yeah. I always save some just in case. It could help pay for community college."

"Community college? But your mother said you were probably going to a big school for fashion design. That you could get scholarships."

"Costume design. I was going to major in costume design. I didn't get far enough in the process to find out about scholarships." I quirked my head as I looked at her. "I thought you'd be glad I wasn't going to major in your demonic whatever."

"That's education—"

"—for me to get a job in costuming."

My aunt stiffened. She was caught in a contradiction, and she knew it. "You don't think costumes are demonic," I said. "Not really."

"Let's not belabor this," she said, which is the kind of thing someone says when they don't have a better rebuttal. She gestured around the room. "How much did you make?"

"Over two thousand dollars."

"That much? In a day?" My aunt stared at me in awe.

"I've never had that happen before," I said. "I've had an online shop for the past couple of years, but I closed it after—"

Stop. Slow down. For a moment I thought I was going to spill everything. I cleared my throat. "Anyway, I guess . . . people saw it reopened and got excited."

Isn't it obvious? the voice in my head said. ***They think you're coming back.***

Shit. It was right.

Aunt Anne Marie looked impressed in spite of herself. "You could almost live off that."

"What about greed?"

My aunt froze. I couldn't fight the smirk on my face. Another contradiction. Then she asked, "Why did you stop making costumes?"

Shit. I'd made a mistake. I'd cornered her too much. Now she was on the offensive.

I shrugged. "Something happened."

"Things happen for a reason. The Good Lord has a plan for everyone. He just wants people to pay attention and not deviate."

I was pretty sure he also wouldn't want me to get lectured if this was part of the plan.

She stooped over to pick up one of the new cosplays I'd sewn for Bo Brightshine, the powerful heroine from *Attack Girl Tokyo*. I'd made a matching one for Dr. Steevius, her arch nemesis and—plot twist!—her creator. "You made this?"

"Yeah. Last night."

"It only took you *one night*?" She brought it close to her face to take in every detail. "The quality . . . the lining . . . this is . . . this is incredible, Alexis."

I warmed on the inside, rubbing the back of my neck. "Uh, thanks." It *had* felt good to sew something again. Muscle memory returning and everything.

She moved to another costume, turning it over in her hands, admiring each stitch. "All for a stranger?"

"They're in a lot of trouble."

"How do you know they're not lying?"

"I just . . . do."

My aunt looked at me with glazed eyes. She embraced me tightly. "I think I was wrong. You're doing the Lord's work with these costumes. These don't look like devil worship. The craftmanship is too fine."

Well, I guess it was a good thing that before she came in, I'd already packed up a costume for *Highway 666*, a horror video game that was like *Us* meets *Silent Hill*. The costumes in that one were super creepy, as was the series, but there was something I loved about how disturbing and wrong it was. Boy-me flirted with danger, embraced the idea of edginess.

Note to self: lock door before working on or selling cosplays for stuff involving demons.

My aunt lingered in the room. "You're an impressive young woman."

I tried not to flinch. Because even though I wasn't a young woman today, the compliment felt genuine. I needed to take what I could get right now.

My aunt stepped back. "I'll go to the post office for you."

"You don't have to—"

"You're doing the Lord's work, helping others in need. The least I can do is take all this to the post office, so you have more time to sew."

"Thanks, Aunt Anne Marie." I wondered if this was her way of finding a loophole, latching onto a reason to like something she'd vehemently opposed. "I was serious before," I added. "At dinner. Maybe sometime you can teach me some more about sewing?" She looked like she was about to cry again, nodding instead of saying anything as she left the room.

Why was my mom so worried about me staying here? I was doing good deeds, and my aunt and uncle seemed genuinely well intentioned. Sure, some of the stuff they believed was a bit out there. But, well, Aunt Anne Marie was at least open-minded enough to revise her opinion of my costume making. That seemed like an encouraging sign. She didn't strike me as a totally unreasonable zealot.

A horrid thought came to my mind—what if the problem *wasn't* them, but Mom and Dad? What if they were the ones who'd distanced themselves from my aunt and uncle instead of the other way around? What if they'd been too quick to judge? What if they'd kept me away from my aunt and uncle intentionally?

You're a selfish jerk to think that.
Look at what they've done for you.
But I guess they love someone as fake as you.
So maybe they're not that great.

The voice was right. That was a horrible, selfish thing of me to think. My parents had been nothing but supportive of me when I chose to reestablish contact with Aunt Anne Marie and Uncle Bryan. There wasn't a cruel or unforgiving bone in Mom's body. I was the horrid one.

To distract myself from the voice, I refocused on the computer. Only then did I realize that there was a catch to reopening my shop—I had to accept messages.

A lot of people used private messages to set up commissions. Sellers also need to communicate with their clients so I couldn't just disable messages. I'd need to read them. But if my items were selling this quickly, I knew what else would be there: messages from friends.

Former friends, I mean.

You selfish jerk.
This money's supposed to help that guy.
Grow a pair. Oh, right. You can't.
Your bravery's about as legit as your masculinity.
aka FAKE.

I took a breath and scanned through the messages. Some were legit, ones I replied to, this time with higher price quotes than what I used to. If I had to make something that reminded me of things that made my heart ache, they'd need to pay.

But the other messages trickled in, each making my skin crawl.

Where'd you disappear to?
Look what the cat dragged in.
Are you mad at me?
Stop being such a drama whore.
What'd I do?

Why are you mad at us?
Real friends don't disappear after conflicts. They confront them.
Are you all right? Somebody told me you ran away.
Talk to me.
Come back.
I miss you.
Send me nudes.

I deleted every message.

I checked the time. Still a lot of stuff to do. I was about to close the window when one message came up that stopped me dead in my tracks.

I'm sorry.

My heart pounded. With a shaking hand, I tried to delete the message, but my index finger wouldn't budge. My tonsils closed up, my chest burned. I started heaving. Hyperventilating.

I couldn't breathe. Couldn't breathe. Couldn't breathe. Breathe. Breathe. Breathe . . .

I curled over my chair, hand still clutching the mouse.

I'm sorry.

I squeezed my eyes shut. It was like it was happening all over again. I was back behind the long table for a panel about *Synthetica*. I seriously was a *huge* fan. I helped moderate online fan communities. I welcomed people with open arms. I wanted to share the passion with someone else, tons of someone elses.

Can't breathe . . . can't breathe . . . no, no, no, no, no . . .
I gripped the back of my head, fingers sliding through, torso rocking back and forth. I couldn't go back. I wouldn't go back.

But I did.

I was there again, behind the long table. I was cosplaying as Jay, the series' *bishonen*—"beautiful boy." I remember laughing with the group, making as many gay jokes as possible because that's what boy-me did, until we got to the end of the panel, the prize giveaway.

I remember all my friends on the panel cheering, "Jay is going to kiss contestants. The person Jay thinks is the best kisser is the winner!"

"What the hell?" I remembered laughing. "That's a terrible idea."

But then I saw their faces. I saw their fingers point. Slowly, my jaw dropped. A line was already forming. There had to be eighty people in it. The full house. All of these strangers, different ages, different identities, in line to kiss the pretty boy over a few stupid manga?

No, I realized with an even sicker feeling in the pit of my stomach. They weren't here to just kiss the beautiful boy. They were here to kiss Jay, a character people wrote off as the *uke*, the effeminate bottom. The one who was shoved against walls, kissed hard, and, as insinuated in one episode, taken without consent . . . just so a bunch of middle-aged white ladies could have wanking material. It spread from there, the fetishization of m/m romance and abuse and—

"You have to do it now," one of my friends said. "Everyone's waiting."

So I did.

I let eighty people shove me against the wall and kiss me, as I squeezed my eyes shut and pretended it was an episode of *Synthetica*, and I was Jay, not Aleks or Alexis, so that meant I wasn't hurt. Soon Ian was going to save me and—

"Is Aleks really okay with this?" I remembered hearing someone say while a stranger held me against a wall.

Where's Ian?

"Definitely," someone else said as a new stranger slid a hand up over my chest, my binder.

Ian is supposed to save Jay. Where is Ian?

"It's a game. Aleks plays hard to get."

What about Aaron? He could save the day.

"He loves this," someone said.

Voices blurred, unidentifiable with my eyes squeezed shut.

Where is everyone?

Surrounded. So many people crowded me, but no one was there. Hands, hands, hands . . .

Why is no one saving Jay?

There was laughter. Familiar. Friendly.

"When this is over, I bet he's going to go in the bathroom and masturbate, or find someone to hook up with."

They were wrong. When it was over, I went in the bathroom and threw up.

Now, I felt on the verge of throwing up again. Those two words moved to the front of my mind: *I'm sorry.*

I'm sorry.

I'm sorry.

I'm sorry.

The voice in my head said, **At least they said sorry.**

Like the voice was trying to console me.
Or make up for wrongdoings.
Or was on my side.
Or didn't know what to do
    and that they knew it was messed up
        but nothing could be done
            and I was screwed, screwed, screwed . . .

I dropped to the floor, lacking the strength to stand, and crawled to the bed. I'd known there would be messages, but I hadn't expected anyone to apologize for real. Halfhearted "we went too far" comments, sure. But actual, legitimate apologies? I didn't know if that made it better or worse—better that they recognized a mistake or worse because they knew what they did was wrong, so wrong.

It was just kissing. You've done way more.
        Just say it's okay and you're done.
    Never have to talk to them again.
They'll stop contacting you.
        Do it.

I forced my body to rise enough to get on the bed. It creaked under my weight. I curled on my side, staring at the wall, distinctly remembering how easy it was in first grade. If you did something wrong, you apologized. If someone apologized to you, you forgave them. Done. End of story.

So what's the problem?

My stomach seized. I knew the problem.

I didn't want to forgive them.

Everyone said forgive and forget, but why did I have to? I bet Aunt Anne Marie and Uncle Bryan would say as much. Forgive and forget, forgive and forget, blah blah blah, Jesus Christ, insert-holy-relevant-thing-here.

How could someone be assaulted by so many people in public without a single person coming to their defense? Why was it a joke when someone had clearly said "no"? Why must the victim be forced to absolve those people of responsibility, be told they should be the bigger person? That was bullshit. Sorry, not sorry.

I *wouldn't* forgive them. Ever.

FROM: Robin, Lee
TO: Yagoda, A.
SUBJECT: Hey

Hey Aleks,
   It's Lee again. I wondered if you didn't reply because I used your other name. I'm trying but you know it's hard to guess online, especially when you haven't seen or talked to someone in a while. Not that I blame you. Although I think it's kind of shitty that you didn't reply to my message on your shop site.
   I think about us constantly. Did you know that? All the time. I think maybe I missed my chance before. Did I? Could we make up lost time?
   It wasn't just me. I know you looked at me the same way. What we had was super special. Hope to hear from you soon.
   Love,
   Lee
   —

Yet if you should forget me for a while
   And afterwards remember, do not grieve:
   For if the darkness and corruption leave
   A vestige of the thoughts that once I had,
Better by far you should forget and smile
   Than that you should remember and be sad.
                    —Christina Rossetti

8 ALEKS

I sat in the absolute last row, in the pew closest to the back exit. I'd been so caught up in making and selling items for Anthony, I forgot that the nonnegotiable part of the ground rules was me attending Mass once a week.

When Aunt Anne Marie had woken me up, flustered about how I wasn't ready yet even though we just had to walk next door, I actually hadn't dreaded it the way Mom feared I might. Well, until I'd remembered I needed to wear a dress and hadn't shaved my legs, so on this hot, humid day, I got to be a sweaty boy in pantyhose. I wished I was brave enough to go natural, but in a town like this, in a *church* like this, if I wanted to be invisible, I'd need to *be* invisible. And I was pretty sure most of the women here shaved their legs.

On the plus side, although I'd be sweaty and itchy from calf stubble, with the pantyhose acting as a barrier, at least there'd be no thigh chafing.

I still didn't know Uncle Bryan that well, and based on what I'd heard through the vents of the confessional, we majorly disagreed on a few things, but Aunt Anne Marie really wasn't so bad. You know, outside of the deliberate misgendering or thinking costumes were part of the Devil's plan until she saw how much money I made then suddenly I was doing the Lord's work, Amen!

I still couldn't wrap my head around that one. But hey, I would take my victories where I could get them.

An envelope full of cash—a thousand dollars freshly withdrawn from the local bank's ATM—was folded and shoved into my purse. I wished I'd thought to buy a new purse before coming here, one that wasn't covered with characters from *Magnetic Us*, but you can't plan for everything, I guess.

I slipped into the very last pew seconds before Mass began. A small choir led the congregation in a song while my uncle, the younger priest from the bake sale, and some altar boys—all wearing white robes—marched up the aisle to the front of the church.

I stumbled through the next half hour—sit, stand, kneel, stand, this was practically an exercise routine with really slow background music—until everyone was sitting again. My uncle began his homily.

There'd been a few tougher confessions over the last few days. Each time, figuring out how to help seemed to get easier and easier. Maybe someone just needed an anonymous letter sent to them telling them not to give up, or that really, they were not going to burn to a crisp because this one time at band camp they'd kissed a girl and liked it.

I rubbed my hands over my knees and glanced at my phone. My uncle had droned for what felt like hours. It was really six minutes. I closed my eyes, tuning him out as best as I could until I heard the word "homosexual." My eyes shot open. I leaned forward, paying more attention now. One of the altar boys stood to the side, eyes downcast, face ransacked with guilt. I spotted the young priest, arms folded over his chest. He was looking into the crowd, seeming to lock eyes on a specific parishioner. I swore even from this distance I could see him roll his eyes. I glanced around the room looking for Sister Bernadette, but from behind, all of the nuns looked the same in their blue habits and white veils.

" . . . and their decisions lead them away from the Lord's will and the Holy Bible. Some are changing their biology. If anyone is plagued by temptation, they must turn to the Lord for help in atoning for their sins."

What. did. he. say?

My fists bunched. So that was what they meant by "guiding me to the light." Now I could see why Mom was hesitant about leaving me alone with them. How could people be so nice and seem to care so much and speak so hatefully against a person's identity?

I shot to my feet and slid out of the pew, noticing a few parishioners glance back at me. Screw the rules. I could feel my uncle's eyes burn into my back as I pushed open the door and stepped into the hot sun. The back of my dress was plastered against my skin from sweat, and those damn pantyhose were itching like hell. I walked around to the back of the church, where I had a view of the cemetery across the road. I had a powerful urge to march over there and start kicking a few upright headstones. Something to show my uncle that I *reallllllly* wasn't okay with what he preached. Mom would probably give me a high five. But that didn't seem remotely respectful to the dead.

A few minutes later the squeaking doors opened. Mass was over. Parishioners spilled out of the church, chatting as they moved toward the back lawn. Mostly their words were a hum, but among the hushed whispers I heard several variations on, "What *was* that homily?" I ducked my head, fighting the urge to say, "That was for me."

A glimmer of blue caught my eye. It was Sister Bernadette. The hem of her habit fluttered just slightly in the breeze as she walked.

Shame she's a nun. She's too pretty to be one—

I cut off the voice in my head. It was one thing when it targeted me. That I could handle. I didn't like it, but I could deal. You get used it when a bunch of real people have told you how fat and ugly you are.

But I wouldn't put up with my inner voice talking shit about other people, spewing gross and crass thoughts at them. As if a pretty person wasn't allowed to be a nun because she should be sexualized, or a person who wasn't conventionally attractive might as well become a nun because no one would want to fuck her anyway.

I crossed over to Sister Bernadette, trying to shake the sickness inside me. A monster that constantly had such bad thoughts running through its head. It possessed me, the cruelty wrapping its tight fingers around me. "Hey."

She smiled brightly. "Hi, Alexis. Did you enjoy your uncle's homily?"

I craned my head. Was she asking me seriously? Was she mocking me? Was she clueless?

"I didn't pay attention until the end."

"Boring?"

"Offensive." I rubbed the back of my neck, then immediately crossed my arms over my chest. If my back was that sweaty, the armpits of my dress were probably drenched. Great. Just great. "I had to leave. I was disgusted."

"You left early?" She seemed genuinely surprised.

"Figured that'd be a less dramatic option than breaking something," I muttered.

Sister Bernadette's smile dissolved. "Was that around when he was saying the homophobic stuff?"

"And transphobic stuff, and everything phobic stuff, and he's-my-uncle-so-he-should-know-better-phobic stuff, too." As soon as I said it, I snapped my lips shut. What was I doing? I was drawing attention to myself again. Why couldn't I have been Alexis? Girl-me was better at staying quiet. But boy-me just *had* to open my big mouth. Again.

"Are you—?" She stopped herself. "It's not my business."

"No, it's not," I said.

"If you are, there's nothing wrong with it."

For real? I snorted. "I know that. Everyone who's studied basic human biology knows that."

"There are differences of opinion."

"There's also being an asshole."

"Honestly, that homily was really abnormal," she said. "Mass has rarely been like that. Father Moore doesn't usually speak with that sort of intolerance."

I wasn't sure I believed her. My mind immediately went to Elizabeth's confession, how she begged for help yet got nothing except a reprimand. I wondered if she had been in attendance today.

"I don't know what I expected," I said. "I haven't seen him in years. I was trying not to make assumptions about his beliefs, you know? Stereotyping goes nowhere."

And there I went again, being a hypocrite. Again. Couldn't I keep my mouth shut for five seconds? Apparently not.

Before she could respond, a woman rushed to her side. I recognized her immediately as Wanda, the first woman I helped. "Sister Bernadette! I have *five* interviews lined up!"

Sister Bernadette's face lit up. "That's wonderful news!"

"I can't believe it! Out of nowhere, all of these places started calling me. Hopefully one makes me an offer."

"I believe it'll happen," Sister Bernadette said. "You've been suffering for a long time. We have to go through many trials and understand how blessed we are. God works in mysterious ways."

Yeah. More like "God" knew how to use a computer. Still, I couldn't keep from ducking my head just a fraction. I'd done it right. I'd pulled off a Raziel successfully. This was, without question, my calling. I'd thought cosplay was my calling, but helping people was way more rewarding than wearing something eye-catching and having people orbit around me.

Wanda grinned. "Wish me luck."

"Wishing you the absolute best. Please let me know how it goes."

As Wanda took off, Sister Bernadette turned back to me. I kind of wished she hadn't. Then I could still pretend I didn't notice how pretty she was.

"Anyway," Sister Bernadette said. "As I was saying. Our doctrine . . . there are many joyous things about it. However, there are many I personally disagree with. I think we hear what we need to. We get different things out of our faith."

"Yeah, well, maybe that's because nobody here hates people like you."

Sister Bernadette rubbed her hands together. "You don't know that."

I flushed. What a stupid thing to say, especially considering how white this congregation was. I couldn't tell whether Sister Bernadette was Latina or—wait, was there a non-racist way to even finish that thought? I was proving her point, standing here trying to guess "what" she was.

"Why are you a nun?" I asked curiously. "It seems like you disagree with some pretty important Catholic views. Why wouldn't you join like another religion that doesn't revolve around suffering?"

"That's between me and God, and us alone," she said, smiling in a weird way I'd never seen before. Lips tugged back in a hard line, eyebrows pinching just the smallest bit. I couldn't tell if it was from pride or sadness or just wanting me to mind my own business. Maybe all three. But what I could tell was that I liked her. Not in the crush sort of way, although she was pretty, but in the I-want-to-know-you sort of way.

Which I guess *was* a crush sort of way.

Ugh. Great. Just *great*.

"Sorry, I have to go," I said to Sister Bernadette.

"Is anything wrong?"

"No. I just have something I need to do." Even though what I wanted to do was stare at her dark eyes for so long I wouldn't blink before the sun set.

As I walked across the grass toward the sidewalk, I noticed the altar boy again, standing in his parents' shadows. Even from afar, I could see sadness on his face, heat over his round cheeks, curly blond hair hiding his eyes. Nearby, I saw the young priest laughing with a guy who looked my age. The guy kept gesturing wildly with his hands like he was telling a story, fingertips accidentally-on-purpose brushing against the priest's cassock.

Gay, the voice in my head said.

I actually laughed out loud before I could hold it in, and both men turned around. Immediately, I backtracked for the sidewalk, jogging as soon as I reached it. I didn't dare look back. Not once.

Good going, idiot.
They're onto you now.

Well, I was onto that guy too. He'd clearly been flirting, hard, the way I often did when I was at anime conventions. It was a tease, a little challenge. One of those "I'm just joking around with you, unless you actually want to hook up, then I'm definitely down for it because you're really hot," sort of things. An Aleks sort of thing.

Shit.

Pretty sure he was barking up the wrong tree, though. Crushing on a priest wasn't going to go anywhere. Just like crushing on a nun.

Damn it.
      Stop it, Aleks.
           You're the worst.
      The absolute
         literal
           worst.

And now I was distracted by queerness and untouchables and rainbows and holy hell, I was out of shape. Or it was ludicrously hot. Both, definitely both. My dress was drenched in sweat and the goddamn pantyhose were tugging and couldn't I rip my uterus out? I'd need a cold shower the second I got back to the rectory, but before then, I needed to get to Anthony's. I wasn't sure how long it would be before he headed home.

Confessions ranged in duration. He'd be longer than others, but what if he was first in line, mowing other parishioners over?

I focused specifically on his mailbox, reminding myself I needed to be fast. Someone else might see me and that'd ruin the whole point. The last thing I needed was for anyone to find out I was listening in on private conversations, even if it was for the greater good.

It *was* for the greater good, I reminded myself. It just *was*.

Sweat was plastering my hair to my scalp. From nerves or fatigue or the heat, hard to say by this point. How did the priests and nuns put up with it? I'd pass out with that many layers on. I only managed with cosplay because I was usually inside overly air-conditioned convention centers and downing Gatorade like no tomorrow.

When I first started going to conventions, I started doing all these workout videos to build up endurance and lose body fat in that hope of lowering my body temperature so I wouldn't melt in costume. But soon that motive changed. I worked out until my hips slimmed down to the point where I felt I could "pass" as male. It was messed up on so many levels—biologically unhealthy (because no matter what, some things wouldn't change since I didn't want to take hormones) and transphobic (like I needed to "pass" in order to be a real guy). I knew it was bad, but when I worked out that hardcore, all my friends commented on how I got hotter as a boy every day.

The constant flow of encouragement made it easy to keep up the routine, although I guess it was pretty shitty for girl-me. No one ever complimented me as Alexis. That was one thing I never got about the people I dated. The girls dated me because I was boy enough for them to "not really be a lesbian" but didn't have a dick so I wasn't threatening. The boys either strayed when they encountered female anatomy or refused to use my male pronouns even if they were the ones all over me when I was in a male cosplay, and spoiler alert: the second that happened, I dumped them.

I hated it. I hated them. Forever.

I didn't have to forgive any of them, and I wouldn't.

You should, the voice reprimanded.

Fuck the voice.

By now I'd reached Anthony's building. With a deep breath, I walked up the front steps. I pulled out the sealed envelope with ANTHONY written on the top. Inside, the cash and a note:

This is to help pay off your debt.
Break up with her. Keep going.
—Raziel

P.S. I will know if you spend it on anything that isn't debt. Don't play me.

As soon as I dropped it into mail slot, the weight lifted from my chest. I could almost forget what my uncle had preached, condemning people like me, people like the altar boy, people like the terribly amused guy who was joking around with the young priest.

My mind shifted to Sister Bernadette. I needed a friend, and it didn't have to matter that I thought she was pretty. Maybe she could know me. Both parts of me. All of me. Maybe I'd permit it. And that would be enough.

†††

"I saw you leave the homily early," Uncle Bryan said at the dinner table in the way that indicated he was trying to be friendly but oh my God, he was *pissed*. And I couldn't really blame him, you know, given that I was in his house and had agreed to go to church every week.

Except, haha, here's something funny: I *did* blame him. If he expected me to sit and take it while he tore people like me apart with not-even-veiled homophobia and transphobia, he had something else coming for him.

I wasn't even sure if I believed in God. I'd identified as agnostic ever since I heard the term when I was in, like, elementary school. Believing in what's been proven by science while being open to the unknown just made sense. It didn't discount people. It acknowledged truths. And it acknowledged things outside our range of perception. Endless possibilities.

That said, if there was a God, and maybe there was—how was I supposed to know?—I didn't think it'd hate people.

So as Uncle Bryan lectured me about responsibility, and appearances, and seeing the light, and sin, and whatever he was rambling on about since I tuned out almost immediately, I stayed quiet. Which was normal for girl-me. But boy-me? Less so. Lately boy-me was taking on a quietness that made me nervous because it *wasn't* me, and if Aleks couldn't say what Alexis thought, my brain would be like a pressure cooker of self-loathing and resentment. I could handle a seven or an eight, but cranked past the max and it was only a matter of time before someone got hurt. And more likely than not, that someone would be me.

There's a lot of stuff about gender on the internet, a lot of great essays and books and everything. Some people want to do away with the concept of gender altogether while some argue that it's critical for spiritual reasons. Is there even a right answer? For me, I see my life in two lenses: female and male. They're not divided by emotions or anything. I'm not magically stoic as a boy or sobbing hysterically as a girl. It's just a construct, a state of mind, whatever consciousness I step into.

So I stayed quiet at the table, sitting on my clenched fists to keep from sticking my middle finger up. I said I'd try not to leave church early again, try being cooperative. Oh, and by the way, could they not insult me in front of the congregation, kthnxbye.

I didn't actually say that last part out loud, even though a part of me, a huge part of me, felt that I should have.

9 ALEXIS

So much for my streak of restful sleep. I tossed and turned the whole night, forcing my eyes to stay shut as best as I could, and wished I had something, anything, to block out my uncle's words. I glanced toward my sewing machine, having a deep urge to create, but I refrained. I'd made money for that Anthony guy, and some for me to save. I didn't need to get into the habit again. I was done with cosplay. Period.

At some point I gave up trying to distract myself and just watched the clock on my phone, waiting for morning.

Around sunrise I heard my aunt and uncle moving around in the bathroom and the kitchen. Once I'd heard the front door open and shut twice, I figured I might as well get up.

I ran my fingers along my femme clothes, settling on a pair of capris and an old tank top. I could have worn something nicer, but I didn't have the energy. Even in the bathroom, I stood at the sink, staring at my cleansers without picking them up. It was stupid, but washing my face seemed like too much.

Just twist the faucet.

    Aleks would do it.

        You can't even do something this simple?

It's "too much"? What does that even mean?
Ugly, ugly girl.

When I walked out of the rectory, I noticed a guy around my age sitting on the steps. He looked up at me with a hazy grin, bottle of Gatorade in hand. I recognized him immediately as the guy who'd been goofing off with the young priest after church. "Are you waiting for my uncle?" I asked politely.

"Nah. I was waiting for you."

I sucked in a breath as he rose to his feet. Who the hell was this guy? He was a lot taller than me, with olive skin, dark hair, and black eyes similar to my own. A gold crucifix around his neck glinted in the sun.

"I'm Dima." He held out his hand.

"Alexis," I replied as I took it. "I don't think I've heard your name before."

"Nickname for Dmitry. Guessing you don't know that many Russians."

"Not as many as I should, considering we might get annexed by Russia any day now," I joked awkwardly. "And considering my dad's got Russian Jewish ancestry."

"Knew it," he said. "I always recognize my peeps."

I fought a little smile. "Did you immigrate here?"

"Me? No. Second generation off the boat, on my dad's side." Dima stretched his back, arms rising above his head. "So you're the infamous niece."

Infamous? I was cringing already. This definitely wasn't a good sign. "Heard of me?"

"Everyone has," he said. My chest tightened. If everyone knew, that meant I wasn't as invisible as I needed to be. My friends—my former friends—from the anime world could find out where I was. It didn't matter that I was avoiding social media if other people talked about me on it. I wouldn't be safe.

But then he started snickering. "Relax. I'm messing with you. Deacon Jameson told me you were coming."

"Who?"

"He's the transitional deacon." When I looked at Dima blankly, he groaned. "Seriously? Your uncle's a priest and you don't know what a deacon is?"

"I know what a deacon is," I lied. Actually, I'd only heard the term in passing. "I just haven't met anyone yet."

"Wow. Don't I seem like a dick now." Dima didn't look embarrassed. He looked amused. At himself, or me because he caught my bluff? Hard to tell. He seemed like the sort of person who made everything a joke. He kind of reminded me of me when I was Aleks. Simultaneously I wanted to get to know him and run away.

"It's fine," I said uneasily. I tried another halfhearted joke. "So what are you doing here? Stalking me?"

"Obviously, except now I can't get away with it since you know." He grinned and I couldn't help but smile back. "I'm actually about to swing by the school," Dima said. "Got roped into extra classes, the *horror.*"

"Like summer school?"

"Sort of. Except I'm not in risk of failing or anything. Collecting a few extra credits, volunteering with summer camp. Kids are freaking adorable. Figure the community service experience can't hurt on applications, if I want to go to a more traditional college instead of straight to seminary."

He grinned at me, like he was cueing me. What was I supposed to say? Not like I had a script. This was live. "Oh. That's . . . cool . . . ?"

"You do know what seminary is, don't you?"

"Like religious school."

"Like religious school," he reiterated, rolling his eyes, pantomiming stabbing himself in the heart. "You're killing me here, Alexis. Legit killing me."

"You want to become a priest?"

"Eh. I don't know. Maybe a permanent lay deacon. Maybe a scholar. Or maybe an architect. I'm just full of surprises, aren't I?"

"I didn't mean it that way."

"I know." He held up a hand in a peace gesture. "My parents are pretty stumped by it too, for what it's worth." He started walking down the steps as he talked, like he assumed I would follow. I guess he wasn't wrong, since I hustled to keep up with his long stride. He was so tall and fit, the type of guy boy-me strived to be. "They're only just getting over the idea of me becoming a practicing Catholic."

"Your family isn't Catholic?"

"My dad's not—originally Russian Orthodox. Technically my mom is Catholic, but lapsed to the max."

"So how did you get so into it?"

He smiled. "When I was in like, second grade, I saw some video of a Catholic choir online and got obsessed. Finally, my mom took me to Saint Martha's. Eye opening. I feel at peace there. Long story short, I got a scholarship to go to the school. Obviously, I've still got a bit of time to decide if I want to go the priest route, but I can tell my parents don't want me to. Honestly I think they just want grandkids. Being an only child means there's a lot of pressure on me all the time. Every time they've brought kids up, I've said, 'Ohhhh, do I have bad news for you.'"

"Because you're gay?" I asked.

Dima stopped dead in his tracks. He turned to me slowly. There was no trace of a smile on his face now. "I meant because I'm in high school."

Immediately I flushed. Great. Great, great, fucking great. I pinned this guy wrong. Big time. And now I was about to witness the moment he revealed himself to be a huge homophobe.

Equally bad option two: he could be gay but not out yet. Outing someone was almost the worst possible thing a person could do.

It's your fault for assuming.

Shouldn't have asked.

Idiot.

I hope he ditches you.

I hope he realizes what trash you are.

Stupid girl. Ugly girl.

"I was just hoping someone would be like me," I spluttered. It was the first thing out of my mouth, and it was partly true. Plus if he was a homophobe, it'd be better to know now than to really like the guy and find out later. Less of a crushing disappointment, you know?

Immediately, his shoulders drooped, like air deflating from a balloon.

I asked, "You don't have a problem with me being queer, do you?"

"It's supposed to be a sin." There was something about the way he spoke that didn't leave me enraged. *Supposed* to be. That changed context. That implied doubt. Maybe his tone wasn't coated with disgust or hatred. Maybe it was self-loathing.

Or fear.

Or maybe I was reading him completely wrong and he was a douchecanoe.

Maybe I was projecting my hope that I wasn't alone in this place.

"It's not a sin. It's as normal as being straight," I countered, waiting for a rebuttal that didn't come. And in that moment of silence, I was absolutely positive that he wasn't a douchecanoe.

Dima shrugged, shifting a bag to his other shoulder. I hadn't even noticed he was carrying one, that's how much presence this guy had. All I could focus on was his face, his dark eyes.

Maybe we could be friends. Especially if he did turn out to be gay. As Aleks, I'd been kind of the go-to guy for my queer friends. I wasn't sure why, but several of them said I was the first person they'd told. What if I developed a similar dynamic with Dima?

He slowed, then stopped, gazing up at something in adoration. It was a tall statue of the Virgin Mary outside of a brick building. "Breathtaking, isn't it?"

I stopped dead in my tracks. Leading me right here when he'd mentioned sin not even two minutes ago. "Son of a bitch."

"What?" Dima turned to me, eyebrow arched.

"You were trying to get me to 'see the light,' weren't you?"

"What?"

I clenched my fists. "I don't need any sort of light. I'm not in the dark. I know what I am, *who* I am. I don't need you saving me—"

"Alexis, I *literally* have no idea what you're going on about."

I paused. "Didn't you pay attention at all at Mass yesterday?"

"A lot of things are said at Mass. If you're cryptic, how am I supposed to know which part you're referring to?"

My lips snapped shut. Having an outburst was an Aleks thing to do. When I was Alexis, it was rare. My throat was raw and dry. I craved water. A cool breeze. An escape.

Dima stood by my side. Faint traces of his cologne tickled my nose. *Realm for Men*. Definitely around my age, but he wasn't a boy. He was a man. Unlike boy-me. Boy-me would never be a man. He would never grow up. This man beside me, he was the type I would gaze at from across the room, the one at the school dances who'd reject me when I shyly asked him to dance. I felt tiny. So tiny.

Right now, I wished I was Aleks. Boy-me always knew what to say and how to say it. Boy-me didn't get tongue-tied. People gravitated toward boy-me like I was their sun. Even this guy, this man, he wouldn't be able to resist Aleks's charms. My stomach churned. I was sick. So sick.

"I thought you were skipping out on me, Dmitry." I turned to a new voice. The young priest approached us, grinning. Like he was up to no good. "You're more than a half-hour late."

Dima straightened his shoulders. "I got held up. Apparently I was trying to trick Alexis here into going to church and seeing the light. Good of her to inform me," Dima said, rolling his eyes. My skin burned with embarrassment.

The young priest looked at me, smiled, and held out his hand. "I think I saw you at the bake sale with Sister Bernadette. Sorry I didn't say hi. I didn't realize you were Father Moore's niece and I had to take a test."

So the priest *was* a student.

"I'm Deacon Jameson."

. . . and apparently *not* a priest. I wondered if being a deacon was like being a baby priest. Deacon Jameson dressed like Uncle Bryan, with the conservative all-black clothes and the white collar, but he didn't seem that much older than us. Early twenties, maybe, like some of my friends at the cons. Former friends, I mean.

"It's, uh . . . it's nice to meet you," I said.

"You left early yesterday," Deacon Jameson said.

I folded my arms over my chest. "I was hoping no one noticed."

"I notice everything." He was still smiling, but not all-out grinning anymore. Something about the way he said it was a little . . . sad. I remembered seeing him during Mass, how his eyes had homed in on a parishioner I couldn't see. "People don't tend to walk out during Mass. Especially if their uncle is giving the homily."

"I'm not Catholic," I said.

"Clearly."

What the hell? Was he trying to challenge me or was he just being blunt? "He said things that offended me. I wasn't going to sit there and listen."

"I'm guessing you're one of the gay rights people."

If I'd been Aleks I would've snarked, *I AM one of the gays, bitch.* But Alexis wasn't as direct as Aleks. Comebacks never worked for girl-me. And I didn't want to be in the closet, but it wasn't closeting if I omitted information, right?

"Yeah," I said. "I'm one of those gay rights people."

Deacon Jameson's expression never changed. It was like he was just making conversation and didn't really care what I said.

What a prick.

"Do you want a tour of the school?" Deacon Jameson offered. I couldn't tell if he was just trying to be polite or if he actually wanted to give one. "Considering how late Dmitry was—"

"Not *that* late."

"—sooooo late," Deacon Jameson continued, pretending to ignore Dima. "No roping you into anything, I promise."

"Don't you want more people to become Catholics?"

"Yeah, if they actually want to be Catholic. Proselytizing isn't a big a hobby of ours."

Dima was grinning ear-to-ear as he interjected, "Then you've got me, whose parents never wanted me to come here."

"I wish I didn't have you," Deacon Jameson said, unable to fully suppress a smile.

Dima fake-gasped. "And after all we've been through. I was going to name my hypothetical future child after you."

Hypothetical children? But hadn't Dima just said—

Deacon Jameson groaned like they'd had this exchange before. "Please don't." He looked at me. "So? How about it, Alexis? Want the tour? It'll spare us both from hearing Dmitry talk nonstop just because he likes hearing himself talk."

"Hey! I resent that!"

"Can you deny it?"

"Eh, not really. I'm a pretty interesting guy."

"I rest my case."

I exhaled. Well, it was summer. There wasn't much for me to do, especially now that I wasn't going to conventions and cosplaying. "No pamphlets, and you've got a deal."

I walked between Deacon Jameson and Dima to the building, holding my breath when passing a RELIGIOUS FREEDOM sign on the outside. If it was literal, it'd be different. A truly beautiful idea—the right to believe in different things. But context meant everything. In this place, "religious freedom" stood for the right to practice bigotry and hatred.

Deacon Jameson held open the door of the school building. I stood just outside, eyes locked on an open field behind the building. A field full of little wooden crosses. A sign right above it read, *Each cross stands for a hundred thousand unborn babies.*

My stomach churned. I pressed my hand to my mouth and backed up. It was impossible to pretend not to notice this—this stunt. This propaganda. A baseless shaming tactic that went against literal science.

"Alexis?" Dima asked. He touched my arm and I slapped it off.

"Sorry, I . . ." No, I corrected myself. No, I *wasn't* sorry. "This is a mistake. Being here. Sorry—"

Stop that. You're not sorry.

Deacon Jameson looked perplexed. "What did I do?"

"It's this. I—I don't want to be a part of this. I'm sorry. I shouldn't have come."

Dima glanced toward the field of crosses. "Oh, that?"

What the hell? How could he be so nonchalant? "Yes. *That.*"

Deacon Jameson said, "A lot of us believe life starts at conception—"

"And a lot of those who believe that don't have a uterus."

Deacon Jameson turned scarlet.

And at that moment, one of the school's front doors opened and Sister Bernadette stepped out. "Alexis? What are you doing here?"

Deacon Jameson rubbed the back of his neck, head ducked like that would make his blush disappear. "I offered to give her the tour. I'm not sure why Dmitry's still here."

"You can't deny me!" Dima said loudly.

"Please go away."

"Yeah, that's going to be a hard pass."

"I'm going to muzzle you."

"Not my kink but hey, I'll try anything once."

I choked. Did he seriously say that? Worse, it looked like Deacon Jameson's cheek disappeared, he was biting it so hard to keep from laughing. Was he allowed to joke that way?

It didn't matter anyway. I folded my arms over my chest. "I'm not a fan of the landscape."

Sister Bernadette looked to the field, then back at me, then Deacon Jameson. She groaned. "Seriously, Joey?"

Huh. Deacon Jameson's name was Joey? For some reason, I thought Jameson was his first name. Unless Joey was a nickname for Jameson. But wouldn't that be James or Jamie? My head whirred. I was dizzy. This was too much.

She continued, hands akimbo, "Out of all the entrances, you *had* to choose that one?"

He lifted his hands defensively. "It was the closest."

"That," she said, gesturing with her chin toward the field of crosses, "shouldn't be there."

"Yeah, well, it's not like it was my idea to put them up," Deacon Jameson said.

"But you did."

"Um, excuse me, but pretty sure you did, too."

My head moved between Sister Bernadette and Deacon Jameson. I was amazed that people who'd taken holy orders could talk to each other like that. It was practically spitfire. It was like they were like a married couple.

. . . oh.

Ohhhh.

Was it possible they liked each other? Their bickering certainly had an affectionate quality to it. Like the way people acted when they were head-over-heels in love, or at least that had been my experience. Snarking with people at a con or online. Trading jabs, insults, anything to distract yourself from the attraction while building it up at the same time, until the tension became so unbearable you couldn't refrain . . .

"You had more say than me," said Sister Bernadette.

"Who said I didn't say anything?"

Sister Bernadette's expression morphed. For a second it looked . . . concerned? Scared?

Deacon Jameson folded his arms over his chest. He stared at his shoes. And I couldn't help but wonder if they were talking about something that had nothing to do with putting up crosses.

"Deacon Jameson, Sister Bernadette." The voice that cut in was deep and firm. Immediately, both the nun and the deacon straightened their pose. A quick glance at Dima showed the bob of his Adam's apple as he swallowed.

The man walking up to us looked like a priest, but now I wondered what anyone even was since I'd totally gotten the deacon wrong. This guy was old, with thin wire-rimmed glasses and thinning hair.

He smiled warmly at me. "You must be Father Moore's niece, Alexis."

"Yes, sir."

Deacon Jameson cleared his throat. His eyes were trained on the ground. "Alexis, this is the Reverend Monsignor Kline."

"It's nice to meet you." I held out my hand. A silence fell over the small group. I knew I'd made some sort of mistake.

Was I not supposed to be that outgoing? But before I could lower my hand and stammer an apology, he clasped both his weathered hands around mine.

"Welcome," he said. "We're happy to have you be a part of our community." Monsignor Kline looked over at Sister Bernadette. "Maybe you can take the time to show Alexis around and give her a run-through of the way we do things here so she can fit in before the school year starts."

School year? What was he talking about? I was going to go to public school in the fall. "Oh, I'm not—"

"I'm happy to do that, Monsignor," Sister Bernadette said, clasping her hand around my bicep, hard. It almost hurt.

Monsignor Kline's smile never wavered. "Deacon Jameson? A word?"

Sister Bernadette yanked my arm, pulling me away from the group. I looked over my shoulder. Deacon Jameson walked with Monsignor Kline into the building, head hanging. He looked condemned. Left outside, Dima slumped against the wall.

"Did I do something wrong?" I asked Sister Bernadette.

"No." She looked over her shoulder as well before hustling forward. "It's probably better you don't think about it."

"The crosses—?"

She hesitated a moment too long. "Forget about this. Okay?"

"What was that with Deacon Jameson? Is he all right?"

"There's nothing about him that you need to know," she said almost harshly.

I withdrew. "He actually seemed sort of nice," I lied.

"He *is* nice." Beneath her breath, she added, "Too nice."

"And Monsignor Kline?"

She stopped walking. I realized we had crossed the church grounds and were standing right in front of the rectory. "You won't agree with his opinions. Any of them. I have to work. Bless you." I couldn't think quickly enough to reply in time. I'd need to shout for her to hear me.

Now I was more confused than when I first got here.

10 ALEKS

I knew this day would be weird the minute I got up in the morning. In my girl clothes, in a bra and not a binder, I already felt like I didn't belong in my skin. An imposter. At least my period was over so that was one less thing to be grouchy about.

When I looked out the front window and saw Dima sitting on the rectory steps again, my predictions for the day were confirmed. It was definitely going to be strange.

I walked to the door and opened it. Dima looked over his shoulder and smiled at me.

"Sup?" he asked, getting to his feet.

"Not much," I said. "What are you doing here?"

"Thought we could hang out. I got bored."

"What? Really?" I was so stunned, of course I said absolutely the wrong thing: "Don't you have like church stuff to do?"

"I mean, I could . . ." Dima's expression faltered for just a second. "Deacon Jameson says there's always work to do . . ."

"I'd love to hang out," I said quickly. "Sorry, you just—I was caught off-guard, that's all."

His shoulders dropped with visible relief, and maybe some guilt for ambushing me. "Cool. Wanna go for a walk around the cemetery?"

"Sounds charming." We walked down the steps and out to the sidewalk. Dima launched into his trademark chatter, totally at ease, like we'd known each other forever.

"I think I pulled a muscle the other day practicing lacrosse," he said, "otherwise I'd suggest going all the way to the swamp, past Deacon Jameson's place. It's a nice walk through the woods, but it's kind of far. He gets to live all the way out there because it's closer to his school."

I remembered the test Deacon Jameson had mentioned. "So he's in school?"

"Seminary," he clarified.

"Oh, right. But I thought he was already a deacon?"

"Yeah, a transitional deacon. That means he's going to become a priest."

Well, that cleared things up. Sort of. "Do you think he'll be a good one?" I asked.

"For sure. I mean, he's only twenty-three—that's super young for a deacon. Had to get special permission to get an early start. Reverend Monsignor Kline really vouched for him with the bishop."

"He gets on with Kline?"

"Yeah, they're pretty tight."

"Really? It looked a little—well—tense."

"You kidding? He totally went to bat for Deacon Jameson. Said he's the type of priest for the next generation. That we need young people like him. And we do. He only became a deacon about two months ago, but the parishioners already love him."

Huh. I must have been really off in my assessment of their dynamic. "You uh, you seem to have a lot of praise for him yourself."

"I like him," Dima said. "He's funny. He's like the Godby to my Swatson."

I blinked. "Hold up. You like *Synthetica*?"

He stopped dead in his tracks. "You actually knew what I was talking about?"

"It's my favorite anime. *Ever.*"

"Shut up!" Dima practically squealed. "Are you serious? I haven't met a single person who's seen it!"

"Super serious. I love it."

"Me too!" His face lit up. "We should watch it sometime. I've got snacks covered."

Lights flashed. **Danger.**

Or was it? He said he wanted to hang out before knowing I liked anime, let alone the same series he did. The anime was just a bonus. Dima seemed cool, fun, harmless.

But so had *he*.

"Maybe sometime," I said, pretending not to notice the way his face fell with disappointment. I cleared my throat. "There's just some stuff . . . fandom stuff. Trying to separate what I love from that, you know?"

"No, I don't know. I've never done any fandom stuff," he said.

"Never? Really?"

He shrugged and resumed walking. "I wouldn't know where to start. I mean, even online, it seems like the hardcore fans know like everything about a series. *Everything.* I don't want to say something and have a thousand people jump on me because I forgot a character's birthday."

"Yeah, well." I paused. "You're not missing out on much."

We'd made it all the way around the cemetery perimeter. Neither of us suggested another lap. By unspoken agreement we headed back across the street toward the rectory.

"Can I ask you something?" Dima glanced at me. "When you watch *Synthetica* . . . you ever feel like you're going to hell for it?"

I couldn't help but laugh. "For a show? No."

"I mean, it's not exactly—it's like really messed up, you know? And the portrayal of the angels and all the stuff they do . . . I kind of wonder how can I like something and be simultaneously offended by it."

"I don't know," I said cautiously. Sure, I knew the series was provocative, with the idea of a failed savior and experiments to play God, but I never really thought of it as offensive. "I just think of it as art, I guess."

Dima sighed. "Forget I said anything."

I wanted to say it was fine. I wanted to encourage him to talk more. But my chest was getting tight. For a moment, it was like Lee was with me.

"I'll see you later," I said hurriedly, hustling up the rectory steps, barely stopping myself from slamming the door. Inside, I closed my eyes. I'd apologize to him later. But for now, I had to steady each breath. I needed to get Lee out of my head before it was too late.

11 ALEKS

When I walked back into my room, for a split-second the mirror seemed to show another me. Beautiful blond boy-me. I blinked. The image vanished. Girl-me stared at me with her dark hair, dark eyes.

Even though I saw her reflection, I knew I wasn't Alexis right now.

In front of the mirror, I stripped, turning my body in every direction to inspect it. Since the last convention, I'd gained a little weight or lost a little muscle or both. I could tell because my hipbones didn't jut out so much and my lower back didn't have such pronounced dimples. My hands pressed my breasts flat to my chest and I got queasy. My eyes drifted to the closet, to the box that had my packer. I could slip on the harness and my binder. No one would see me in there, so by that logic I'd still be safe . . .

No.

That'd lead to bad habits. I wouldn't be able to refrain from taking a few selfies, uploading them all over social media just for a few likes and comments. *You're so hot. Sexxxxxxayy. Heart eyes forever.* Seeking likes was an addiction. An alcoholic is always an alcoholic even if sober. Addiction to praise was similar, though not always as deadly.

Not for the first time, I had to remind myself without the eye of social media that I was valid.

I am a boy even if I don't look the way I want to sometimes.

I am a boy even if I don't like the way I look when I'm undressed.

I am a boy. I am a girl. I am both.

You're lying to yourself.

Faux trans.

Ugly girl.

Hate. Hate. Hate.

Boy-me could stand to learn some humility. Huh. Maybe I'd actually learned something about Catholicism that I really liked, besides Sister Bernadette.

You're doing it again.

STOP!

What is WRONG with you?

I rubbed my hand over my face and redressed quickly. A lot was wrong with me, that was for sure. No one would deny that. Even in the cosplay world where I was king, people knew I wasn't all right. Whispers I wasn't meant to hear, group messages I wasn't meant to see, the way people would look at me.

Before coming to Aunt Anne Marie and Uncle Bryan's home, I'd never give a second thought to the idea of "impurity." My parents were pretty chill and sex positive. "Wasn't like we were virgins when we got together," Dad said once, and after I did my obligatory "ew," he and Mom proceeded to tell me stories that were so wildly TMI, I half-wondered if they were making them up. But they made sure that I never viewed desire as abnormal or shameful.

Now? I felt filthy. Gross. I thought about making out and more, fooling around in costume because that's what the characters did. Realizing I wasn't viewed as more than a character was . . . disgusting. But how could it be disgusting if for a few moments I wanted, craved, the idea of objectification?

I thought about the way Lee and I kissed. I don't mean the fan service sort of kissing in costume while tons of people took pictures to make their dreams come to life. Sure, we did a lot of that in front of the camera. But I mean the first time we weren't in cosplay, when we both were leaving a convention, our hotel rooms down the hall from each other. And the wheels on his suitcase got caught on the carpet, tipping over, but he kept walking. And I dropped my bags as I closed in, arms wrapping around his shoulders. We kissed tentatively at first, then with a ferociousness I never knew existed. We shoved each other against the wall, clawing at everything we could. Hair. Clothes. My hand snaked to his fly as he pinned me and bit my neck—

A flash of light. We turned our heads. My friends laughed.

We parted, his lips red and swollen, my shoulders and neck and back aching.

We got our suitcases, not exchanging a glance. Before I got to Mom's car, when I kissed my friends adieu, I pretended I didn't notice how their fingers drifted over my body. I pretended not to care that after catching us so reckless and wild, they got more rough and handsy. And I kept on pretending until the beginning of this summer, when—

My phone started buzzing. It'd been awhile. I trekked to the bed, looked at the screen. A Skype call: Dad! I answered quickly.

"Hey, sport," he said, image and sound a little grainy through the app. "Which pronouns today?"

"He and his." I never got mad at Dad for asking. He wasn't able to see me on a daily basis, and I'd rather someone ask what I preferred than assume, even if they asked me multiple times a day. Online, some people who are nonbinary get frustrated by this, and maybe I'm weird. But although I think most people wish their friends would know immediately, my parents' caution—their consistent efforts not to hurt me—meant everything. "Where in Iraq are you?"

Dad hesitated. That was never good.

"Spit it out, Dad."

He sighed. "You know, most people ask 'how are you' before interrogation."

"How are you? Where the hell are you?"

"My son, folks," Dad said, turning his head away from the screen as he gestured elsewhere. "Forget a polygraph, he's got the best bullshit meter out there." In the background, I heard people laughing. Then, to the screen, to me: "It's actually my last day here. We're off to Kuwait."

"What? Seriously?"

"You know I wouldn't joke."

"No, I meant, I was hoping you were coming home soon," I said as I sat on the bed.

"I know," Dad said. "But I need to provide for you and your mother."

"Make me feel a bit more guilty, why don't you?" I said, only half-joking.

"Don't you dare."

"I dared."

"You know, you're just like that gif thing you sent me."

"You gotta be more specific than that, Dad. I send you gifs all the time."

"The one with the cat touching the fish while being told not to touch it. The 'no touch the fishy' or whatever it was, and it kept touching the fish and really being a pain in the ass."

"Wow. You sure know how to give your son a compliment."

"Damn right I do." He chuckled. "So how are things with your aunt and uncle?"

"Fine."

"Uh-huh." He sounded distinctly unconvinced. "Look, I know I said I wouldn't push, but I really wish you'd tell me what brought all this on."

"You don't want to know."

"Of course I do. I'm your dad."

"No, really. You don't want to know."

"Aleks, seriously, I'm worried. It's not like you to be this withdrawn."

"That's my problem. Not yours. You've got enough to worry about in Kuwait."

"Hey, I've still got a few more hours in Iraq. And by the way, you know what I worry about more than getting shot at? You."

"Dad . . ."

"If you won't talk to *me*, have you seen a therapist about whatever this is?"

Immediately, my chest tightened. This certainly wasn't the first time he'd suggested therapy. My mind went to the cognitive-behavioral therapist I tried during a rough patch in eighth grade. How scolding myself for feelings made me hurt more. "Not yet. I'm not ready."

"That's usually code for 'I need to go.'"

I snorted. "Or for not wanting you to waste money if I can't get the words out."

"Okay. Now I'm more than worried. Do you want me to ask for emergency leave?"

"Dad, don't." I cleared my throat. "Chill out. Please. I'm actually enjoying myself here."

"In that house of crazy?"

"They're nice to me. Well, Aunt Anne Marie's nice to me." I thought about mentioning a few of the things that were bothering me—the demonic costumes that my aunt and uncle argued about, the homophobia and transphobia at the church— but decided against it. Dad would tune out the good parts, the parts that I actually liked about being here. "There's a nun who's really cool. Sister Bernadette. She's really funny, pretty—"

Shit. There I went again. Before I could distract him, Dad was all over it.

"Pretty? Nun? Same sentence?"

"Don't go there."

"You've got to be kidding."

"I said, don't go there," I warned Dad, but it was too late, and I knew in a minute I'd be gripping my sides from laughing so hard it hurt.

Dramatically, Dad said, "Out of anyone in the whole world, you decide to get a crush on a *nun*?"

"Better than when I used to have a crush on Hal Jordan."

"Who sucks."

"He does not."

"He seriously does, Aleks. If you're going to have a crush on a Green Lantern, obviously the right answer is John Stewart."

In the background, I heard a soldier yell, "Guy Gardner for the win!" Before I could speak, Dad looked over his shoulder.

"Great, now you've done it. My kid's going to email me a five-thousand-page dissertation about why Guy Gardner's the worst Green Lantern ever."

"Hey," I said, "that dissertation is only two thousand pages, and it's not my fault that he sucks."

"Like Hal Jordan?"

"Like you."

Dad laughed, then sighed. "I wish I could talk longer."

My chest ached. "You have to go already?"

"Unfortunately. I pulled every favor I could to get a Skype call. Don't tell your mom. She'll get jealous."

"Secret's safe with me."

"Which means you're totally telling her. That's my boy."

I gave him a thumbs up.

"I love you, kiddo," Dad said.

I braved a smile even as tears slid down my cheeks. "Be safe. Love you, too."

"I'll try my best."

"Come home soon."

"I'll try."

"Don't get yourself killed."

"And use deodorant, I know, I know," Dad said.

When the call ended, I flopped on my back on my pillows. I missed Dad so much. And talking to him made me miss Mom even more.

I curled up, hugging my pillow to my chest, face buried in it. I wanted Dad to be home, to be with Mom, for all three of us to have a home together. Maybe one close enough to my aunt and uncle so that I could get to know more of the good in them—mostly Aunt Anne Marie, since Uncle Bryan still didn't seem to like me—

"Thanks for seeing me so late at night, Father."

I pinched the bridge of my nose. Greeeeeeeeeeaaaaaat. This was the absolute worst time for anyone to confess. Couldn't their sins wait until morning when I wouldn't be cocooned in blankets wanting to hide from the world?

What would Raziel do?

Help them.

Raziel's not selfish, like you.

Reluctantly I pulled out my notebook, wiped my eyes, and waited.

"It seemed urgent," my uncle said. "Urgent enough that I have a suspicion about what happened." There was a long pause, a little annoyance in his voice. "Whenever you're ready."

"Okay," the man in the confessional said, sucking in a deep breath. "I confess to God and to blessed Mary ever-Virgin, to blessed Michael the Archangel and blessed John the Baptist and to the holy apostles Peter and Paul, and to blessed Leutherius and Cassian and blessed Juvenal along with all the saints and you, Father. Through my fault, I have sinned by pride in my abundant evil iniquitous and heinous thought, speech, pollution, suggestion, delectation, consent, word and deed, in perjury, adultery, sacrilege, murder, theft, false witness. I have sinned by sight, hearing, taste, smell, and touch and in my behavior, my evil vices. I beg blessed Mary ever-Virgin and all the saints and you, Father, to pray and intercede for me a sinner to our Lord Jesus Christ."

Damn. Whoever this guy was, he sure was covering his bases. I was pretty sure he would've included Mickey Mouse if he could.

My uncle sighed heavily. "Go on."

There was another long pause, then a shaky breath. "I thought about it again."

"Color me not surprised."

Ouch. That was brutal.

"I'm trying my best, Father."

"Trying isn't enough. You have to stop doing that."

"Stop thinking? How do I stop thinking? Isn't it enough that I didn't act on anything?"

"Did you really? Not once?"

"Never."

"*Truly?*"

The voice shook a bit more. Quaking with a mixture of anger and fear. "I'm not going to lie in confession."

"Well, that's a relief. But only partly. You're still thinking those wicked thoughts. It's all over your face."

I held my pen poised over my paper. I had no clue what they were talking about. It was so cryptic. That said, I knew my uncle was needlessly being a dick, so whatever the guy did must be both bad and frequent.

Masturbator, the voice in my head chirped mockingly. ***He's totally a masturbator.***

I had to bite the inside of my cheek to keep from laughing. Because oh my God, that did seem plausible.

Bitterly, the confessing man said, "There are those in higher positions who do worse."

My amusement dissolved. Higher positions? Worse?

"Do you wish to restate your last comment?" my uncle's voice deepened, dangerously so. I could almost feel the other person tremble.

"I—I didn't say anything."

What the hell? The guy literally just said he wouldn't lie in confession, yet—

"I thought so," my uncle said. Weird. Why was he encouraging a lie?

"Is . . ." The guy's voice hitched a little. "Is it so bad to love someone? You're married. Surely you know love."

It took a while for my uncle to speak. Then he sighed heavily, like he didn't have an answer. "Maybe priesthood isn't for you, Joey."

My eyes widened. Joey? The transitional deacon?

It hit me like a semi. He must be in love with Sister Bernadette. That made total sense, and for some reason also it made me feel so hollow.

"You can't tell Monsignor," Deacon Jameson said, desperation filling his voice.

"Joey—"

"I want it so badly, Father. This relationship with God, our savior Jesus Christ." He wept harder. "You don't understand. I'd do anything. *Anything*."

A vice clamped around my heart, squeezing until I was gasping, clawing at my chest for some sort of release. I needed air. Needed to breathe.

Help me. Help me. Help me.

Help *him*.

Although I never prayed, I tried to will my thoughts into reality: Help him, help him, *help him*. I pictured Deacon Jameson and Sister Bernadette praying together, walking hand-in-hand. I pictured them smiling in the sun, talking about their love for God and each other. It should have been a beautiful image, but somehow at this moment I could think of nothing sadder.

Hopelessly, I set down my notebook. I didn't see how I could help on this one. A nun and a transitional deacon on his way to priesthood were going to be rigid about their vows, and even without that complication, matchmaking in general made my stomach turn. My two most serious relationships were ones I'd tried because my friends, I mean ex-friends, pushed me into them. I let people convince me that maybe I was being too harsh, maybe they weren't *that* bad. Except the boy I dated when I was fifteen was an asshole, and the girl I dated a few months later punched me. Setting other people up felt gross and intrusive—and that was without throwing in the eternal damnation for good measure.

I hugged my pillow tightly, helplessly. I'd gotten cocky, too cocky. Sinning from pride and the smug satisfaction I got from helping others. Maybe I needed to stop listening to the confessions. They were making my head spin, making me feel even more stressed and guilty and mixed-up than usual. I hated myself enough as was. Last thing I needed was a reason to feel worse about myself. I mean, for fuck's sake, I'd just accused myself of sinning against a god I didn't even believe in.

"Get a grip, Aleks," I said out loud, just to hear my voice. My words didn't sound like me, or what I thought "me" was. Distorted through the continuous prayers in the confessional below, it was like another stranger in the room.

Get a grip, Aleks, Alexis said to me.

And, for the first time, I felt like I didn't know her.

FROM: Robin, Lee
TO: Yagoda, A.
SUBJECT: . . .

Hey Ale/xis/ks or whatever stupid name you're using,
    I know you've been online. The shop and every-
thing. How stupid do you think I am? Did you forget
about that app you showed me? You know the one
where you could tell if a message had been read?
    Surprise, bitch.
    Why are you avoiding me? I tried to apologize. All
I wanted was one little reply, that was it. You could
have said you were angry, asked me to give you
space, but you're just giving me the silent treatment.
Coward.
    I wonder why I bother. Probably because I love
you. It's weird. I love you but I don't like you. You're
mean. Both parts of you. You're mean, you're
standoffish, you're an asshole. All of us have been
so worried about you and you couldn't even send a
courtesy note.
    But I love you. As much as I hate you, I love you.
We complete each other. It's why the hate-shippers
like us so much.
    We hate. We love.
    You need to call me. Or email me back. Or ANY-
THING. You owe me that much.

I hate you, Alexis. Aleks. Whoever the fuck you're pretending to be this time. I don't know why I'm bothering. You're the worst.
Hate/Love,
Lee
—

There is no magic anymore
  We meet as other people do,
You work no miracle for me
  Nor I for you.

You were the wind and I the sea—
  There is no splendor any more,
I have grown listless as the pool
  Beside the shore.

But though the pool is safe from the storm
  And from the tide has found surcease,
It grows more bitter than the sea,
  For all its peace.
                    —Sara Teasdale, "After Love"

12 ALEXIS

My phone woke me up. I didn't remember falling asleep, but at some point I must have set down the notepad and pen on my desk, along with my phone. I rolled on my side, back to the phone, as I waited for the ringtone to play out. That ringtone made me sad. I wished I'd remembered to change it. It was the opening theme song for *Synthetica*.

Note to self: Change ringtone. Way too early to get kicked right in the feels.

Maybe I'd change it to the opening of *Attack Girl Tokyo*. Maybe it'd help me forgive myself for not leaving sooner, for putting up with the jokes, the derogatory comments, for my inability to walk through a convention without someone grabbing my ass. My inability to tell people to back off, that I didn't feel like it or just plain didn't want it.

You know what's the worst part? These people weren't all strangers. These were people I knew, people I thought were friends. I figured I'd hurt their feelings if I told them. And what if in the future I *wanted* them to treat me like that? To objectify me as something sexy, something desirable? If I said no once, they wouldn't get that out of their heads, would accuse me of sending mixed signals.

So I didn't say anything. Not one word. Nothing. Disappearing without a goodbye or a hint about where I'd be.

My phone stopped ringing. About three seconds later, the ringtone started again. Three times in a row meant it was important. I dragged myself out of bed and padded across the room. I blinked a few times at the name on the screen before I picked up the phone and pressed it to my ear. "Mom?"

"Took you long enough," she said.

"Sorry, just woke up."

"That's a relief."

"Why?"

"I was starting to wonder if they locked you in the church to pray the Devil out of you."

"Nah, that'd be way too much effort," I said. "They want me to see the light on my own."

"Woof. That bad?"

"Eh. They have their moments."

"Uh huh."

"Honestly, Mom, they've been fine overall. Aunt Anne Marie actually took some of my cosplay to the post office."

"The post office? Why are you shipping your cosplay? Are you going to a convention?"

"No. No, definitely no." I paused. "I, uh, I sold some."

". . . You sold your cosplays?"

"Some."

"Oh my God. You're not going to regret this in a few weeks, are you?"

"Mom, no. I won't. I made a lot of new things with fabric I had. Sorted through some old."

"You spent so long making them."

"I didn't sell *everything*. And even if I did, it's fine. I'm not going to be cosplaying again."

"But if you change your mind—?"

"Hypothetically *if* I change my mind, I'll make new ones that don't have bad associations with them. A fresh start."

We were quiet for several seconds. Mom eventually sighed. "I hope you at least made some decent money on them."

"I did," I said, omitting the part about giving a thousand dollars to that Anthony guy. "It was a good move. I needed to do this for me."

"If you say so."

"So how are you?" I asked, trying to change the topic.

"Tired," she said. "Still working on a transfer. I started peeking at some other jobs online. Thought maybe I could find something."

"You're on your way to pension, though."

"You're more important."

"Mom, don't you dare quit it because of me," I said. "Remember, I'm going to college next year. I wouldn't be home anyway."

"Are you really going to last that long at your aunt and uncle's?"

"Of course," I said although my tone was strangely unsure. "Why wouldn't I?"

"You know they're going to make you go to Catholic school next year, right?"

"Uh . . . ?" My exchange with Reverend Monsignor Kline surfaced in my mind. Maybe that was another term of my staying here my aunt and uncle had failed to mention to me.

"If your uncle's the one making the final call, you're not going to be going to public school," Mom said flatly. "And

Catholic school's a lot of work. Tons of homework. Uniforms. No sense of individuality."

So I'd be invisible. Perfect. "I could live with that for a year." Worst case, there were other options too, like taking the GED so I could get my high school diploma and still go to college, or taking as many credits as I could to graduate earlier.

I could picture Mom pacing the kitchen the way she always did when she was on the phone, no matter the type of call. "Have you made friends?"

"Sort of. There's this nun, Sister Bernadette, who talks with me a bit. And this guy Dima. They're both pretty nice. They seem pretty open-minded."

"Do they know?"

"No. I mean, Dima sort of. I don't know." I rubbed the back of my neck. "Sorry, I'm kind of out of it today. Still adjusting to all this."

"Oh. Then let me let you get a move on."

"I didn't mean—"

"I know," Mom said. "You're just having a day, aren't you?" By her tone, I could tell she was smiling. That put me at ease but wow, it made me think about how much I wished she was here.

"I miss you."

"I miss you too. Cross fingers that I get a transfer soon."

"Crossing my eyes and toes, too. But I mean it. Don't quit your job because of me or I'll never, ever forgive you."

"Oh, come on."

"I swear, I'll convert if you do."

Mom burst out laughing on the line. "Threatening your own mother. What would your father think?"

"He'd think it was hilarious."

"He would, wouldn't he?" Mom took a breath. "Love you."

"Love you, too."

We hung up. I realized that for the first time in ages, she hadn't asked whether I was Alexis or Aleks. Did she know by the way I spoke or did it not matter because I was me no matter which gender? And if it didn't matter, why should I suddenly feel as hollow as I did?

I sagged into my desk chair way more exhausted and drained than when I first woke up. Mom had me thinking about things I didn't want to, like my attachment to my cosplay and maybe some regret. But I wasn't going to cosplay anymore, and selling my stuff was for a good deed, and it had gotten me enough money for some classes at a community college. And if I ever wanted to try again . . . well. I was good at sewing. And fast. I could always make something new. Set aside a couple hours, then bam. Done.

There was a tap at my door.

"Come in," I said.

Aunt Anne Marie walked in. "I thought I heard you on the phone with your mom."

Crap. Was she eavesdropping? "Uh, yeah. Just a short catch-up."

"Figured you'd be awake." Aunt Anne Marie folded her arms as she peered around. "I don't see any costumes out."

"I sold out."

"Sold out?"

"Yeah. The first day, really. It was weird."

"Wow. The Lord works in mysterious ways, doesn't he?"

I didn't answer. What was I supposed to say? *I'm pretty sure the internet doesn't do the Lord's bidding, but thanks anyway!*

"Are you making any new costumes?" she asked.

"Don't you hate those?"

"You make them for different purposes than demon worship. I thought . . . I thought maybe I could learn about how you do it."

I looked over her face. She really *was* trying. That much, I was certain of. "Well . . ." I picked up my phone and started to scroll through my saved photos. It was hard to find a costume based on something that didn't have some kind of religious connotation, since those costumes tended to be more elaborate and I liked making interesting things. I found one of a schoolgirl outfit. "If I were to make something like this, I'd do the blouse, then the square collar, and a pleated skirt. Might do a mockup for the cutouts and to get better A-seams. And here," I added, using my index finger and thumb to zoom in the picture, "I'd use my embroidery setting to stitch the seal."

"How'd you figure this out?" Aunt Anne Marie asked. "This is really hard to do."

"Practice, I guess. Trial and error. I'm not the best, not even close. If you look at some of the professional cosplayers in Japan—*they* have impressive stuff."

I could tell I was losing her, so I stopped talking. This wasn't like talking to my parents. They both had a nerdy side—Mom with sci-fi, Dad with comics—so they sort of got cosplay and anime fandom. Kind of. This was new territory for my aunt.

"I'm, uh, I'm talking a lot about myself," I said. "Sorry."

"You were excited. Nothing wrong with that. And I doubt I have much to say that would interest you."

"That's not true," I said even though I agreed with her.

"I'm serious. Ask me anything."

Crap. Now I had to think fast. It wasn't that I wasn't curious about Aunt Anne Marie. But maybe because I spent so much energy trying to put a positive spin on her actions and beliefs, I wasn't sure I wanted to know more about her. I suspected that the more I found out, the less I would like her. That all her niceness would be outweighed by hatefulness.

Surely I could think of one question. "Why did Uncle Bryan become a priest?"

Wow. My question for her wasn't even about her but her husband. Top-notch work.

My aunt's smile waned. "The Good Lord called him to the ministry when he was very young. He was already studying to be an Episcopal priest when I met him. And then later on, he realized God wanted him to be a Catholic priest."

"Yeah, but I mean, why? Like, you're married. I thought the whole point of being a Catholic priest was celibacy and everything."

"It's not common, true," my aunt said. "But this was his calling. God was telling us this was his plan when he gave me ovarian cancer."

My eyes shot wide open. For real? Did she seriously believe she'd gotten cancer so her husband could become a Catholic priest? I didn't know if it was the most messed up or most depressing thing I'd heard in my life. Maybe both.

"It's in remission," she said. "Which happened right after he started the conversion process. If that isn't a sign, I don't know what a sign is."

She gazed at me like I was supposed to say something profound, but how was I supposed to answer?

a. Sorry you got cancer. That blows. Want to go bungee jumping?
b. I'm truly sorry you believe God gave you cancer. Have you considered getting a new god?

    c. Congrats on the remission! Hope it sticks!

    d. None of the above. Literally there's nothing to say. Every answer will be wrong.

"I think I need to go on a walk," I said, swallowing hard. "It's—it's nice talking to you, but that's a lot to take in."

She nodded. "There's a lovely park a few minutes' walk from the school. With a lake that I think is technically just a pond, but everyone here calls it the lake. Just be careful not to go too far out or you'll end up in the swamp." She stopped and cleared her throat. "Well, I'm rambling. I'll see you later." She left the room, closing the door behind her. It still seemed like she was disappointed in me. No. Disappointed was the wrong word, but I didn't know what else could fit.

I walked to my closet and pulled out jeans and a T-shirt from the left side of the closet. As I dressed, I looked at myself in the mirror. I twisted my body, sucking in my stomach as if I'd like what I saw better. Hideousness looked right back at me.

Maybe you can just work out a little bit more, Aleks's voice said in my head.

"Great pep talk, Aleks," I grumbled as I pulled on shoes and headed out.

†††

How do geocachers do it? Seriously. *How?* Without using my phone as a map, I felt instantly lost in the woodsy area near the church. My chest kept pounding with each step I took away from familiar territory. I couldn't imagine anyone voluntarily going off into the wilderness just so they could hide a toy in a lunchbox under a rock near a snake pit in a field of poison ivy and were those vultures overhead? I swore I saw vultures.

I'd barely set foot in the park when I was hit with the urge to turn around and head right back to the rectory. As I turned, though, I stopped in my tracks.

Sister Bernadette and Deacon Jameson stood near a group of children—the summer camp?—as the kids ran around, sometimes splashing into the water at the edge of the "lake." They were both laughing. I watched with an open mouth. It was still weird to me that people in positions of power in the Catholic church were allowed to have fun. I kept expecting them to be stern like in all the movies.

There was a shriek and a few yelps. I recognized Dima, holding a huge Super Soaker, drenching Deacon Jameson. "Who's going to yell at me for being late again?" Dima cackled.

What the actual hell?

I must have blinked, because the next thing I knew Dima was sprinting across the grass. His hands flailed in the air in total over-the-top camp. Deacon Jameson was right on his heels with the Super Soaker, pumping jets of water at Dima's back as the summer camp kids cheered and laughed. Sister Bernadette overdramatically face-palmed as she called, "Deacon Jameson, you're giving me a migraine!"

I couldn't help it. I pulled out my phone and started recording. This was literally the best thing I'd seen in my entire life. A deacon. With a Super Soaker. Going after a dude who probably was regretting every single one of his life choices right about then.

"Ahem."

I turned and faced Sister Bernadette. Immediately, I stopped recording. "Sorry, I—"

"Don't," she said, and I winced, prepared to be berated, until she continued, "you dare *not* text me that video."

I blinked. "You're not mad?"

"About Joey being a moron?" Sister Bernadette laughed.

Wow. I felt so much lighter. Her smile was radiant. Warm. It made me want to smile like some love-struck idiot. But if I did, I'd need to accept that yes, I had a crush on a nun. And yikes.

And then the shadow of the overheard confession hit me.

"I don't know how you do it," I said softly, smile vanishing from my face as Deacon Jameson and Dima ran off into the trees.

"What do you mean?"

"Like with Deacon Jameson. Being around him all the time. I don't think I could if I were you."

Sister Bernadette's eyebrows rose. ". . . Okay?"

"You know," I said.

"Can't say I follow."

I rubbed the back of my neck. "I mean because you like each other. And you're not allowed to be together with all the celibacy stuff."

Sister Bernadette gawked. "Are you implying that there's something romantic between us?"

"Well, it's kind of obvious."

"Not obvious to me." She laughed. Hard. I flinched. Was Sister Bernadette a great liar, in denial, or totally unaware that Deacon Jameson was in love with her? It wasn't like I could tell her what I'd overheard in the confessional and that yes, he *did* like her. A lot. "I'm sorry," she said between giggles. "But . . . but have you never had a friend that you were just silly with?"

Was she intentionally deflecting? I didn't think she was. "What do you mean?"

"That's literally what I mean. Someone you joke around with. Don't you have that?"

"Uh . . . no. Pretty sure not."

"Close your eyes. Think harder. Surely there's been someone."

I barely suppressed a groan. Evidently this was my penance for listening in on confessions instead of, you know, minding my own business as Sister Bernadette would say. I closed my eyes, reluctantly thinking back to my anime conventions and the people I hung out with.

Everyone was a blur. Well, everyone except Lee.

Forget him, forget him, forget him.

My eyes snapped back open. "What's your number so I can send you the video?" I said, anything to change the subject. And that's how I got Sister Bernadette's phone number. She didn't press me further on the friendship question, although she hovered over my shoulder to make sure I hit *send*.

Then she stepped away from me. "I better get back to the kids or else instead of a day at the park, we're going to have *Gold Riot*."

"You know *Gold Riot*?" I asked, shocked. It was a super obscure, super old series. People had to team up and survive a ton of obstacles over a thirty-day span, and if they survived, they'd get enough gold to last a lifetime. It started out great until power-lust took over and soon it was all-out war with zombies. (No, really). How were there so many nerds at Saint Martha's?

The way she smiled at me made me question everything I thought I knew about her. "I'm a nun. Not a hermit."

I watched Sister Bernadette leave, heart pounding. I wanted to stay, ask if I could volunteer just so I'd be near her. But I made myself walk. Someone like me wasn't qualified to volunteer to help a bunch of Catholic kids.

As I got to the footpath, I noticed the abandoned Super Soaker. I stooped down to pick it up. A bird cawed. I lifted my head in time to see the black. My eyes traveled up to Deacon Jameson's lip-locked face. His back was pressed to a tree, arms wrapped around someone's back.

They kissed hard, oblivious to everyone in the world except each other. And it was beautiful and sweet and everything both parts of me would dream of because it was something I'd never find.

Quietly, I set down the water gun and slipped back. I didn't need to go through the foliage to realize yet again how wrong I'd been. Because it wasn't Sister Bernadette who Deacon Jameson was in love with.

It was Dima.

13 ALEKS

If there was one thing I never thought I'd expect, it was to be excited about going to Mass. I absolutely, positively could. not. wait.

Not because of my uncle preaching about unborn innocent babies and abominations and all that bullshit. No way. I was there to see Sister Bernadette. I'd do just about anything to talk to her, especially knowing that Deacon Jameson was just a friend, for real. Also I absolutely needed to see what happened next in the Dima and Deacon Jameson saga. I pictured them casting secret glances at each other throughout Mass, trying to stifle laughs when my uncle talked about "the gays," then them just saying, "screw it" and making out, right there, to the horror of all the homophobes.

Bet you'd never guess that I watched a lot of movies.

But that was the problem with my imagination. Reality could never live up to it.

First off, staring at Sister Bernadette proved to be impossible. From behind, I couldn't distinguish her from the other blue-robed, white-veiled nuns she was sitting with.

And for another thing, my uncle wasn't even running the show today. Reverend Monsignor Kline led the procession up to the altar and stood center-stage while Uncle Bryan stayed respectfully off to one side. "Peace be with you," Kline said to the congregation, and when the crowd chorused back, "And with your spirit," they sounded extra hearty. "It's a pleasure to be with you today," Kline added. There wasn't a scripted response for that, more just a low hum of enthusiasm from the parishioners. I could sense everyone paying close attention as Kline said, "Let us pray," and started reading from the book that the blond altar boy held out to him.

One person who *didn't* look blissed out was Deacon Jameson. I hoped that he'd be beaming, ecstatic over his hookup with Dima. Instead he seemed fully focused, a grimace on his face, like he was praying extra hard. For some reason, that made me tremendously sad. I had a feeling he'd be confessing to my uncle tonight when everyone was long gone and it felt safe. I was certain of that. And I needed to get headphones or something, because that was one confession I *didn't* want to hear.

There was a flash of motion. Dima sat down next to me. "Hey," he whispered. "I got a flat. I hope I didn't miss too much." He was smiling like always, only this time his smile was like glass, a fissure in its corner. Soon it would spider-web out and finally shatter.

"Hey," I replied, looking from him to Deacon Jameson and back. Deacon Jameson's eyes darted toward him once before returning to where Monsignor Kline preached. Clearly, something had happened since I saw them kiss. Something bad. "You all right?"

"Yeah," he said in the way that suggested the opposite.

We sat as people stepped up for Communion. Dima didn't budge.

"Aren't you going to go up?"

"Can't. Not until I confess. I don't deserve Communion today," he said without looking at me.

The urge to comfort him hit me hard. Gently, quietly, I said, "What you did wasn't bad."

"How do you know what I did?"

I froze up.

He tilted his head up, eyes rolling back. "The park. Of course. It was the stupid park."

"I left as soon as I saw," I said. "I didn't tell anyone."

"You wouldn't. Because you're like me, right?" He twisted toward me in the pew.

I hesitated. I wasn't prepared for this. "It's complicated, but sort of."

"Sort of? What do you mean 'sort of'?" His voice dropped to a softer whisper. "Like you . . . like both?"

Not quite, I wanted to say. But I didn't. Someone a few pews down glanced at us. I lowered my voice and leaned toward his ear. "Can I explain somewhere that's not here? Trying to stay on the downlow."

"Ah, so no one knows?" he asked breathlessly, almost eagerly. Like we'd share some big secret.

I winced. I couldn't lie to him. Not about that. "They know. Just—later? Is that okay?"

He nodded vigorously. Then he reached out, his large hand closing around mine with obvious desperation. I squeezed back. I couldn't remember the last time I'd held hands with someone I wasn't dating. As kids, we did it all the time. Everything was simple then. But we got older, and suddenly holding hands was only permitted for couples. Nothing to do with comfort. A few times at conventions, people reached for mine, but I evaded their touch.

Except with Lee. I always made exceptions for him.

I ran my thumb over the back of Dima's hand, marveling at each vein, each boney knuckle, and how warm he was. How a platonic gesture could be so intimate. We stayed silent. He seemed comforted, and for once I felt needed as Alexis. Dima didn't know about boy-me. And although my ego took a hit, there was something comforting about that. A few gay cis-guys had issues when they found out what I was born with. They recoiled. They questioned their identity. They wouldn't accept me either way.

Keeping Aleks a secret from Dima was the safest thing for me to do. Even if it made me a liar. And Alexis finally had a friend. Alexis finally could help someone. I couldn't ruin that. So what if I said I'd explain my deal later and then changed my mind? I hadn't committed to anything, had I? Would he even remember to ask me about myself when his mind was so clouded with grief, when he was stuck between loving someone and being true to his beliefs? Maybe he'd forget. Then I wouldn't have to lie.

By the time Mass was over, a line was already forming by the confessional. Dima squeezed my hand as he stood up, his intent clear.

"You didn't do anything wrong," I repeated.

"Yeah, I did. I talked him into it."

"It looked really mutual."

He snorted. "Like that makes it okay."

"Dima—"

"Look, you don't get it." His voice turned harsh. "You know what, just leave me alone." With that, he pulled away from me to insert himself in the line.

My body moved of its own accord as I slipped out of the

church. I stared across the road toward the cemetery, half-wishing I were a trapped spirit among the headstones.

Someone bumped into me. "Sorry," he muttered, not slowing his pace. It was the blond altar boy. He looked just as dead as I felt. He crossed the yard directly to where Deacon Jameson was standing. Side by side, they walked away from the church parishioners.

As they moved, heads bowed together to whisper, Deacon Jameson clenched his fists. His hands gripped the boy's shoulders, digging in as he bent over, looking him dead in the eye as he said something. It was intense. I needed to get closer. I needed to hear. Biting my lip, I started to edge toward them.

I felt a hand close around my wrist. I turned to Sister Bernadette. For once, she looked furious. "That is not your business."

"That kid, the altar boy—"

"That is *not* your business," she reiterated, possibly even more harshly than before. "That's between Michael, Deacon Jameson, and God."

So the altar boy had a name. Michael. It was weird hearing her say Deacon Jameson when not around the kids. She'd so easily called him Joey. But this degree of anger, of ferociousness . . .

I looked down. "Sorry. I wanted to help."

Sister Bernadette took a quick breath. I could almost hear her counting to ten to calm herself. "You need to give people their privacy. There needs to be trust in this community."

I thought about listening in to the confessions and shuddered. If she knew . . .

She added, "Sometimes there are things you can't fix, Alexis."

My mouth was so dry, my tongue felt too large to fit in it. I was barely aware of speaking. "Aleks. My name today is Aleks."

She cocked her head, the veil gaping just enough for me to see a bit of her black, curly hair. I wanted to tug a lock free and twist it around my finger. I tried to shove my hands in my pockets, remembering then that I was wearing a dress. I felt way more out of place and ugly than I had before.

"I was going to tell you before but, uh—well. This is weird." I took a deep breath. It wasn't like I hadn't told people I was bigender before, but she was different. Her opinion seemed to matter so much more. That meant my explanation had to be that much clearer. There wasn't room for error. "So I'm bigender. Before you ask, it means that sometimes I'm a girl and sometimes I'm a guy. Today I'm a guy. Aleks."

She kept quiet for a while. "So it's sort of like being transgender?"

"Kind of."

"How do I know when you're a boy or girl?"

I paused. I'd never actually been asked that question before. A lot of times people asked me how *I* knew but not how *they* were supposed to. "Um." Well. How *was* anyone here supposed to know? It wasn't like Sister Bernadette was going to see me in my guy clothes.

"You could ask," I said. "I don't expect people to just instinctively figure it out. It's not like I get super butch when I'm a guy, you know?"

"I don't know. That's why I asked."

I flushed a bit. I didn't have the answers she needed, and everyone varied so drastically. If I was the first bigender person she'd met, would she assume anyone who was bigender was just like me? Would I become the default? I didn't want to be anyone's default. Ever. If I was her primary frame of reference, I wouldn't be invisible. I needed to be safe. "So are you going to talk about me needing to see the light? Because if so, I'm really not interested. I'm happy."

But that wasn't the right word. Content? Not right either. Was there even a word to describe how I felt?

"I'm not pushing my faith on you," she said. "Trust me on that. My relationship with God is mine, yours is different. It's as simple as that." She paused. "Does your uncle know?"

"Yeah. Part of the deal with me coming here was that they knew and they wouldn't push me to change. I guess it doesn't count as 'not pushing' if it's in a homily."

"Why do you come to Mass?" she asked. "If it offends you all the time, why do you bother?"

"I have to. Part of the terms of me staying here."

"Probably explains why he's been preaching extra about gender roles and sexuality," she murmured. After another moment she added, "Thank you. For telling me."

"Of course," I said. Because what else was there *to* say? Exude confidence. Ride it out. Be everything Alexis is not. Ignore the self-loathing. "I'm just glad you don't—hate me."

"I don't think I could hate you. But none of that sneaking around listening to people's private business, understood?"

Kind of hard not to, I refrained from saying. A little lie wouldn't hurt. And was it a lie if I was just omitting some details that may or may not have been relevant? She didn't need to know why I listened to people's sins. I didn't want credit for playing Raziel. Anonymity was the key. It was a little secret just for me.

She smiled, but not for long. It was like her eyes lost focus on me. She gazed into the distance. "I need to go. God bless." She left me in a hurry, fabric of her skirt whipping behind her as she pattered along the walkway that led back toward the church entrance.

Reverend Monsignor Kline was surrounded by a growing crowd, smiling as he squeezed hands, presumably blessing people. There was an emotion radiating off of Sister Bernadette. It was so strong, it was unmistakable: fear.

I hugged my waist, having a pretty good idea about what the fear stemmed from—talking with a "sinner" like me. If anyone else here found out I was bigender and queer, she'd probably be judged for associating with me. Church leaders might even reprimand her. Although Reverend Monsignor Kline had been friendly to my face, Sister Bernadette had essentially warned me that he believed in the right to hate people like me.

There was a time when I used to crave hate. How messed up is that? It wasn't long after I had the bigender revelation. I must have been thirteen, fourteen. I wore my boy-clothes, bound my chest, wore my packer. I just *had* to pass as male on those days. There was no other option. I'd add a lisp and be as goddamn fucking fabulous as I could be. I'd look people in the eye in the school hallways or the mall food court, daring them to scoff, grinning perversely whenever someone shoved into me saying "faggot" in my ear. That meant I passed. I was part of the club. I was real enough to be hated in a group instead of ignored as an individual.

Now it made me sick. I was so naïve then, such a baby enby. I didn't know about internalized transphobia, and even now I still struggled with that same body dysmorphia. My decision to not present as male didn't weaken that need. If anything, it became stronger. Fiercer. The voice in my head way meaner.

Through the parishioners orbiting around him, Reverend Monsignor Kline spotted me. A broad smile spread across his face. How much did he know? Had my uncle told him about me, or was I just Alexis to him?

The Reverend Monsignor wove through the crowd before extending his hand. "Alexis, how did you like the homily today?" he asked with such tenderness I was taken aback. An aura of warmth surrounded him. It was impossible not to smile back, and impossible not to wonder why Sister Bernadette and Deacon Jameson seemed so off-balance around him. Could they have misjudged him?

I took his hand, not sure how to answer his question since I'd tuned out my uncle as best as I could. "I, uh, didn't realize you'd be doing it instead of my uncle. It was—you're a really good speaker."

He actually laughed. "Maybe someday soon you'll be taking Communion."

"Uh. I'm not Catholic."

"Yet."

"I'm, uh, I'm not a good candidate for it. Really. But, uh, good for you all. You do you."

Reverend Monsignor Kline laughed again as he released my hand after a tight squeeze. "You really are something else, Alexis. Your uncle wasn't joking when he said you were different."

He looked me in the eye. Although the energy around him was still warm, goosebumps rose on my arms.

Stop being so paranoid.
You're looking for reasons to be miserable.
Such an Alexis thing to do.
I'm disappointed in you.
Coward.
Faux-trans.
Fool.

"I'm going to greet the others," Kline said. "I'm glad you're here, Alexis. Truly. I know your uncle and aunt are as well. They're blessed to have you in their home. Peace be with you and God bless."

I took in the crowd. Everyone seemed happy and far away from me. As soon as the Monsignor left my side, I became invisible, which was what I wanted. And inexplicably lonely, which I didn't want quite so much. The chill never left. It got worse despite the hot summer sun. I was in a group, a large group, and yet I was so alone. So disconnected, it physically hurt.

Suddenly Dima stormed out through the church doors, face red. He was too far away for me to call out for him. My limbs felt too heavy to run after him, to ask for his number so I could at least text him and see how I could help. Because one thing was clear: confession with my uncle had *not* gone well.

I turned around. Sister Bernadette had disappeared in a sea of blue habits. With her back to me, she was indistinguishable.

Something didn't feel right. The peacefulness of the morning felt as fragile as porcelain, like it'd only be a matter of time before everything was smashed to pieces.

14 ALEKS

Aunt Anne Marie tapped on my door and poked her head in. "Alexis?"

Aleks, I wanted to say. I didn't bother. There was no point in trying. No matter how many times I corrected her, she would misgender me twice as much in response.

"You have a visitor." Her tone was polite but less than thrilled.

I sat upright on my bed. Aunt Anne Marie stepped aside and there he was in the doorframe: Dima. In his hands, a plushie of Haniel, the archangel of joy from *Synthetica*. It was absolutely adorable, with outstretched arms that made her look ready to give anyone a hug. He walked in and handed it to me. "This is for you."

I looked at him, perplexed. "Wha—"

"I'm sorry," he said. "About what I said right after Mass . . ." His voice trailed off. I followed his eyes to the bedroom door, where my aunt hovered.

I cleared my throat. "Can we, uh, can we have a little privacy, Aunt Anne Marie?"

"I'm not sure how appropriate it is for a young woman and young man to hang out together in a bedroom," Aunt Anne

138

Marie said guardedly. Was that a part of Catholicism or a part of her? Had she always been so . . . rigid? How would she act if she knew I'd had sex before? Or that my parents were cool with it?

Dima glanced over his shoulder at my aunt. "If it's any comfort, Mrs. Moore, I can promise that I'd *never* be interested in dating your niece."

Niece—a reminder that he didn't know.

Never interested—something that made my aunt look like she wanted to puke.

Shockingly, Aunt Anne Marie shut the door. I gestured to the bed and Dima sat on the end of it, flopping back.

"It's hard, you know? The . . ." he struggled. "The gay stuff. It's hard. You know what that's like, right?"

"Honestly?" I rubbed my hands. "It's probably not what you're going to want to hear, but not really. My parents are pretty chill about me being queer and bigender. My aunt and uncle—"

"Bigender?"

I flinched. Damn. I'd half-hoped we wouldn't actually get into this. But I'd said the word anyway, I hadn't just said *queer*, and it didn't seem fair to either of us to try to walk that back now.

I took a deep breath. "Sometimes I'm a girl, sometimes I'm a guy. When I'm a guy, I use the name Aleks. A-L-E-K-S."

"That's Russian." He looked more surprised by that than by the gender reveal.

"I know."

"Huh. Why'd you go with that instead of just A-L-E-X?"

Random question, but okay. "A lot of girls are Alex with an X. I felt like I needed something else to distinguish me.

Insecurity, I guess. Most of the bigender people I've met online do the same. My dad thought I was a bit dramatic. I kind of am."

"That's cool," Dima said. "Also we spell it way better." He turned on his side. We were so close, I could almost feel his breath. It was absolutely incredible to have this amount of intimacy despite a lack of physical contact. Was this what a healthy friendship was supposed to be? "So why did you come here? If your parents are cool with you—I mean, I swear, your aunt was about ready to chase me out until she saw I had something for you. Then I think she hoped I was trying to date you. It'd be a great cover-up."

Oh no . . . please please please don't let this be about me becoming a beard . . .

"I don't do cover-ups," I said.

"Neither do I. But you have to admit, it'd be a great one." That hazy smirk came to his face before his eyes snagged on something. Before I could ask what, he was on his feet, rummaging through the open closet door.

"Hey! Don't—"

"This is cosplay," he said. "You do cosplay?"

Shit. I knew exactly where he was going with this. Since it's for fun, you'd make me stuff for free, right? No? You charge what? It's cheaper from China. Don't I get a friend discount?

"Did. Not anymore."

"You've got a sewing machine."

"So does my aunt."

"You know, I've always wanted to cosplay."

"It's kind of expensive and—"

"Dude, relax. I've got a job. I could afford it. But sort of seems . . ." He frowned. "I don't know. I don't think I'd want to go alone. None of my friends are into that. And Joey—Deacon Jameson—I don't think he'd want to. Not that he's ever free. He's always working or doing homework or writing papers or in class or volunteering at prisons."

I frowned. "I kind of assumed you hung out a lot. I mean, you looked really familiar with each other."

Dima smiled, but it was bitter. "We used to hang out a lot more. He helped out with some stuff at school, different music programs, chorus."

"He sings?"

"Yeah. He's all right," Dima said in the way that suggested Deacon Jameson was incredible. "Plays lute because why stick to only guitar when you can be that extra?"

"So he likes showing off?"

"He likes showing off to me." He smiled. It was wistful. "He's obsessed with Gregorian chants. If I tell him I like a song, even casually in passing, I know I'll get a text with audio of him covering it as a Gregorian chant. Cool party trick."

Curious now, I asked, "Do you sing?"

That same smirk crossed his face. "Oh, yeah. Except no one wants to hear me sing. Even Joey—Deacon Jameson. He kept trying to suggest I do something that was for 'the less musically inclined.' But if I did that, that'd mean I'd never get to see him."

"So what'd you do?"

"Obviously I signed up for every single music class he was involved in."

I couldn't help it. I burst out laughing. "You did not."

"Swear, I did!" Dima pressed his hand over his heart, laughing hard. "He got me back once he realized I was trolling him. He told me I was the first chair for the triangle."

"No way."

"Swear to God."

"First chair too? Out of how many people?"

"That's the best part. It was *only* me." Dima's face lit up. "I decided to do a mean-ass solo once. He cut me off partway through and announced to the class that I was permanently demoted to wood block."

I couldn't help it. I howled laughing. My sides ached as I gasped for breath. "What—what could you do in a band with—with that?"

"Absolutely *nothing*. Clergy members seriously are the best trolls ever." He returned to the bed, dropping onto it. "Sorry, I shouldn't be . . . I shouldn't gush."

"It's fine," I said. And that was true. It was actually pretty nice hearing someone talk about being in love and that love being healthy. Aside from the fact that both parties involved considered that love a sin. "So you two—has it been going on for a while?"

"Depends on what you mean by a while." He flopped onto his back. "He actually transferred me out of his classes last year because he said we were too close. Forced me to take different electives. I didn't want to, but he told me to look him in the eye and tell him if I truly wanted to be a musician. I couldn't lie to him, so I just reminded him the legal age of consent here is sixteen. Obviously that didn't help my case. And it's not like he was wrong. It was tough to be alone with him. Every little touch was electrifying."

I shifted uncomfortably on the bed. "Did he try anything?"

"You're kidding, right?"

"You said *touch*."

"Oh, God, no. Not like that. Like bumping into each other, or him pointing to my sheet music when my hand was

142

right there." He laughed bitterly. "I asked him for a kiss on my eighteenth birthday. He said no. Who does that? Denying my birthday kiss, phsh."

My heart pounded, the pulse throbbing in my ears, hard and loud. Like the drumming of thunder.

It's just a kiss . . .

"Then in the park—I don't know how it started."

It just . . . happened.

"Which is weird when I think about it. How do you not remember something so intimate?"

We were walking . . . weren't we?

"I mean, I've only ever kissed three other people but I remember all those first kisses. What was said, what was worn. With him? I can't remember how it started. It really bugs me."

His mouth was warm . . . so warm.

Dima flushed. "That makes no sense, probably. Anything like that ever happen to you?"

His fingers were cold . . .

My stomach turned. I couldn't speak but nodded.

Don't ask, don't ask, don't ask, please don't ask . . .

"Okay, that's a relief," Dima said.

He didn't ask. *That* was a relief.

"Confession really sucked," Dima said, continuing without a breath. "Your uncle wanted me to say who. I didn't. God's not going to be happy with me for that one."

"Maybe that's God's problem and not yours," I said.

"I don't think that's how it works." He sighed. "Maybe it would help to have something else to focus on besides my sins. What do you think?"

I forced myself to look at Dima. Really look. He was seeking something from me. I wasn't sure what.

"Maybe we could go to a con," Dima said. "Like you and me. I've always wanted to go to one."

Danger.

Dima sat upright and pulled out his phone. Before I could wrap my mind around the hairpin turn this conversation had taken, he was searching away. "Looks like there are a few next weekend . . ."

"No," I said, surprised at how harsh the word came out. I cleared my throat. I knew exactly which one was this weekend. Seeing the perplexed look on his face, I said, "I can't go to Ureshii-con. Personal reason."

"Ureshii-con?" He raised his eyebrow, glancing at his phone then back at me. "That's like five hours from here."

"So?"

"Why would anyone drive five hours to a convention?"

It took a moment to recollect myself. Right. He'd never been to a convention. He'd never cosplayed. There was no way for him to know. Did that mean that he didn't have many friends? That was hard to imagine since he was so gregarious, ludicrously attractive, and funny.

"That's . . . literally what all of us do," I said gently. "I mean did."

". . . drive five hours . . . to go to a convention?"

"Yup."

"But *why*?"

"We just . . . do." A wave of embarrassment washed over me, as well as the need to defend myself. "We see friends there. There are panels, viewings, a dealer's room and artist alley. Usually my friends and I would just hang out in cosplay.

Sometimes we'd roleplay and call each other by our character names the entire weekend."

"Sorry, I missed all of that because I still can't get over the five-hour drive part," he admitted. "Five hours, *seriously*? Then you'd need a hotel and all of these other expenses."

"I told you, it wasn't cheap."

"Like making a costume. *That* I get because you have something to keep. Like how much is fabric anyway?"

"Depends on what you're making."

"Okay, so . . ." He got up and walked to my closet, making himself at home yet again.

"Dima, come on—"

He rummaged through the packed collection before pulling out one of my cosplays for Jay from *Synthetica*. My blood went cold.

Not that one. Any costume except that.

My chest was tight, pulse so strong it throbbed in my neck as I eyed the torn white shirt, bandage-wrapped pants, and harness with mechanical wings. Why hadn't I put it up for sale on my store? Why had I kept it?

"So like, how much would something like this cost?"

I couldn't speak.

He ran his hand over the costume. My esophagus tightened. *Stop.* He traced and studied each seam, like he was trying to figure out the mechanics. *Stop.* His hand moved to the harness, to the broken wings.

"Like this can't be one of those ones you see online for ninety bucks, right?"

"No way," I had said, voice hitching with a nervous laugh.

Chants had echoed back at me. "You have to! You have to!"

So I did.

There was a tap on the door. Aunt Anne Marie poked her head in. I'd never felt so relieved. "Everything going okay?"

"Everything's fine," Dima said. "Was asking Aleks about a convention next weekend. I didn't know he cosplayed."

I closed my eyes. If they were shut, I didn't need to see him hold the costume. Then I could consider his words. He'd gotten the name and pronoun right the first go. And to say that to my aunt's face, knowing what she was like . . .

"Does that mean you and Alexis will be making new costumes?"

My eyes shot open. Dima was no longer holding the costume. It must have disappeared back in my closet. And my aunt was there, some sort of eagerness on her face. No trace of the wariness she'd shown toward Dima just a few minutes ago.

"If we go, do you think there'd be time to make something?" Dima asked her. "I've got work and I need to help out Deacon Jameson."

"Maybe I could help." She was so timid, I thought I must have misheard her.

"That'd be awesome." Dima's face lit up, and so did my aunt's.

Could a person flip that quickly? Wasn't it only last week that she believed costumes were demonic?

Maybe she was so desperately lonely that any sort of friendliness won her over. It wasn't like she had much company here. The other priests didn't have wives for her to hang out with. And parishioners probably weren't too keen on gossiping or sharing secrets with her, in case it all got back to Uncle Bryan. She hadn't mentioned any friends, any hobbies or activities outside attending church. Maybe she was happy just to be included in something.

Dima looked at me. "Well? Are you in? I was thinking this one. It's only a half hour drive." He handed me his phone, and I looked at the page he'd pulled up. It was the homepage for a convention I'd never heard of.

Think. I needed to think. This con that Dima had suggested was something very local. Small. Relatively dinky. Maybe a college event.

That wasn't the sort of place any of my friends, I mean former friends, would know about. They wouldn't go. Especially not when a big con was happening the exact same weekend.

He would be at Ureshii-con, not here.

"Okay," I said. *Just once. It'll be okay.*

15 ALEXIS

Mom and Dad took me to my first convention when I was fourteen. Apparently Mom used to go to them when she was in her early twenties, but they weren't on the same scale. Like small sci-fi ones, I think.

For my first convention, I was nervous about the idea of cosplaying, but my parents encouraged me. They said we'd do it all together, one of the rare times when Dad was home for a few months, us three versus the world. I was the Grim Reaper from *What You Sow*, an anime revolving around the relationship between a young, nameless girl and the reaper who was to take her to the unknown. My costume took about a month to make. I had enormous retractable wings on my back that I'd made with a pulley system, and I created low stilts for height. The inside of my hood was lined with luminescent bulbs and el wire that I could operate with a handheld remote control.

I thought Mom and Dad would dress up as other characters from the show since they saw my process and periodically helped out with tools. But no. I was mistaken. Rather than do a serious cosplay, Mom and Dad decided they'd go as Bruce Wayne's dead parents. They thought it was *hilarious* to photobomb every Batman photoshoot by shouting, "Bruuuuuuuuce!"

and diving on the floor, pretending to be dead while I loomed above them. Honestly it was pretty funny and most of the Batmans would crack up.

I wasn't as good a stitcher back then, but I was good enough to get the attention of a small group of people, some with rainbow bands around their wrists. And they approached us cautiously, cells and cameras in hand as they asked permission to take our pictures. They lingered after taking the photos and I was clueless until Dad whispered, "They want to talk to you."

So I talked to them.

They asked me everything. Was I a boy or girl? Bigender? What's that? You're a really beautiful boy. That's a compliment! You want to hang out with us? Let's friend each other. You're so cool. And they talked so, so much that I didn't realize my parents had drifted off until they came back, asking if I wanted to stop by the dealer's room because they were closing in thirty minutes.

I couldn't stop laughing and smiling and I was so, so, so happy.

For the first time in my life, I belonged.

I could be anyone. I could pretend.

So for every convention after that, I'd pretended that I was their permanent *bishonen*—the beautiful boy—and all the girls thought I was cute, so cute. When I was a boy, I mean.

> **Exploitation.**
> **It was exploitation.**
> **You were viewed as a sexual object.**
> **It's not right.**

Was the voice actually being supportive?

Well, it was wrong. For me, at those moments, people's reactions felt so right. I *liked* being viewed as a sexual object. Being seen as a beautiful boy. Not an ugly girl, or someone who was completely incompetent when straddling the gray space of binary gender roles.

> **You're allowed to change your mind.**
> **That's Consent 101.**
>
> **Idiot.**

There. That sounded more like the voice I was used to.

†††

I'd forgotten the magic of a first convention. By the time Dima and I arrived at the small hotel where the con was happening, I was rolling my eyes at some of the cheaply made costumes. In our *Synthetica* cosplays—me as Raziel, Dima as Aaron Swatson—we'd easily outshine the people who used hot glue on the seams or bought cheap, premade things from China. But Dima practically leaped out of the car the second he parked. He sprinted across the parking lot before I could stop him, arms waving wildly. "EXCUSE ME! CAN I TAKE MY PICTURE WITH YOU?"

I got out of the car more slowly, checked myself in the mirrors to make sure my costume was fitted, then walked to Dima's side. These people's costumes were poorly constructed with broadcloth and cheap linen. I could see where they'd used permanent marker to trace the pattern instead of chalk. The closure was Velcro. And—

"Aren't they amazing?" Dima asked me excitedly. "They made Bo Brightshine and Dr. Steevius by themselves!"

"Your costumes are so much better," one girl said shyly.

"Pfft, they don't count." My head snapped to Dima. Did he just insult my work after I busted my ass sewing costumes for two instead of one? "Alexis has been at this for so long, it was like hiring a professional. I couldn't even begin to do something like this."

So he wasn't insulting my work. He complimented me, *and* he complimented someone else.

I looked at the girls, taking in their costumes. They'd improvised with what they had, clearly with limited resources and skills. The attention to detail, however, was spot on. There was love poured into every inch of those costumes. Pride. Like they were the people who truly loved *Attack Girl Tokyo* more than anyone because they'd done everything they could to be the *character*, not everything they could to be the *best*.

Shame swept over me as I compared that to my Raziel cosplay, with its elaborate theatrical pieces, its monstrous wings with eyes. I'd spent so much time trying to make everything perfect, I hadn't encouraged Dima to embellish more on his own. He could have. He probably would have had more fun too, even though he'd been perfectly content sitting next to me or Aunt Anne Marie, watching the whir of the machine, captivated by our work and occasionally trying it on for a better fit.

Maybe this was what I'd been missing out on with my cosplay group. The chance to just enjoy the experience, instead of constantly performing.

Maybe with a friend like Dima, I could learn.

†††

151

I stepped out of the bathroom. Great. Dima was *not* waiting outside like he'd said he would. I spotted him down the hall, phone out, grabbing selfies. Oblivious to the hoard of girls pressed up to him. Or at least pretending to be oblivious. It was hard to tell.

Someone bumped into me. "Sorry," they said. I twisted to let them past when something caught the corner of my eye. That fabric—

Time stopped.

My chest rattling with each breath like I'd swallowed gravel. Thunder in my ears.

I stared at the cosplayer's back. Slowly, they turned around. Brown skin. Not white. A girl, not an overwhelmingly cis-het boy. A stranger.

Not Lee.

There was pressure on my side. I yelped and spun around, fists raised defensively, prepared to strike. "Whoa, easy!" Dima said, stepping back.

My heart still raced. "Don't *do* that. Sneak up on me like that. Jesus."

"Yeah, okay. Got it. Do you have the phone charger? I'm running low. Do you wanna go to the *Fever 33* panel in twenty minutes? Man, I wish Joey were here too. I can't wait to show him all of the pics. I'd text him but I think I should upload them to social media first and see how long before he notices. He always pretends he doesn't use it ever, but I think he's faking it. What do you think about that?"

"Sounds . . . okay . . ." I murmured. But really, I wasn't sure. My mind was still on the cosplayer, the one who'd reminded me so much of Lee.

"Hey." Dima looked concerned now. "What's wrong?"

"It's stupid."

"Obviously not that stupid because you're upset. Talk to me."

I hesitated. The idea of even vocalizing it . . . "I kind of wonder if this was a mistake. Coming here."

"What? Why? I thought you were having a good time," Dima said, shocked. "Is it because I ditched you when you were in the bathroom? Because I thought with the wings you'd take longer and I totally got carried away and there were so many people with amazing costumes—"

"No. No, it's not . . ." I sighed. "I've just got a lot of bad memories and, well . . ." I squirmed. "I thought it'd get better. And that was stupid. No matter how much I try to run away, to get away from it, it's lingering there."

"I don't think I understand," Dima said.

"It's like—if there's something that's toxic . . . a lot of people put up with it. They say they won't get caught up in it. But they can't avoid it. Maybe it's sort of like being an alcoholic. You can't just drink occasionally and not be an addict anymore. You have to cut it out, completely. Be sober. Abstain. Like . . . you get what I'm saying?"

I could see the excitement dissolve from Dima's face with each word I said. His mood crashed visibly. "Maybe we should go," he said.

I thought about the panel he wanted to go to, but I didn't have it in me to suggest we stay longer. We walked to his car in silence, Dima not really looking at me. In the car, he turned up his music before I could say a word. I rested my head against the window as the scenery passed.

Remorse swept through me. I shouldn't have said anything. Maybe I'd had a traumatic experience, but he hadn't. This was his first con. I'd yanked away the magic of the experience.

And beyond that—Dima might have been the first person I'd met who was relatively well-adjusted, who was *safe*, and who was into the same things I was into. If I kept my mouth shut, maybe we could have geeked out more. I could have learned to really love something for what it was instead of focusing solely on proving myself. We could've had fun together. One of those platonic relationships I'd never really experienced. Friendship.

But by the time he dropped me off at the front doors of the rectory, barely replying when I thanked him for the trip, I knew that I'd missed my chance. Before I could say so much as "sorry," he was gone.

16 ALEXIS

Sleep was my go-to when things got tough. Being unconscious meant there were fewer hours to be awake and depressed. Dreamless sleep was the best, although rare for me. It'd take hours out of the day, shortening the emotional storm that was brewing.

But since we'd gotten back from the con, I'd been sleeping worse than usual. I kept thinking about opening my online shop and immediately getting that message: *I'm sorry.*

I dreamed about walking into that cosplayer. Except in my dream, it wasn't some random person.

It was Lee.

Lee was . . . I don't even know what Lee was. One day, he was just there. He integrated with our group perfectly. The one who spoke our language. The "woke" white cis-het dude who was the "good guy," the "ally." No one could remember a time without him, even though once I looked online and there wasn't a trace of him before February of last year.

The winter comic convention: my friends were infiltrating it in their anime cosplays because it was *so* funny (Narrator: *It was NOT funny*), but I thought I'd fit the theme for once. So at the hotel, when I pulled out my surprise Ice Siren costume, my friends didn't know what to think.

"But she's a girl."

So?

"Why are you going as a woman?"

I felt like I should have given them a multiple-choice answer sheet:

a. The costume is super cool.
b. I didn't want to freeze my ass off during outdoor photoshoots.
c. Ice Siren is absolutely fierce, except holy hell, did she have the worst boyfriend EVER with Fire Night.
d. I want to. Leave me alone.

I guess they wouldn't have been okay with any of those answers. Internalized sexism, internalized homophobia, who knows what sort of issues they triggered. Nope, they couldn't handle me as female because that'd mean the girls weren't as straight as they thought they were, or they couldn't handle me suddenly not being attractive to them.

So I separated from my group for the first time in at least a year. I didn't want to deal with their whining about how I wasn't being a team player. In my toasty cosplay, I trekked through the snow outside, away from the traditional photoshoot area.

That's when I saw him. Dressed as Fire Night and goofing off with a couple of his friends as they ran around in the snow, knocking each other over, taking turns with their phones to record it. They were making a CMV—cosplay music video—or just some silly takes for fun. We barely made eye contact when he said, "Hey, Alexis! Or uh, Aleks? Sorry, I should have asked first," and, "Want to help with our video?" I had so much fun as we posed for photos, goofing off wildly. Then Lee brought me to their hotel room, where he'd smuggled in alcohol to make jungle juice, and that was it.

I think.

With Lee, one could never be too sure. There were always a few little things that were off. Like how he'd slide his hand on my hip. How he'd tug me away from my other friends into small, quiet halls. The way he'd block my path, maintaining as much eye contact as possible so I would see him, *only* him, in whatever cosplay he was in, as whatever character he was. "I love you," he'd say. When I'd return it, he'd say more loudly, "No. Really. I *love* you."

He told me that he needed me. That I was his best friend. That he couldn't believe how amazing I was, how talented. Sometimes we sat next to each other on the floor, backs to the wall, watching cosplayers pass as we held hands, fingers linked together. Silent, almost invisible. Until someone would glance down and squeal about fan service and Lee would grin and say, "It's show time."

He's socially awkward.

He doesn't get boundaries.

It's not like you said "no."

Weren't you dating?

I'm positive you were dating.

I don't remember who, but somebody told me, "He's not your friend." Funny how that was probably the most important social advice I'd ever received, and now I couldn't remember who'd sent that message.

But I remembered the other messages. The ones my friends showed me after the fact.

LEE: Did you know Alexis is MTF? Pre-op.
PERSON 1: Wowwwww. Uh, are you aware of how transphobic that is?
PERSON 2: Also bullshit. Aleks/Alexis wasn't born cismale, you cockweed.
LEE: Swear to God. She told me herself.
LEE: I'm only telling you for your protection.
PERSON 1: WTF, Lee?
LEE: She told me that once she had her surgery, she wanted me to be the first dick inside her pussy. How am I supposed to say no?

I didn't believe it until my friends—former friends— showed me the screen caps. And for a split-second I thought, *Someone thought I was MTF instead of FTM? That's a first!*

And then the humiliation set in. And it all came crashing down, down, down . . .

Rustling sounds on the other side of the wall vent drew my attention. I glanced at my phone for the time. Two in the morning. I squeezed my eyes shut. Who had done something so bad they just couldn't wait until morning to confess? After getting reprimanded by Sister Bernadette, the last thing I wanted was to hear a confession. Couldn't I cry in peace? Couldn't I have some degree of privacy?

"Father, forgive me, for I have sinned," a voice whispered in a low register. It was almost impossible to distinguish the words.

Ignore it.

Mind your own business.

But there was something about the tone . . .

Unable to resist, I slid beneath the bed, putting my ear to the grate instead of remaining in bed. If anything could distract me from Lee, this would be it. If I helped enough people, he'd be erased from my mind.

"You need to stop doing this." A voice. My uncle.

"I'm trying my best."

"Try harder, please."

Please? My uncle, the man who regularly tore people to shreds, said *please?*

"I'm here, aren't I?"

My uncle made a sound like he was sucking in a breath. I tried to picture his face, the grave disappointment that surely was there. Why was he so hesitant? My uncle was the type to eviscerate people for their sins. He was blunt, impatient, even angry. A priest's version of tough love. "What happened?"

"I did it again."

"Say it. God can't forgive you otherwise."

There was a long pause. "I engaged in a lustful encounter."

Lustful encounter? That seemed pretty tame in comparison to some confessions. My uncle sucked in another breath. It was almost like he was scared. "It was more than an encounter."

"I know."

"You need to acknowledge that."

Silence.

My uncle's voice definitely quavered. "Tell me what happened. Please."

"He wanted it," the person said. "I could tell he did."

Goosebumps rose on my skin.

You wanted it.

        You were asking for it.
You never said no.

"He was just so pretty, and right there . . ."
Pretty boy.
"What happened?" my uncle asked softly.
"I gave him Communion."
A copper taste rubbed over my tongue. Bitter. Thick.
"What do you mean by Communion?" my uncle asked. My palms were sweaty. I was pretty sure he wasn't talking about wafers and wine.
Beautiful boy.
"Do we really need to do this again?"
My uncle hesitated. *Again.* Unmistakable fear in his voice. "This is a huge sin. You need to be fully honest with me so I can help you."
"I am. You know exactly how I gave him Communion."
I envisioned drinking wine, taking a wafer on the tongue. Accepting the body and blood of Jesus Christ and the Holy Spirit. "The same way I give Communion to the best boys," the voice continued.
And suddenly I realized just what the sinner meant by Communion.
Fists balled up, I choked on bile. Sweat coated my back, slick and wet.
A priest. The man talking to my uncle was a fellow priest. A priest who'd . . .
"He's not even fourteen," my uncle said, voice quivering.
No. No, this was not happening. Not here. This wasn't like the places in the news. This was a place with some cool people,

like Sister Bernadette, Dima, and Deacon Jameson. And . . .
And . . .

My mind spun like a tilt-a-whirl. And I hated carnival rides
to begin with.

I waited for my uncle to say this guy needed to turn himself in to the police. Probably quietly, but still. I'd look up
arrest records. There were online memberships to sites that
did background checks, and surely that information was public. And once I found it, it'd be everywhere. To hell with my
avoidance of social media. I'd make it go viral. I'd use my
cosplay accounts. I'd make sure no one was near this abuser
again.

Instead, my uncle said, "I see your remorse. God forgives
you for this grievous sin, but you need to stop doing this. You
have to stop."

Forgiveness? Wait, what?

I scrambled out from beneath the bed too quickly, smash-
ing my head against the metal frame. I staggered, disoriented
and practically wild with fury. My head throbbed. Forgiveness?
My uncle was offering a predator *forgiveness*? He hadn't for-
given Elizabeth for hitting her brother in desperation, he hadn't
offered to help her find an organization or outside resources for
help, yet he forgave a priest for abusing a thirteen-year-old?
Letting a criminal walk away, absolved . . .

No. No way. I wasn't going to let that happen. Maybe my
uncle was a coward, but I wasn't.

I opened my bedroom door. In my socks, I took off toward
the back door. I only managed to get halfway there when my
aunt appeared in front of me. "Where are you going?"

I froze. "I. Uh. Just wanted some fresh air."

"It's two in the morning."

"Yeah. I just—I need some air. That's all." And to see the face of the guilty person so I could kick his ass.

My aunt looked like a brick wall. "It's not appropriate for young ladies to go out after midnight. Especially dressed like that."

I glanced down at my boxers and tank top. This was bad. I was running out of time.

"There's a window in your room."

The window!

I raced back to my room, locking the door behind me. If she wasn't going to let me out, this was the next best thing. But by the time I yanked the window open and leaned out, the sidewalk outside the church was empty.

Maybe the confessor hadn't left yet? I scrambled back to my bed and slid beneath it, ear to the vent, but I only heard silence.

I was too late. They were long gone.

✝✝✝

What are you supposed to do when you find out something horrible? Something so bad, there isn't an adequate word for it. What are you supposed to do when someone you care for is in the wrong? When he could have done something but chose not to?

I used to think that if a person knew about a crime but didn't commit it, that was some sort of lesser crime. Now that I'd discovered what my uncle was covering up, I wondered if instead it was way worse. He had the potential to stop it and for whatever reason, he chose not to. More than that, my uncle *absolved* this person, a person who molested teens. Abuse of power in so many ways.

Something this heinous definitely could be the reason why my parents severed ties with my aunt and uncle if they knew. But if they knew my uncle was enabling a sexual predator, surely they would've spoken up.

And if my parents thought Uncle Bryan was dangerous in any way, they would've never let me move in in the first place. I was certain of that. They must not know.

Did my aunt know? As twisted as her "God gave me ovarian cancer" story was, I couldn't believe she would be fucked up enough to make excuses for sexual abuse.

My aunt and uncle couldn't actually be okay with this. Both parts of me needed to believe that. There had to be another reason Uncle Bryan was keeping this under wraps.

What if my uncle was being blackmailed somehow, forced to keep quiet, like the victims of mobsters in old movies? Hell, maybe he'd deliberately put me in the room next door so I could bring the perps to justice. Maybe he'd even figured out that I was Raziel, the guardian angel looking after his most desperate parishioners. Maybe he actually hoped I'd intervene and do the right thing, seek the justice he was afraid to pursue.

The only problem was that I didn't know how.

17 ALEKS

Wearily, I lay in bed staring at the ceiling, fists clenching and releasing with each breath. I didn't budge as the sun rose. Or when Aunt Anne Marie knocked on the door and asked was I all right and I said I didn't feel well. There was no way in hell I was coming down for breakfast or going anywhere near my uncle. I didn't want to see his mug outside of prison.

Coming here was a mistake. From day one, it all was a mistake. I shouldn't have run after that anime convention. I should have told someone what happened. I should have told my parents. I shouldn't have moved here. I shouldn't have tried hide. I shouldn't be here.

I wondered if I was the only person besides the two men in the confessional who knew what was going on. I knew there were a couple of other priests working at Saint Martha's, living in a separate apartment from ours. Were they in on the secret? Sister Bernadette and Deacon Jameson couldn't be involved, could they? Sister Bernadette said she believed in science. She implied she was pro-choice and had been chill about my identity. And Deacon Jameson—

I paused.

What if the confessor—the sinner—the abuser—was Deacon Jameson?

No. He was in love with Dima, and Dima was eighteen, not thirteen.

Unless Dima wasn't the only one. Deacon Jameson spent time with that altar boy too, didn't he?

I heard him confess the first time. My uncle didn't seem to believe him when he said he hadn't acted on his attraction. And then I caught him making out with Dima. Dima said he couldn't even remember how that had started.

Even though it had been Dima pinning Deacon Jameson to the tree, Deacon Jameson was older, and he was an authority figure. Last year, we'd had a substitute for sex education once. He talked about grooming, an older person getting a younger person to trust and idolize them so that their abuse would seem like the victim's decision and the victim would believe it was real love. The substitute said not all predators were crusty old men. It was just as likely to be dudes in their twenties victimizing young teens.

I'd scoffed at the time. There were age gaps in the cosplay world—and in a lot of anime, fifteen-year-olds got with much older people. It wasn't a big deal then.

Except I told you it was, the voice in my head said.

So was it remotely possible that Deacon Jameson was a sexual predator and that Dima had been one of his victims? That he'd groomed Dima when Dima was younger, so that Dima would think of their relationship as good and normal? Could I find out? If I asked Dima, would he tell me?

No. Wait. He'd defended Deacon Jameson, said he needed to confess because their kiss was *his* fault, not Deacon Jameson's.

Which is exactly what a grooming victim would believe . . .

My stomach roiled. Oh God. This was a nightmare. It had to be Deacon Jameson. The snake in the Garden of Eden.

I pulled out my phone. I flipped through the videos to pull up the one of Deacon Jameson chasing Dima with the Super Soaker. They laughed and yelled.

Was that the voice I heard in the confessional?

I couldn't tell. The confessor had been whispering.

But he hadn't gone through a grocery list of saints to pray to for forgiveness, like Deacon Jameson had the previous time I heard him confess. And the tone had been very different.

That didn't necessarily mean it wasn't Deacon Jameson, though. He might have been in an especially penitent mood the first time I overheard his confession. Maybe Deacon Jameson didn't always include every saint he could think of. Maybe sometimes he just got right to the point.

The point being that he was a predator.

With effort, I sat up in bed. Lying around doing nothing wasn't going to help me. That much was obvious. My penance for eavesdropping would be solving this. Fast.

I pulled out my notebook, tapping my pen against it like that'd help me think of solutions.

The obvious idea would be to wait until another confession happened, record it, and go to the police, turning over my phone as evidence. I didn't need my phone anyway. It wasn't like I had friends to talk to anymore.

But there were several huge-ass problems with that plan. One, it meant I'd need to allow abuse to happen again, to let someone get hurt again, before I did anything about it. Two, I wasn't sure if it was legal to record conversations without someone's consent. On TV trial shows, the "judge" usually dismissed cases where a person overheard a conversation but

didn't physically see the people involved, as that was hearsay. Wasn't this the same thing?

And three, I wasn't one hundred percent sure who the priest was, even though preliminary evidence pointed to Deacon Jameson. If I got the police involved but it turned out that my evidence was inadmissible, that would alert the abuser to the fact that someone was on to them. It might alert the church, including my uncle, who'd absolved the criminal and might help him cover the whole thing up.

I scratched my pen through option one. No, I couldn't go to the police.

The second obvious choice would be to talk to Aunt Anne Marie. She was married to Uncle Bryan, she deserved to know that he was absolving terrible people of their sins. And maybe, through her, I could find out who the abuser was and go to the police, and *then* he'd go to jail.

Unless Uncle Bryan was an undercover cop. Shit! He easily could be one. It would explain why he became a Catholic priest after marriage—

And what if my aunt never had cancer? Maybe they weren't actually religious at all. Maybe she was an undercover cop, too. What if they were both FBI agents who'd worked on this case for years in an attempt to bring a huge ring of pedophiles down?

But would anyone in the FBI lie about having ovarian cancer to her niece? Or spend years as an Episcopal priest before converting?

I wrote *unlikely* above that theory.

What if it was worse? What if my aunt knew or suspected that my uncle was committing a huge crime but was living in denial? What if I told her and she kicked me out? My stomach

turned with nausea. I couldn't let myself get kicked out. Then I'd be powerless to help anyone, powerless to stop the monsters. Or face mine.

Okay. Right. Not that.

Think faster, moron.

What else was there?

You know exactly what you could do.

I could tell my parents.

Yes!

No. No, the voice was wrong. That wasn't an option, either.

Mom would swoop me away from harm, but she wouldn't be able to help me get justice. And the last thing I wanted was for Dad to worry about what was happening here when he was now in Kuwait.

I scratched that out so hard with my pen, I tore a hole in the paper.

So what was I supposed to do? I had to tell someone. That much I knew. I had to tell someone because otherwise the abuse wouldn't stop. I thought about the anime convention, how out of eighty people no one had stepped in the way to protect me. After the fact, no one had consoled me, no one had offered to go with me to the police or even the con's organizers, no one had done anything.

And Lee . . . his betrayal had hurt almost more than the actual assault.

So I ran.

I ran where I thought my past wouldn't haunt me.

I ran to get away from my trauma yet somehow got tangled up in someone else's.

I looked at my notebook and the scratched out whole page.

You're getting off track.

Focus, Aleks.

If you want to be the hero, you need to be the hero.

There was that strange shift in the voice again, like it was actually on my side.

No time to dwell on it. If I was going to help, I needed to be prepared.

Think, Aleks. *Think.* Pretending I was Raziel could only get me so far. I needed to be me, and I needed to be clever, and fast.

I needed to find Dima.

FROM: Robin, Lee
TO: Yagoda, A.
SUBJECT: Please don't read the last email I sent.

Hey Alexis/Aleks,

I hope you didn't read the last email. If you didn't get to it, delete it. I shouldn't have hit send. I was in a bad mood. A lot of stuff's going on at home and I didn't get into any college I wanted to.

If you did read it . . . I am so, so, so sorry.

I went to a convention last weekend. I kept thinking I saw you again. I ran up to so many strangers, ready to hug them, only to realize they weren't you.

I'd recognize your cosplays anywhere. And in the shop—I guess I was in denial when I saw you sold them.

I guess this means you're done. For real.

I can't accept that. You can't just leave. I need you. I need you more than I've ever needed anyone, even my parents. You're the light in the dark. Everything good in my life happened because of you. I'm spiraling out of control without you there to ground me.

I love you. I mean it. I. Love. You.

Sincerely,

Lee

—

I'm so horrible, I don't deserve to be witty and use a poem in my signature. Alexis/Aleks, I'm so sorry. Forgive me. Please. I'm begging you. I love you.

18 ALEKS

Why was it impossible to find someone when you needed to see them? Foolproof way to ensure no one's around. Every. Single. Time.

I hadn't seen one glimpse of Dima since the convention, and now he wasn't replying to my texts. He was elusive. A ghost.

In the morning, I trudged down the steps and into the kitchen. My eyes burned from lack of sleep and how many times I'd rubbed them. They were probably red and baggy. "You're up early," said Aunt Anne Marie, who was sitting at the table with her Bible.

"Yeah. I've got stuff to do."

"More of your costumes?"

"I wish," I muttered. That certainly would be a lot more fun. She was quiet for several seconds before clearing her throat. I realized she meant for me to continue. "I'm going to find Dima. Do you know where he lives?"

She grimaced as she set the Bible on the table. "No. Even if I did, I wouldn't tell you."

"Why?"

"I don't like that boy," she said.

"You helped him make a cosplay."

"Yes, because I hoped that you two . . ."

"Hoped that we'd *what*, exactly?"

She flinched. "Trust me. It's for your own good."

"Why?" I asked. "I thought you'd like anyone who was considering becoming a priest."

There was a strange sort of pause. I glanced at her. Too close to home?

"Not all people who want to become priests should." Huh. Interesting word choice there.

I decided to go out on a limb. "What about Deacon Jameson?"

"Deacon Jameson loves what he does." By the tone of her voice, I could tell she was damning him with faint praise. And also that she did *not* feel comfortable with that sort of opinion. Definitely interesting.

"But I think it's best if you spend less time with Dima," she said briskly, before I could consider whether she had her own suspicions about Deacon Jameson.

"You still haven't explained why, though," I said, feeling even more on edge now.

She got up from the table and moved aimlessly toward the sink. "It's because of who he is."

Although I knew why, the masochist in me wanted to hear her say it. "You mean because he's Russian?"

She leaned against the sink and sighed. "I mean because he's a sodomite."

I closed my eyes as I took a breath. Then another. Reopened my eyes, my vision clearing on Aunt Anne Marie. "Do you think all queer people go to hell?"

Her skin paled. "You're not like him."

"Yes, I am," I said. I tried to keep my face from scrunching up but couldn't hold back my tears. She extended her hand, but I stepped back.

"Alexis, please."

"My name's Aleks," I said.

"You don't need to keep that up," Aunt Anne Marie said. "You're a girl."

"Not always."

"It's just pretend. I don't know why your mother let you get it in your head."

"Don't talk about Mom like that."

"This is my home. You are my guest."

"Well maybe I shouldn't be anymore, since you clearly hate me."

"I don't hate you."

"Yeah, you do. I'm just like Dima. You just won't admit it because that makes you the bad guy."

I didn't wait for her to answer before I stalked outside. I half-thought she might follow, but she didn't.

Well, that charming exchange definitely ruled out confiding in her about anything. I was on my own.

My first stop was the church since I was right here.

Everything was quiet. A few people prayed. My uncle walked into the confessional.

No trace of Dima. No laughter, no looming guy with a smug smirk on his face, thumbs hooked in his front pockets, gold crucifix glinting in the sun.

Next, I swung by the school. The RELIGIOUS FREEDOM sign stared at me, but I ignored it and walked into the building.

It looked like an ordinary school: fluorescent overhead lights, bulletin boards on the walls. I walked quickly past the front office and started roaming the halls, trying not to think about how creepy I was being. I glanced through the windows in the classroom doors. The kids were working on projects in one room. In another, Deacon Jameson wrote notes on a whiteboard.

"Alexis, welcome!"

I whirled around, ready to yell, "It's Aleks!" when I came face-to-face with Reverend Monsignor Kline. "Oh!" Good thing I didn't raise my voice. I was supposed to be on the down-low anyway, even though I was breaking all of my rules. Some people had a better grasp of their emotions. Not me. I never had. Not as Aleks. When I was Alexis, I had more restraint. "Uh. Sorry. I should have asked before I came in."

"Nonsense," he said. "What brings you here?"

"I was looking for Dima."

Reverend Monsignor Kline smiled. "Ah. Are you his girlfriend?"

"Me? Oh. No. Definitely no."

"Good-looking guy like him with a good-looking girl like you? Come on."

Great. This dude was trying to act like the "cool priest" even though he was way too old and the way he spoke made the hair on the back of my neck rise. I was pretty sure that this conversation was the equivalent of being stuck in Purgatory.

"He's my friend," I said. Then, to get Reverend Monsignor Kline off my back, I added, "I'm not really over my last relationship." It wasn't a lie. I'd never called him my boyfriend, but to deny that I had a relationship with Lee . . . The way he held my hand, the way he looked at me, the way he touched my hip . . . *You're so beautiful, you're so beautiful.*

The way we kissed . . .

Denial's a good motivator, I guess. Easier in hindsight to pretend I didn't like Lee that way, ever. Because at one point, I did like him. A lot. And then, one day, I hated him.

"Ah." Reverend Monsignor Kline gave a broad gesture with his arm. "I'm afraid you just missed him, but please feel free to continue touring the school."

My chest tightened. What if Dima was just like me, running from something horrific? "Do you know where he went?" I asked.

"I'm not at liberty to say."

That was weird. It made his absence almost . . . suspicious.

"Um. Okay. Do, uh, do you know when he'll be back?"

"That depends on Dmitry." He squeezed my shoulder and walked past me. "He's on a retreat."

"Retreat? Like a vacation? Or—"

"Don't worry about him. Maybe by the time he's back, you'll be ready for another relationship."

Reverend Monsignor Kline walked a few steps down the hall. With his back to me, he said, "Eavesdropping doesn't suit you, Deacon Jameson."

I turned around. The transitional deacon stood just outside his classroom, still gripping the doorknob. He dampened his lips with his tongue before he released the door, allowing it to swing shut slowly as he stepped into the hall. Without so much as a word, he slipped past me and walked down the hall with Kline. I stared at Deacon Jameson's back like my eyes would burn holes through the fabric.

After hearing his confession about liking men, witnessing him and Dima make out in the woods, and factoring in Dima's sudden disappearing act the day after I heard the latest confession, I didn't see how the predator couldn't be Deacon Jameson.

He had guilt written all over his body. Even showing up in the hallway, spying on me. I just needed proof and I'd get that piece of shit behind bars.

As I left the building, I cast a glance to the side. Near the field of crosses was a boy. The blonde altar boy—Michael, wasn't it? He knelt before one of the crosses, face mostly hidden by the thick curls. Although it made my stomach churn to go near them, I did. I needed to see his face. I needed answers. I needed to channel Raziel.

I stopped beside him. "You're Michael, right?"

He lifted his head. I barely kept from gasping. His eyes were practically lifeless, begging me to put him out of his misery.

I knelt on the grass. "I'm Aleks," I said. "I'm going to help you."

"I'm fine."

My stomach clenched like I was about to dry heave. This boy was dead. His eyes, his expression, his posture. Even his voice sounded dead.

"No. You're not." I touched his back. He flinched. I pulled back my hand and cleared my throat. "I—I know what's going on with you. I know what's happening."

He met my eyes warily. There was no denial.

"I can't imagine how awful it is, or how terrifying. But it'll be okay. I'm going to help you, Michael. Okay? I'm going to make it better."

He turned his face away from me. "Leave me alone. You can't make it stop."

"Yes, I can."

Once again, I had his attention. "How?"

"We're going to contact the police and tell them what Deacon Jameson did."

He gripped my shirt by the collar, looking almost wild. "You know what he tried to do?"

I blinked a little. Was that the confirmation I needed? Why didn't I have the recording app turned on my phone? "You mean what he did?"

"I mean you know what we talked about?"

Talked? What . . .

My confusion must have made my expression blank, because Michael released my collar and abruptly stood, face scrunched in disgust. "You're a liar."

"Bad guys deserve to be punished," I said gently.

"He's gay. Not a bad guy."

Deacon Jameson told him that? Despite sounding so ashamed in confession? Or was that Michael's logic, his coping mechanism to make it all safe?

"I—I know that makes him—look, it's normal to protect your abuser at first. To be in denial."

His eyes burned. "Normal?"

"I—I didn't mean it like that."

"Have you been hurt?"

I stalled. Yes. Yes, I had, but I couldn't say it out loud. Not to this boy I was trying to help. I'd make things worse. He'd compare himself to me and . . .

"I thought so," he said gruffly, breaking my train of thought. "I hate you," he added. "I don't know you but I hate you. And I'll *never* forgive you if you get Deacon Jameson in trouble."

"Why are you so hell-bent on protecting him?" I burst out before I could soften it.

"Because he's trying to stop him."

Stop him? Stop who?

Before I could ask more, the altar boy stalked off into the grass, rigid against the summer breeze. A chill rushed through my body like it had holes in it, one near my heart, one by the back of my skull. And I could tell by the way I got numb that I was about to disappear.

Nonononono. Not now, not now, please not now. But it was too late.

Goodbye, Aleks.

Hello, Alexis.

19 ALEXIS

Changing gender in the middle of the day was always tough. It hurt. Like a door slamming in my face. It was disorienting. Afterward I'd be easily distracted, or two intense, or a weird mixture of both.

Today was no different except the transition was slower than it usually was. Often I noticed in the blink of an eye, a moment of lost consciousness, but today I could feel Aleks evaporate. Sometimes he clung hard to my head, demanding he not be erased. *I am here, I am here.* But today, he gave up. Boy-me stood with his arms spread like a cross, inviting girl-me to take him away.

And girl-me was mad. How dare he leave when things got tough? How dare he abandon me to deal with this shit on my own? I didn't sign up for him to cause a stir and leave me with his messes. Alexis wouldn't have made out with Lee in the hallway, practically dry humping in public. Alexis wouldn't have alienated a victim.

I walked aimlessly for hours, letting the summer sun set. My feet blistered and my throat was so parched it stung but I didn't care. Nothing hurt as much as the altar boy, Michael, saying he hated me.

I had messed up our whole interaction. I knew a lot of people protected their abusers, conditioned to believe it was love, or that it was something to be ashamed of. But Michael has said Deacon Jameson was trying to stop someone else—protect Michael from someone else.

Who was the other person? Did another person exist or was it just in Michael's head?

I was doing a last loop of the lake when I heard crying. Quietly, I moved toward the sound, keeping to the shadows. There was something about the sound, a desperation that I didn't know could be conveyed just through tears, but there it was.

Under the moonlight, I could make out the shadowy figures of Sister Bernadette and Deacon Jameson. They sat on the bank, Sister Bernadette's arm around Deacon Jameson's shoulders as he wept.

"You didn't know," Sister Bernadette said gently.

"I should have known. I'm a deacon."

"This isn't your fault."

"Of course it's my fault. I didn't think he'd feel so horrible after it."

I sucked in a breath. A confession. My chest tightened. I stepped closer, unable to keep more distance. My hand moved to my pocket, pulling out my cell and hitting record on the audio app. I had him in my grasp. I wouldn't be too late this time. I'd save Michael.

"I should be the one getting locked away," he continued. "That place is hell."

Yeah, which is where you're going once I turn this recording over to the police.

"Joey, don't," Sister Bernadette said sharply. "You're making it sound like the camp *isn't* voluntary."

The camp? Did they mean the summer camp? I took another step closer.

Sister Bernadette continued, "Dima wanted to go."

Wait. Dima? I thought they were talking about Michael.

Reverend Monsignor Kline made it sound like Dima was on vacation. Unless this camp was a recovery place for victims. Reverend Monsignor Kline *did* keep a close eye on Deacon Jameson. Maybe he'd encouraged Dima to get help—privately, secretly, without exposing Deacon Jameson to any consequences. I could vomit.

"But why?"

"Really, Joey? Do you really need to ask why?"

My heart drummed faster against my ribs. I trembled as I took another step closer. How much did Sister Bernadette know?

"He asked me to sin for him," he said.

My fist tightened. I thought of the confession I heard. *He wanted it.* Bullshit.

"He kept asking and I kept saying no and no and no until I finally said one kiss. Just one. Then I made him promise that he had to stop asking me."

"And?" Sister Bernadette said.

Deacon Jameson flopped on his back in the grass. "You ever look at the sky? Like right now. You see the faint wisps of the Milky Way."

Sister Bernadette lay beside him. I scooted closer. "Yeah, so?"

"It was just like that. The kiss." He turned on his side. "I've never felt closer to God. Bernie, how can it be wrong?"

"Because there are a lot of translations of the Bible over time," she said. "Joey, your feelings are not sins. You know that."

"No, I don't."

"You're getting emotional."

"Of course I'm emotional! How could he ask me to give up my integrity and then go to that place?"

"Deep breaths—"

"Stop patronizing me. How would you feel if you were in my shoes?"

"You're all over the place. Just one day at a time. Okay?"

"You're avoiding the question."

"Because that's none of your business."

Deacon Jameson got to his feet. "You don't respect me, *Sister*."

Sister Bernadette could have been on fire as she stood up, getting right in his face. "Well, maybe you're not meant for priesthood, *Transitional* Deacon Jameson."

His temper flared. He looked almost ferocious as he snarled, "I guess not, because I love him."

As quickly as the flames came, they were extinguished. Deacon Jameson practically crumpled, so fast Sister Bernadette barely got her arms around him. "You're right. I shouldn't be a priest."

I turned the recording app off.

"No, Joey. No. I was—I was mad. I shouldn't have said that. The celibacy thing—it was *one* slip. You're going to be a great priest. I'm so sorry."

As quietly as I could, I took a step back, then another and another until I touched pavement. I walked quickly, head low, hoping I was still unseen. Even though I tried to be quiet, I felt like I crunched every stone and snapped every twig. I didn't look over my shoulder to check. If they saw me, if Sister Bernadette specifically saw me spying . . .

My stomach flipped. How could I have assumed Deacon

Jameson was a sexual predator? Because I knew he liked men? Because he was twenty-three and Dima was eighteen? Because I saw him with thirteen-year-old Michael looking distraught? I'd assumed. I was no better than the others.

But the way he talked about *giving up his integrity* to kiss Dima—those weren't the words of a predator. Which meant someone *else* was the abuser.

Just like Michael told you, the voice reprimanded. **You weren't listening.**

One of the other priests at Saint Martha's. Or maybe even a priest from a neighboring parish, someplace within driving distance, but close enough that he might still have access to a victim here . . .

I needed to fix this. I needed to make amends for suspecting Deacon Jameson, and I needed to figure out who the real abuser was. I had a lot of work to do.

✝✝✝

As I stepped into the rectory, Aunt Anne Marie almost knocked me over, like she'd been waiting just inside the door the whole time. "You weren't here for dinner."

"Wasn't hungry."

"We eat together at six."

"I said I wasn't hungry."

"Your uncle waited for you—"

"I bet he did," I said, walking around Aunt Anne Marie.

"What's gotten into you?" she called after me.

"I suspect you don't want to know."

"Alexis, I'm concerned about you. You weren't interested in sinning before."

Interested in sinning? I couldn't help it. Not today. Any day but today, I could have held my tongue. But after judging a man because he was the easy target, spying on him and the woman I had a crush on, bulldozing an abused kid instead of letting him talk to me on his own terms . . . I was supposed to be doing better. Maybe I wasn't acting like a jackass the way I had in the cosplay world, but if anything, I was worse.

And yet Aunt Anne Marie didn't care about that. She was worried about something I hadn't chosen, something that didn't hurt anyone.

I faced my aunt. "Can't be a sinner if you don't believe in sin. But if you insist, sure. I'll bite. I love it. I love sinning."

My aunt gasped like I'd mortally wounded her. "You watch your mouth. This is *our* home."

"Then maybe I should leave, since you hate me."

"I don't hate you."

"Of course you do," I said, a cruelty creeping into my voice that I thought I'd buried. "You think queer people are going to hell. Well, guess what? I'm queer. You knew that. Me not dressing in my boy clothes doesn't change that. You called my friend a slur. I *am* that. That means you hate me by default."

I went in my room and barely kept from slamming the door. I turned the lock, grabbed my pillow, and screamed into it. I was bad. The worst. The literal worst.

I wasn't meant to be Raziel. I wasn't strong enough. I'd fooled myself, like I did with cosplay. Professional pretender, that's all I was. That and an idiot. I was wrong more often than I was right. I thought I knew everything, I thought I could be the hero. I couldn't. I was never meant to be one. I was the loser. I was the one who had no friends, desperately lonely, until I got into cosplay.

I could put my friends' past transgressions behind me. I could go right back where I was.

I booted up my computer and logged into all of my social media accounts. Tons of notifications popped up. Yes. This was it. This was what I needed. Forget about this horrible mess. It never happened. I'd go back home, say everything was taken care of. I'd make new cosplays and go to conventions with those same friends.

A window popped up at the bottom of my screen. I didn't need to read the name. I knew.

Lee: Why are you ignoring me?

I'd do it. I'd confront him. I started to type:

You're an asshole, Lee.

No. Stop. Delete. Better idea. I'd *apologize*.

Yes. That was it. I'd apologize. I'd ask did he really mean it, could he take it back. I'd ask if we could do our cosplays together, comics or anime, I didn't care. We could hold hands. We could make out. Behind a closed door at a convention hotel or hell, out in public, in cosplay, under the glare of camera flashes.

Coward.

Faux-trans.

Is this what you came for?

What about Michael?

Are you that stupid?

Don't you learn?

Do something.

DO SOMETHING.

I started crying. *Shut up, shut up, shut up.*

I won't shut up.
    You're a disgrace.
        A disappointment.
           Failure.
This is why people hate you.
              This is why I hate you.

I gripped my hair, torso bowing forward as I dug my fingers across my scalp. *Shut up, shut up, shut up.* The noise was so loud. Buzzing in my ears. Like mosquitos. Mosquitos who fed off my failures and insecurities.

Where's your backbone?
        Piece of shit.
Why are you crying?
      Why are you curled up like that?
          Are you fucking giving up?
Look in the goddamn mirror.
Do it!
Look in the mirror.
           Think long and hard.
     Then you can reply.

I trembled as I dragged myself to the mirror. Dark circles were below my eyes, nose swollen and puffy, skin sickly pale, almost a jaundice hue. I stripped, twisting my body. There were no back dimples anymore. My stomach had a small paunch. Breasts small and low.

Ugly girl.
    Ugly, ugly girl.

The back of my throat stung.

I pinched my hip. A curve I hated. My inner thigh. Despicable. Every trace of something female, hideous. Just like my friends, former friends, said. Ugly girl, ugly girl. But such a beautiful boy. And they were so trans-inclusive, didn't I know that? Couldn't I tell when they told me I was holding myself back from my full potential? It'd be easy to get HRT with parents as supportive and cool as mine. Why are you wimping out? Are you scared? We'll support you. You're such a beautiful boy. Such a beautiful, beautiful boy.

I dropped to my knees, like I was held up by a cord that snapped. They were right. I was a hideous girl. I was also a beautiful boy. But I couldn't be a beautiful boy all the time. And if everyone wanted me to be a boy, why did Lee tell people I was a girl?

No. *Not* a girl. A slur.

My body rolled to the side, arms wrapped around my knees as I wheezed. My hand slid between my legs. I couldn't bear to touch what I knew was there. I was disgusting.

I pictured Lee's smiling face. *I love you. Really. I do. You're beautiful.*

I pictured my cosplay friends saying how much I loved it. That I wanted to be objectified. That I'd have told them years ago if I didn't really want it.

I gazed at my reflection. If I wanted to be objectified at one point, did that mean I was bound to it? Did it mean my former friends were good people or bad people? If they didn't know, was it still bad? If they really thought I liked it, did that nullify everything?

You have the right to change your mind.

187

The voice was right. I couldn't go back to the life I had before. Maybe at one time I was welcome, or at least half of me was welcome, but I wasn't safe there anymore. I wasn't safe anywhere, but especially not there.

Now, I was in a new place. It was me at fault. I made a mistake. I made a horrible judgment. Now Dima was MIA, and it seemed unlikely that I'd get Michael to open up now that I'd blown my chance to just shut up and listen, the way I hoped people would listen to me and they never did.

Refocus.

You had a plan.

Can't you amend it?

Yes. Yes, of course I could amend it!

First, I would keep my phone within reach at all times. The abusive priest would be back, and I would be ready with my recording app. Maybe I'd get in trouble, but I needed evidence in order to help others. Someone had to risk it and it might as well be me. I wasn't going to major in costume design anymore, I didn't have friends except Dima, who was at some camp, and I didn't have a lot of prospects.

Second, I would need to get Michael to trust me. That would be hard, especially since I'd alienated him, thinking Deacon Jameson was his abuser when instead Deacon Jameson was trying to save him.

Third, I needed someone on my side. I needed an insider, a person who believed in justice over vows of silence. I didn't need to waste another second. I knew exactly who I needed to confide in and ask for help in solving the crime.

20 ALEXIS

"Sister Bernadette!"

She turned to face me, smiling. For a second, my breath caught in my throat. She was even more beautiful than usual. The early morning sun's glare looked like a halo around her. My chest thumped harder as she approached. My mind whirred.

"Alexis, you're up early," she said. "Or is it Aleks today? I hope that's still okay to ask. I'm not sure how to tell otherwise."

I opened my mouth to speak but nothing came out. The words froze around my vocal cords.

The smile slid off her face. She stepped closer. "Something's wrong."

I nodded and coughed, trying to clear my throat. Everything was so dry, even my tear ducts. I swallowed, like saliva would wet my parched mouth. It did nothing. After last night's revelations, I didn't go to sleep. Now, it was six in the morning and my mind had whirred nonstop. Information sickness, wasn't it called that? In a gravelly whisper, I said, "I need to talk to you."

Her lips twisted to one side in hesitation. She glanced over her shoulder. "I'm guessing it's not safe to talk here?"

I shook my head.

"Okay. Where can we talk?"

"Somewhere no one will find us."

"There aren't many places like that around," Sister Bernadette said. My shoulders dropped until she snapped her fingers. "How would you like to go for a drive?"

"You have a car?"

"You have a lot of weird thoughts about nuns, don't you?"

I flushed as I walked beside her. Nun, not prehistoric, right. "You got me there."

She patted my shoulder. "You're not the only one, unfortunately. A lot of people assume we're like the Amish. The two years in poverty to learn how to become humble can be rough, but even then, we have access to vehicles if there's an emergency." She pulled out her keys and beeped the doors to a dark blue jeep. A crucifix hung over the rearview mirror. I climbed in.

"How steady a driver are you?" I asked once we were a few blocks away from the church.

"Because I'm a nun?"

"No. Because I'm about to tell you something horrible and I don't want you to run off the road."

"That bad?"

"If it wasn't that bad, I wouldn't have made you drive all the way out wherever we are."

She turned the jeep down a fork in the road. "I've got my foot right by the brake."

"You're gonna need it."

"What did you do?"

"Okay, so try not to be mad at me and hear me out. Because a lot of this is out of my control." I took a deep breath. It was time for me to do my own confessing. "My room—it's right next to the confessional."

Tires screeched. She pulled the jeep over to the side of the road so quickly that I grabbed my seatbelt for support. "You've been listening to people's confessions?"

"There's a vent in the wall—"

"Those are private conversations between a person—"

"—and a priest and God. Yeah, I know." Because I sure heard all about it over the past couple weeks.

Her face flushed with anger. "Just because you don't believe in it doesn't mean you have any right to listen. These are people's most painful secrets."

Her anger, as deserved as it was, stung. "I told you, *I know*," I said. "For what it's worth, I wasn't eavesdropping on purpose. I was trying to sleep and I heard it through the vent. I was going to plug it up but then this woman started talking about stealing food for her children. And I just . . . I got so sad. I thought maybe I could help her, you know?"

She re-gripped the steering wheel. "You tried to fix things for people."

I nodded. "I did. Fix things, I mean. A lot of things. I wasn't just trying to get gossip or anything."

I watched her fingers stretch out before tightening again on the wheel, clenching and unclenching repeatedly. It was like I could see the gears in her mind on overdrive. She dampened her lips a few times. I swore there was the faint sheen of lip gloss. "Did you have anything to do with Wanda getting a job?"

I sucked in a breath. Sister Bernadette was about a thousand times more perceptive than I gave her credit for. And already I knew she was smart. I gripped my thighs, fingers digging into my jeans.

"Her information was all public online," I said quietly. People talked about feeling lighter once they cleared the air, like getting their secrets out made everything so much better. "I just . . . spruced up a resume with what I could find. Hers was so, so bad, there was no way anyone would hire her. I posted the new one on some job seeker websites. I figured anything would be better than nothing. I mean, kids were involved."

Sister Bernadette inhaled slowly through her nose like she was trying to process everything. "There's more?"

"This guy—his girlfriend racked up all of this debt. So I—I tried to help."

"The cash." She looked over at me, her expression hard to read. "Anthony said the Archangel Raziel left an envelope for him specifically to pay off debt."

"Yeah. I sold a lot of my cosplays and made some new ones."

"I don't understand," she said, shaking her head, bewildered. "He was a stranger."

"He needed help." I looked at my lap. "Someone confessed to abusing their brother."

Sister Bernadette's eyes hardened again. "Elizabeth Mackell's brother was taken to a hospital. Involuntary stay. It's not been going well."

"Is that really the worst thing?" I asked. "If she couldn't take care of him on her own, is it so bad that he's in a place that can?"

"I think something that extreme would make anyone even more scared and panicked."

"I'm not saying it's ideal. But doing nothing would've been worse. I'd do it all over again if I needed to."

Sister Bernadette seemed to be literally biting her tongue. She still didn't agree with me. Not even remotely. "Was there more?" she asked after a moment.

I squirmed a little. "I found out about Deacon Jameson and Dima."

Sister Bernadette blinked. "What?"

I paused. "You know, because they're in love?"

Sister Bernadette snorted. "Unbelievable. First you think Joey's in love with me, now you think he's in love with Dima?"

"Why are you lying to me?" I asked, hurt.

"I'm not—"

"I heard you and Deacon Jameson talking about Dima. On the lawn. You talked about the kiss."

Sister Bernadette paled. "You were spying on me?"

"That's beside the point."

Sister Bernadette sighed heavily. She looked . . . disappointed, maybe? I wasn't sure. She tapped her fingers on the wheel. "Surely that's not why you're here though."

"No. It's not." I took a deep breath. Now or never. "The other night, a priest went to my uncle for confession. I didn't realize priests actually went, you know? I just thought . . . I thought it was all like once you become a priest, you get a free pass, or you confess to yourself, or whatever. But he said . . ."

My chest ached. I half-hiccupped, tears springing from my eyes. "He said he's molesting one of the altar boys. It was—it's Michael."

Sister Bernadette's eyes widened. "Which priest?"

"I don't know," I said, even as a chill went through me. She didn't say *what* like she was in disbelief. She specifically asked *who*. "I didn't recognize his voice. And I couldn't get to the door in time to see who it was."

Her face softened. For a second, I thought she might cry. "I'm sorry. That's . . ." She shook her head. "I'm stunned. I've seen a lot of stuff. I've heard a lot of stuff. But this . . . abuse of power from a position of authority over a minor at *our* church . . ." Tears slid down her cheeks. She seemed devastated, and yet, at the same time, she didn't really seem surprised. "So you haven't talked to your uncle about this?"

"No way. I mean, he absolved this dude. Pretty much let him off the hook with the whole 'don't do it again' routine. He actually said *please*. I didn't know what to do so I came to you."

"I don't know what I *can* do," she said honestly.

My heart sank. "Someone's in danger. We have to do something."

"I'm not saying this should go unpunished. It has to be stopped at all costs. I just literally don't know what *I* can do."

I didn't understand. "Can't you go to the police?"

Sister Bernadette's lips pursed. I didn't know whether that meant she couldn't or wouldn't or what.

"If only we could find out who the priest was, it'd be easier," I said.

"Not necessarily," said Sister Bernadette.

"What do you mean?"

"Canon law. Vows. Priests often absolve each other of sin. It's not so uncommon—"

"That's illegal."

"We believe in forgiveness."

"For pedophiles?"

I could see the tension running along her jaw as she clenched it. "Look. There's a small percentage of bad people in the world. Some are Catholic. Do the math."

"Okay, fine. The math is telling me that there's at least one sexual predator at Saint Martha's, and thanks to canon law he's getting away with it."

Sister Bernadette continued to tap her fingers on the

steering wheel. She then reached over to grab a plain black handbag from the glove box. I repressed my surprise that she even had a purse. She fished through it and pulled out her phone.

"What are you doing?" I asked, chest tight. "You're not calling my uncle, are you?"

"Shh," she said, gesturing at me to keep quiet. Through the speaker, I could barely hear a muffled "Hello?"

Sister Bernadette suddenly recited:

"We believe in one holy Catholic and Apostolic church.
We affirm one baptism for the forgiveness of sins.
We look forward to the resurrection of the dead,
And to life in the world to come. Amen."

The reply was muffled against Sister Bernadette's ear. Quietly, she said, "Alexis." I craned my head. "She knows about Michael." She continued to listen as I strained to hear what was being said, though soon she nodded. "Always."

She hung up the phone and pulled the car on the road.

"What was that?" I asked.

"The Nicene Creed," she said, turning down a side road. "Sometimes it's too dangerous to talk."

"So it was code?" She didn't say a word, neither confirming or denying it. I struggled to remember how to breathe. There was only one reason for a code to be created to signal an abuse of power.

This had happened before.

"Who were you talking to?" I asked quietly.

"Probably best that you don't know."

"But Michael?" I pressed.

"It'll be taken care of."

"Really?"

"Really."

I reached to rest my hand over hers on the clutch. She turned her palm up, fingers linking with mine. Although she didn't look at me, she smiled. The stress washed off my body. "I love you," I told her.

Her smile never faltered. A rosy tint came to her cheeks, or maybe that was just in my head, as she looked away from me and said, "I know."

21 ALEKS

You know that feeling of dread you can't shake? Like when something's just not right and you don't know what it is or what it could be and you start wondering and your day's just off because of it? Sometimes it turns out to be nothing and you realize at the end of the day that you're unsatisfied without a resolution but how can there be a resolution when there's no known problem? And when it gets in your head and stays in there and oh my God, what's happening? Shut up, shut up, shut up. No, don't shut up. If the voice goes away, then there'd be no one.

How messed up is that? Was I so addicted to misery that I couldn't let something go right?

Yesterday was a win. Sister Bernadette had made that phone call and promised the sexual abuse at Saint Martha's would be taken care of. Michael would be safe. My conscience was clear.

Well, almost. I owed Deacon Jameson an apology. Or some other subtle way of making amends, because he didn't even know I'd suspected him. I could get him some kind of gift, maybe get him a really cool Super Soaker, or see if there was some Gregorian chant album that he didn't own. I'd ask Sister Bernadette what else he liked.

Thinking of her made me smile. Didn't he call her Bernie? Was I allowed to call her that, too, now that I'd told her I loved her and her response wasn't to push me away but say, "I know?" Was I allowed to think of her as Bernie when she linked her fingers with mine so intimately? The slight sheen on her lips—had that been lip gloss? Had it been it for me? Was she hoping I'd kiss her the way I wanted to kiss her? How old was she anyway? She looked my age, but she seemed more mature. Probably a little older. If she was nineteen did that mean I had to wait a few more months before I could crush on her? Or twenty? Or twenty-three, like Deacon Jameson, at which point the age gap might just be gross?

Thoughts of gross age gaps took me back down a dark path.

I should have gotten up feeling light, feeling relieved. But this whole thing still didn't feel right.

I kept biting my lip, stomach turning from nerves. My anxieties shot out in all directions. I thought about Dad in Kuwait. Was he safe? I grabbed my phone and dialed Mom. She answered on the third ring.

"Hey, kid. Long time no talk."

"Sorry, I've been busy." I wasn't sure why I held back from telling her about Michael. Maybe because I didn't know who the abuser was, or because Sister Bernadette said it'd be taken care of. I trusted her and the weird phone call she made. No need to get Mom riled up over something that was already being resolved.

"Have you heard from Dad since he got to Kuwait?" I asked anxiously.

"Briefly," she said. Instantly my shoulders relaxed.

"He tipped me off about you liking a nun."

"Oh my God. It's not a big deal."

"Aleks." Mom's voice took on a slightly stern edge that surprised me. It never ceased to amaze me that even over the phone, she knew what was up. "How old is she?"

"I don't know."

"You know the magic rule I used with your father?"

"What are you even talking about?"

"Half your age, plus seven. That's the youngest you can date."

I wished I was on Facetime so Mom could see my expression. "Yeah, that'd be super helpful—if she was younger than me."

"Oh. Crap. Right. Okay, so, that means we have to do math."

"Oh, come on. It's summer."

"It's good for you. Okay so if X divided by two plus seven equals seventeen, you . . ." She made a sound like a drumroll.

I groaned, grabbing my notebook and pen as I scribbled down:

$$X/2 + 7 = 17$$
$$X/2 + 7 - 7 = 17 - 7$$
$$X/2 = 10$$
$$X/2 \times 2 = 10 \times 2$$
$$X = 20$$

"Okay, so by that logic, no older than twenty."

"Twenty! Are you sure? That's way too old."

"Oh my God. Mom, seriously. She's a nun, remember? Nothing's going to happen. Just let me have this stupid little crush."

Mom pretended to wail, "MY BABY'S ALL GROWN UP AND CRUSHING ON A NUN."

"Keep it down. If Uncle Bryan and Aunt Anne Marie hear about this, I'm going to blame you."

"Ugh," she said, no longer amused. "They would definitely not be on board with that. They'd probably want to send you to the camp."

I paused. "What's the camp?"

"It's so unbelievably stupid."

"That's not exactly answering my question."

"It's this stupid place for quote-unquote *sinners* to quote-unquote *change their ways*. I did my research before I agreed to let you live with these people, and I made it clear to my sister that if she even mentions it to you, I will torch the rectory. It's so stupid and terrible and criminal and ugh."

My heart stopped pumping. "You mean it's gay conversion therapy?"

"Yeah, why?" Immediately, Mom's breathing became louder on the phone. "Did your aunt and uncle bring it up? I swear, I went over it with them—"

"No! Nothing like that." I rubbed the back of my neck. "I made a friend . . . and apparently he went there."

"Oh, shit. Parents are the worst—"

"Voluntarily."

Mom choked up on the other end. "Oh, Aleks. I am so, so sorry."

"Yeah. Me too." In my head, I heard my own words at the convention, my disconnected ramblings about how the only way to overcome something toxic is to cut it out of your life. Had Dima applied those words to himself, to being gay? Had I inadvertently pushed him further into the well of self-hatred he'd been struggling with, to the point that he'd taken this sudden, drastic action?

I sighed and pulled the phone away from my ear enough to check the time. "I better go."

"Yeah, of course. I love you."

"I love you, too."

"If you need anyone to sneak your friend out of the camp—"

"What part of voluntary didn't you understand?"

"Just saying, I do parkour."

I tried to smile against the threat of tears. "Yeah, like one class."

"Hey! I did *not* take just one class. I took two."

I smiled for real. "Bye, Mom."

"Talk soon, Aleks. Love you."

We hung up. I walked to the closet, hovering by the right side with my masculine clothes. It was so tempting to go to the box above to get my binder, compression shorts, and packer. Was I really trying to stay invisible anymore? Did it matter?

I compromised with myself. Capris, sneakers, and one of my band shirts. With the men's sizing, even the small hung off my shoulders. I kept meaning to do some alterations, but for some reason it was easier to spend the time on cosplay rather than daily wear.

I emerged from my room, pausing when I noticed the silence. "Aunt Anne Marie?"

Nothing.

I peered around, poking my head in each room. Kitchen. Dining room. Living room. Empty.

That's when I saw the blue and red lights.

Slowly, I approached the front door and opened it. A police car was parked on the street.

My chest was tight. I walked around the front of the rectory toward the church doors. Several nuns stood outside, including Sister Bernadette, who seemed dazed. Two other priests were there too, plus a couple people who I was pretty sure did admin work in the rectory office. My uncle stood near my aunt, hands trembling as he nervously clasped and unclasped them, while my aunt brought the rosary to her moving lips.

I zeroed in on two men in suits speaking with Reverend Monsignor Kline. Detectives.

They'd caught the abuser, I realized with a gasp. They'd caught him, whoever it was, and this was over.

I walked toward the groups, unsure of where I was headed. I just knew I had to keep going. Something tugged me forward, like an invisible chain. "Sister Bernadette?" I asked softly. She didn't budge. Cautiously, I reached for her hand. The second my fingers brushed against her palm, she jerked away, alert.

"What are you doing here?"

"I live here." I swallowed hard. "Who was it?"

Sister Bernadette didn't answer. I looked around the assembled people. Something wasn't right.

I closed my hand over my mouth to keep from throwing up. Because there was someone missing from the group: Deacon Jameson.

Deacon Jameson was Sister Bernadette's friend. She said she'd take care of the problem. A day later, he wasn't here. Cops were everywhere. And here I was ready to forgive him, thinking I owed him one.

"I'm sorry you had to do that," I whispered to Sister Bernadette.

"You should be."

I took a step back, caught off guard by the fury in her voice.

"You did the right thing."

"Did I?"

"Alexis, go inside," my uncle said roughly. Where had he come from? He was supposed to be talking with police, wasn't he?

Aleks, the voice in my head said. **Tell him it's Aleks.**

Instead, I said, "What's going on?"

"Go inside. Now." He looked toward the street, then shook his head. A news truck was rolling up. I sucked in a breath. This was huge. Like with the original reveal in the *Boston Globe* way back. "Shit," Uncle Bryan swore under his breath, shocking me. Could priests curse? "Go back inside. Do not talk to anyone."

"What happened?"

"Go. Inside. *Now.*"

His tone put me even more on edge. Well, sooner or later I'd find out the extent of what had happened with Deacon Jameson. I didn't really need to be here.

As I turned, I swore I felt fingers brush against my forearm. Sister Bernadette? I wasn't sure. I didn't look back as I walked away.

As I passed the open door of the church, I was struck by the echoing boom of sobs. I paused, eyes widening, then stepped inside. Before the altar, under a statue of Jesus being crucified, Deacon Jameson prayed. His body heaved as he whispered, "In your mercy and love, blot out the sins he has committed through human weakness. Let him live with you forever. I beg you, Christ. Save his soul."

Again . . . and again . . . and again . . .

I didn't turn when I heard footsteps behind me. Didn't flinch when I felt the hand on my shoulder either. "What did I tell you about letting people have their privacy?" Sister Bernadette said.

"It's not my problem his voice is echoing." I turned on her. "What did you do?"

"Exactly what you wanted."

"I asked you to intervene. You said you'd take care of it. Why isn't he in the back of a police car?"

"Don't talk like that—"

"Stop covering for him! What the hell did he do to Michael?"

"Shut up!" At the sound of Deacon Jameson's voice, I spun toward the altar. Deacon Jameson was on his feet, voice echoing off the arched ceiling. "Shut up."

"What did you do to him?" I demanded.

"You just had to interfere. You just had to mess things up," Deacon Jameson said.

As he stepped forward, I took a step back. "Stay away from me, creep." But he kept coming.

"First you drove Dima away." Somehow, it felt more intimate and terrifying to hear Deacon Jameson use his nickname when I'd only heard him use Dmitry before.

I fought to keep my nerve, to keep a brave face. "He went to the camp because of *you*. Not me." Whether that was completely true was irrelevant right now. Anything I'd said to Dima at the convention that might have influenced him paled in comparison to what Deacon Jameson had done. "What happened with Michael?"

Deacon Jameson's voice hitched. "Why couldn't you leave things alone?" Tears streaked down his cheeks.

"Oh, cut the bullshit! I heard your confession."

Deacon Jameson stared at me blankly. "W-what?"

"I heard you. The *special Communion*. I heard everything."

"Special Communion . . ." Deacon Jameson said, voice shaking. "Do you—do you actually know what happened?"

"I *heard* your confession. And you know what sucks?

I thought I was just paranoid to suspect you. I thought I misjudged you, pervert."

"I don't have time for this," Deacon Jameson said, getting back on his knees.

"Fortunately you'll have plenty of time once you go to jail."

"What is wrong with you?" Sister Bernadette hissed. "How dare you!"

"What's wrong with *me*? What's wrong with *you*?" I asked hoarsely as Sister Bernadette knelt down next to Deacon Jameson. "The police are right outside. If you cover for him, you're just as culpable as him—"

"Cover for me?" Deacon Jameson's voice raised in pitch. He half-laughed, half-sobbed, hysterically. "Michael is *dead*."

My blood stopped pumping. He bowed forward, prayers broken up by sobs, Sister Bernadette by his side. "What?"

Silence.

This didn't make sense. Michael was dead? Sister Bernadette told me she'd take care of it. She made a phone call. Everything was supposed to be fixed.

Did Michael kill himself? Rather than acknowledge what Deacon Jameson did, he took his life? I envisioned Michael's eyes, already dead when I spoke to him.

My mind moved to the street, the reporters. I yanked my phone out of my capris and pulled up my news app. The headline glared at me:

LOCAL BOY FOUND MURDERED IN SWAMP

Michael . . .
Take care of it . . .
Did that mean . . .

205

Was it possible? Had Sister Bernadette and Deacon Jameson killed Michael?

"Oh my God . . ." I barely got the syllables out as my vision blurred. I thought I could faintly hear someone shouting my name but everything merged together. A symphony of chaos. Devastation. Guilt.

It's your fault, it's your fault, the voice in my head shouted seconds before my head crashed against the pew and the lights went out.

22 ALEXIS

Everything was blurry. Streaks of color through the corner of my eye—green, brown, blue—until I realized they were objects I could barely see. I sat upright slowly. I was in the backseat of a moving car, a crucifix swayed in the rearview mirror. Sister Bernadette was behind the wheel, but it wasn't her car. Deacon Jameson sat in the passenger seat. Was this his car? My throat was dry. Oh and, twist, I was suddenly girl-me.

"Where are we going?" I got out hoarsely.

Sister Bernadette turned on the radio. A sermon was on. The crucifix around the rearview mirror bounced with each bump in the road.

I blinked a few times groggily, trying to make sense of everything. Michael was dead? Michael was murdered? And now I was in the backseat of a car? Was this a kidnapping?

No. A nun and a deacon would *not* kidnap the priest's niece.

I thought about the previous day, Sister Bernadette reciting the Nicene Creed. How not long afterward she smiled and said it'd be taken care of. Now, neither of them were smiling.

Possibly because they'd just murdered someone. "You killed him," I blurted out.

In the rearview mirror, I saw Sister Bernadette's eyes widen. Deacon Jameson whipped around in his seat. His eyes were blood-shot, haunted. "Are you serious? You think *we* killed Michael?"

"What am I supposed to think?" I shouted. Or tried to shout. My throat felt raw.

"Jesus Christ," said Sister Bernadette without looking away from the road. I wasn't sure if a nun who took the Lord's name in vain was more trustworthy or less so. "We tried to help him. We tried to protect him. We failed."

Her words hit me like a blow to the face.

Lies? The lies of a murderer?

But if they did kill Michael, why would they have been so upset about his death? The tears, the anger they'd directed at me . . .

Think, stupid. Think.

I went over her words again. *We tried to help him. We.*

"It was you on the phone yesterday," I said to Deacon Jameson. "The person she talked to in code. It was you."

"No shit," Deacon Jameson said.

"Joey, stop," Sister Bernadette said. She turned up the volume on the sermon.

I tried to process it. It would make sense—a twisted, sickening kind of sense, at least—that whoever was abusing Michael ended up killing him. If Deacon Jameson *wasn't* Michael's abuser, that probably meant he wasn't Michael's killer either. Instead, Deacon Jameson and Sister Bernadette had been trying to help Michael, but something had gone wrong. Horribly wrong.

"Why *couldn't* you protect him, then?" I asked softly, on the verge of tears. "Why didn't you turn in whoever did this to him?"

"You have no idea what we're up against," Deacon Jameson said, no rage left in his voice. So exhausted there was a little slur in his words.

"But you do know who the predator is."

"I don't want to talk about this in the car," said Sister Bernadette firmly. "Can you just be quiet for another five minutes?"

Deacon Jameson reached over, plugging in his MP3 player. The sermon cut off. Instead there was a Gregorian cover of Metallica's "The Unforgiven." Hadn't Dima said something about his passion for Gregorian chants? If it were any other time, I'd comment on how much I liked this song and ask if he listened to the originals or just Gregorian chant versions.

I could barely see his face from the backseat, but I was certain he was crying again when Sister Bernadette rested her hand on his knee. He jerked but she kept it there.

Finally, she pulled into a small, gravel driveway. There was a little cottage that looked a bit run down. The garden outside needed weeding but must have been magnificent in its prime. I followed them to the door and watched her pull out keys.

"What is this place?" I finally asked. Anything to break the haunting silence.

"This," she said, going through each key, "is my grandma's home."

"Is she here?"

"No." She paused just as the key slid into the lock. "She's dead."

The hair on the back of my neck rose. She swung the door in, gesturing for us to enter. Deacon Jameson pushed me in before him. Once he entered, he closed the door and turned the lock.

"So . . . what now?"

"Now," Sister Bernadette said, "You tell us *exactly* what you overheard in the confessional."

I hugged my sides. "Just what I told you before. A priest confessed that he screwed a minor. Then my uncle fucking forgave him."

"And you assumed it was Joey because he's gay," Sister Bernadette said. She waited for me to deny it, but I couldn't. Then she sighed heavily and mumbled, "God damn it." I hadn't thought nuns were allowed to swear. Judging by Deacon Jameson's expression, I wondered if he was surprised too. Definitely he was hurt by my assumptions about him.

"Well, who was it?" I asked again.

They looked at each other but didn't say anything.

I took a deep breath, trying not to explode. Normally that was easier for girl-me, but not right now. I tried a different tack. "How did Michael get killed?"

"Strangulation," Deacon Jameson said, staring ahead at the wall.

"How do you know that?"

Deacon Jameson didn't speak.

"Can't they get DNA?" I asked. "From the—body?"

"The wrong DNA," he mumbled.

"I think we need to stop the cryptic stuff, Joey," Sister Bernadette said gently. She looked at me. "Michael stayed at Joey's overnight."

What the hell? "Why?"

"Because I was supposed to protect him," Deacon Jameson said like a broken record. "You wanted it taken care of. I thought it was the safest place for him to be."

Memories flashed through my mind: those hotel rooms a bunch of us shared during cons, no adult supervision, anything goes. Maybe I wasn't the best judge of what was appropriate. But still— "You couldn't let him stay home with his parents?"

"Michael's parents trust . . . the predator." Deacon Jameson squirmed. "They've given the predator access to Michael before, not knowing what was happening. And Michael wasn't willing to tell them, he wasn't ready yet."

"Why didn't *you* tell his parents?"

"I swore I wouldn't tell a soul. It's difficult to even say this now."

I struggled to keep my temper under control again. "Okay, okay, but clearly he didn't end up being any safer there. What happened?"

Deacon Jameson folded his arms, clearly not willing to go there. Sister Bernadette stepped in. "Well, for one thing, Joey confessed that he was going to turn the predator in to the police."

"Are you serious?" I gawked. "You *confessed* that you were going to turn a criminal in . . . *to* the criminal?"

"Not directly," Deacon Jameson muttered.

Anger flared up, deep in my lungs, like the first sparks of a fire. "You confessed to my uncle—"

"I never thought he would break the sanctity of the confessional," he said, resigned. "What's said in confession is supposed to stay in confession."

"But why confess it *at all*?"

"I needed to get right with God. You don't understand."

"I understand someone's dead," I snarled. "And my uncle's involved, and that means you were too by proxy."

"Cool it," Sister Bernadette said, hand closed over Deacon Jameson's knee. It was trembling. I studied his face. Deacon Jameson's red eyes might have been glazed, but for a split-second they looked like Michael's: dead.

"Oh shit," I said softly, feeling my heart shudder with each pulse. "You were a victim, too, weren't you?"

I waited for him to deny it. He didn't. I looked to Sister Bernadette, but she remained silent. *Shit.*

"Am," he mumbled.

"Huh?"

"I should have aged out. But sometimes, still . . ." He trailed off, and I realized what he meant. *Am a victim. Still.*

I fought the urge to cry, to scream. I remembered Michael's brief words with me, his fierce defense of Deacon Jameson. Kindred spirits bound together by terror.

Focus.

Don't fall apart now, you idiot.

"Did my uncle . . . ?" I couldn't finish the question.

Sister Bernadette grimaced. "He absolved people of sin. He's not a criminal himself."

"He's covering it up. That absolutely makes him a criminal." Although I couldn't help but feel a little bit relieved that Uncle Bryan wasn't molesting kids. Talk about a low bar.

I dampened my lips as I fixed my attention on Deacon Jameson. "If you can't say who did it to Michael, can you say who did it to you?"

Deacon Jameson got to his feet. "No." He backed up, eyes darting around the room as if seeking an escape.

"Joey—" Sister Bernadette said, rising as well.

"No. I'm not doing it."

Sister Bernadette glanced at me then back at him. "Forgive me, Joey."

"For—"

"You've got five seconds to say or I'm saying it for you."

He became rigid. "You swore you wouldn't."

"Maybe if I'd told, this wouldn't have happened. Four seconds."

"So you're blaming me now?"

"I'm not. Three seconds."

"That is not your call," he practically shrieked, that same hysteria from the church returning as he hyperventilated.

"Two."

"I'm not saying it."

"One."

Deacon Jameson dropped to his knees. "Bernie, please. I'm begging you. Please."

My heart started to shatter. I didn't see a man before me. I didn't see a transitional deacon, a person with authority and power. I saw the face of a young boy, one who'd never fully grown up. One who'd never felt safe, who constantly lived in fear.

Sister Bernadette's eyes softened. "Forgive me." She turned to me, took a deep breath, and said, "Reverend Monsignor Kline. He's Joey's abuser, and he's the priest whose confession you heard."

My head snapped toward her, eyes widening. Reverend Monsignor Kline? The *big* boss?

Deacon Jameson's body deflated, almost like his soul was emptying out of it. Disconnecting. Leaving an empty husk.

I opened my mouth to speak but nothing came out. Something had put me on edge about Reverend Monsignor Kline, but he he'd always been friendly to me. I'd assumed the bad taste in my mouth was only from his staunch views, not a sixth sense.

I thought about each time I'd seen the Monsignor. About how Sister Bernadette rushed to his side that morning after Mass. I'd mistaken the fear in her eyes for fear of me, of my sinfulness, when really it had been fear of Kline. Had she been placing herself between him and Deacon Jameson? The few times we were together, the deacon had barely been able to speak, mostly staring at us.

No. Not us.

Me.

My stomach churned more. God, I was so stupid. Appearing in the hallway at the school, interrupting my conversation with Kline . . . I thought he was trying to cover up his guilt and make sure I'd stay silent when really he was probably trying to protect me. Maybe Sister Bernadette or Dima had told him I was bigender, or he figured out on his own that I was a boy sometimes. Or maybe he worried that Reverend Monsignor Kline would go after me regardless.

"Okay," I said softly, gently, as if I might spook him. "I get how hard this is. I do. But he hurt Michael too. He . . . *killed* Michael, I'm guessing. And the police were there today. Couldn't you tell them?"

"If I talk to police now, they're going to blame me."

"But DNA—"

"He died in my apartment," Deacon Jameson said, still

sounding broken, weary, and dead. "Wearing my spare paja-mas. If police find DNA, it could easily be mine."

Fuuuuuck. This must be what confessions felt like for my uncle. Hearing shit you wished you could un-hear. Assigning penance and offering absolution so you wouldn't have to think about it anymore.

Because I didn't really want to know. And I sure as hell hoped that didn't make me a bad person, just like my uncle.

Deacon Jameson dropped his head into his hands. "He should have slept in the bedroom. I should have taken the couch. Then I'd have heard. I'd . . ." His voice broke.

This was getting worse by the second. "But you saw his body—after?"

"I saw enough," he spat. I could practically taste the bitterness. "You know how this will look? Thirteen-year-old boy found strangled to death in a gay deacon's house?"

"You think that's better than 'thirteen-year-old boy found murdered and dumped in a swamp after being strangled to death in gay deacon's house'?"

"I *didn't* dump Michael in the swamp," he snapped. "I'm the scapegoat, don't you understand?"

"You know who did move him?" I pressed, almost hopeful.

"People came. People left." He didn't look at me. "I went straight to the church right afterward. Confession. Then I prayed. I didn't leave until you passed out."

He's lying, the voice in my head said. *He knows exactly who did it.* And considering everything I'd heard through the walls, plus all Deacon Jameson's evasions, I had a guess about who'd helped Kline hide his victim's body: my uncle. Why, after all this, was Deacon Jameson still protecting people?

I wanted to ask them how Michael was found. Wouldn't

Kline want it to take a while? No, of course not—if Michael's body was found right away with Deacon Jameson's DNA on him, with clothes that could be traced back to Deacon Jameson, he really would be the perfect scapegoat. I was slowly starting to understand why they kept saying again and again and again that they *couldn't* talk.

"We need a plan," Sister Bernadette said. "Because honestly, I don't know what more we can do."

"All this happened, and you're still saying you're not able to help?"

"You misunderstood," she said carefully. "I don't know what *we* can do."

We.

As in Sister Bernadette and Deacon Jameson.

Not me.

They stared at me. I swallowed. "You have an idea."

Sister Bernadette cleared her throat. "It's a bad idea."

"Please tell me."

"It's dangerous."

"Then maybe we can work with it to make it not-dangerous."

She seemed to mull over it, exchanging a silent look with Deacon Jameson. "So, you're bigender."

"Yeah. So?"

"You used to go out presenting as male? Like sometimes? And you have costumes, right?"

"What does that have to do with anything?" The question was barely out of my mouth when I processed her words. "Oh."

Because there was one thing I knew from documentaries and books: predators preyed again.

"It's a bad idea," she said again. "Forget I suggested it. We'll think of something else."

"It'd work," Deacon Jameson said. "It'd work, and you know it."

"Don't push her."

"She owes me."

"Don't go there, Joey."

He winced. Pain spread through my body. They were fighting over my body. My rights.

Aleks was the beautiful boy. He always looked younger than he was. His face was like a cherub's, while Alexis's just looked ugly. He was fearless, unlike Alexis. And he was being objectified, like he had been at the conventions.

Sister Bernadette studied me. "Joey, can you give us a moment?"

"You've got to be joking—"

"Please?"

He threw up his hands in defeat and stood, dragging his feet as he slipped into another room. Sister Bernadette stepped toward me. Soon my arms were wrapped around her tightly. She rubbed my back gently. "I'm sorry. We'll come up with another idea. Something that doesn't put you in danger."

"It's not that." I sucked in a few deep breaths. "I swore I'd never present as male again."

"Why?" she asked quietly.

I gripped her more tightly. "Because when I'm Aleks, everyone likes me, everyone wants to sleep with me, Aleks is the beautiful boy, Aleks gets the attention. And girl-me . . . I'm . . . not."

"Alexis—"

"I hate Aleks," I blurted out. "I hate that he's easy. I hate that he can have whoever he wants, whenever he wants. I hate that. And I really hate that I wish I was him all the time."

Words I'd never once uttered out loud slipped off my lips like water. Feelings I never wanted to admit or acknowledge, because it meant the cosplay girls were right all along. Beautiful boy, ugly girl. Be the beautiful boy instead.

"I'm not sure I understand. I thought you said you *didn't* want to be him."

"I don't want to be him because I was assaulted as him," I said. "As Alexis, I'm so ugly, I'm invisible. No one would try anything. It's safer to have no one notice me than . . . than let it happen again."

"Alexis," Bernadette said strongly. She took my chin in her fingers and forced my head up. "Being assaulted *isn't* your fault. It has nothing to do with how you look or how you present yourself or how you dress. It has everything to do with the person who assaulted you."

"But—"

"And this idea that someone can be too 'ugly' to be assaulted—you know that's not true. Anyone can be assaulted. Hiding who you are isn't going to change that."

Reverend Monsignor Kline's face loomed in my vision. Had I been safe with him as a girl? Not really.

I wasn't safe anywhere, as anyone.

"But maybe more troubling to me," Sister Bernadette went on, "is how you see yourself."

"I'm hideous."

"You're beautiful."

"You're just saying that."

"No, I'm not." Bernadette shook her head. "Don't you notice that everyone watches you?"

"If I'm beautiful why couldn't I get a single person to ask me to dance when I was Alexis?" The words felt ridiculous as soon as they left my mouth—such a flimsy way of expressing the weight I carried inside me.

"Because you look like you hate people."

"You're saying I owe people a smile?"

"No, but if you don't look like you want to be bothered, do you think people would bug you?"

"Beautiful girls are bugged all the time."

"Look, trust me, walk down the street in certain neighborhoods I know, and if you're a female between the ages of eleven and seventy, you'll get catcalled even if you look like the Phantom of the Opera."

Under other circumstances I would've chuckled.

"But if you're talking about being *liked*, being seen as approachable . . . You don't make eye contact when you're Alexis. Did you know that?"

"That's not—I—" But as I spoke, I found I looked at her lips, her cheek, her nose.

"You also are really fast to pick fights."

"You mean because I'm defending my opinion?" I winced as soon as the words escaped my lips. I was proving her point any time I opened my mouth.

"Because you assume."

I tried to make eye contact but couldn't. I didn't deserve to look at someone so incredible, so divine. I didn't want to see in her eyes that she was lying. Or for her to see into my soul and hate everything she found. "You really think I'm pretty?" I asked quietly.

"Yes. I do. I only wish you could see it too."

I brushed my thumb against her cheek, hardly aware of what I was doing until I felt a handful of fabric in my hand. Her veil.

"Alexis, stop," she said, moving my hands away. "This isn't right."

"I'm sorry." I looked at my lap, ashamed that I'd made a move without getting her consent first.

"A nun's about the worst possible person for you to get a crush on," she said.

"So I've been told."

"I'm in a committed relationship with God."

"How can you say you're in a committed relationship with God when the priests you work with are covering up sexual abuse?"

"Because my God knows that's unacceptable. Because my practice of Catholicism is not like theirs. The connection I feel with my God when I'm in the church at prayer, by myself on walks, everywhere—I'm happy. I feel blessed."

"And now we're going after the people the Church is protecting."

She nodded. "I've been silent too long and I'm not going to sit back and allow some people to tarnish what I hold most dear. Not anymore." She paused, struggling a moment before continuing. "I like you, Alexis. I really do. I also like you as Aleks. But you have to understand, I took a vow. If I break away from that, I need to know it's the *right* thing to do. I need to know it's not just because of this mess so I don't hurt you. And so I don't get hurt either."

I stared at Sister Bernadette. My admiration for her, separate from my crush, shot through the roof. She was everything I wanted to be. Fearless, tough, strong in her convictions. Things I'd thought that Aleks was. Things I'd thought Alexis wasn't.

I hugged my sides, nodding. "I'll go undercover."

She blinked, surprised at the shift. "Are you sure?"

I nodded. "I could use a recording app on my phone. With audio, it'd be enough evidence to go to the police."

"You're really willing to do this?"

"If it's our best chance of catching this bastard, then yes."

She eyed me thoughtfully. "On one condition."

"You're giving me a condition when it was your idea?"

"Absolutely," Sister Bernadette said. "I want you to promise that when this is over, you'll work on learning to love yourself as Alexis. Not just Aleks."

I frowned. "How do I do that?"

"That's up to you. But if I were you, I'd start from the beginning." I couldn't see what Sister Bernadette saw in me. Any time I looked in the mirror as girl-me, I saw someone who was ugly. Scared.

I pulled up my phone app and put it in selfie mode.

"Hello, Alexis," I said to my reflection. "You are beautiful."

And while I'd never felt more stupid, the voice in my head shocked me by saying, **Yes, you are.**

"You're crying," Sister Bernadette said.

Was I?

Deacon Jameson walked back in. "Well?"

"I'll do it," I said, shoving my phone in my pocket.

I forced myself to make eye contact with the deacon, although I didn't want to. He didn't seem angry with me. He seemed hurt and unsure. "And I think I owe you an apology," I added quietly. "I really misjudged you, Deacon Jameson. And I'm so, so sorry."

He grimaced, like my words were daggers in his heart. Softly, he said, "I forgive you."

Forgive and forget. The way everyone was expected to

behave. Be the better person, let bygones be bygones. Forgive my friends at the anime convention.

Forgive Lee.

But I could tell Deacon Jameson didn't fully forgive me. The words stuck in his mouth. Sooner or later his anger and resentment would boil over. And when they did, I wouldn't fight it. I'd accept his words, harsh as they'd be. I'd accept him pushing me away. And, if I needed to, I'd accept the inevitable: if she had to choose between us, Sister Bernadette would stick with her longtime friend. Not me. The same with Dima whenever he left the camp.

And as much as that sucked, I accepted it.

Sister Bernadette's hand slipped in mine, squeezing. I gave a gentle squeeze back then let go. Okay. I could do this. "We'd better get back. Sooner we can catch Kline, the better. And I can't do it if I don't have access to my stuff. So let's not waste any more time."

"Amen," she said as we left the house, ready for the long trek home.

23 NO ONE

It had been so long since I wore a binder, I forgot how much of a pain in the ass it was to get on. Everyone bitched at conventions, arguing over brands. Double front compression with smooth seams but a snugness that was like a medieval torture device, versus an under-the-armpit Velcro that took tons of attempts to tighten and readjust. Then there were the people who used surgical vests with double rows of hooks and eyes and—

I bit the inside of my cheek to keep from screaming. If I was at a convention, I might have used a full body compressor designed to be pulled up over the hips and then the shoulders, but for this, I needed more mobility.

I grunted as I wriggled my shoulders, gasping in pain as the fabric scraped my skin. I'd been at it for five minutes and I still couldn't get my arms through the holes. I caught a glimpse of myself in the mirror, studied the small swell of my breasts and the harsh red lines indenting them.

Then I remembered my alternate binder.

I pulled off the painful white piece and hurled it across the room, then started rummaging through my box for the gray binder. It looked more like a sports bra with a zipper down the front. But the flat panels worked incredibly well as they compressed me, and the short line over my ribs allowed my waist to be free and made it easier for me to breathe. Snugness in general freaked me out, especially on my stomach. And maybe I wasn't as smooth as I once was, but a lot of cis guys put on some weight in their stomachs. It'd distract from my hips because there was only so much I could do.

Next, I pulled out my packer, harness, and compression shorts. I didn't always wear a packer when I went out. Really, it wasn't like people were staring at my crotch. At least I didn't think they were staring at my crotch. I *hoped* they weren't staring at my crotch. As Aleks, as Alexis, I didn't want that.

But now? Who was I?

I'd been Aleks when I woke up yesterday, and then I'd been Alexis after I passed out. But ever since my talk with Deacon Jameson and Sister Bernadette, I'd felt adrift. Empty. Like I was trapped in my body but not connected to it. Like part of my brain had shut off.

Like I was no one.

It was easier that way. If you were a machine, you didn't feel. To turn off the emotional aspect meant it would be easier to do a task that would make anyone's stomach turn.

For Michael, the voice reminded me any time I started feeling queasy. *For Deacon Jameson.*

You owe them.

Don't back out now.

This was your call.

I slipped my legs through the holes, tightened the straps, and readjusted. A lot of people wore packers too high when they first started. I know I certainly did—I must've looked like that idiot who got high on meth and decided to steal puppies by shoving them down his pants (note to self: don't do meth). I had to really pull it between my legs and keep it low. I tightened up the straps further. The silicone felt alien against my skin.

The compression shorts came on next, another layer of protection to keep my packer in place and slim my thighs and hips. I looked at myself in the mirror, turning from side to side. Definitely a little softer than I used to be without my workouts, but I still looked good. Different, but good.

"You've got this, Aleks," I said to my reflection, but that felt like a lie. "You can pull it off, Alexis," I tried again, but that also didn't feel honest. My heart thudded with fear. I wasn't a machine because I could still feel. But both parts of me were gone, leaving me like the skin of a cicada.

I was nothing. I was no one.

I waited for the voice to berate me, but it was silent. Like it had left me too. And that silence was so unbearable. Devastating. Isolating.

I got the message loud and clear. Not only was I no one, but I was completely on my own. Atonement for my sins. Not the normal seven deadly sins that people preach about, not the sins I overheard in my room beside the confessional. But the real sins of life and friendship:

Doubt.

Assumption.

Willful ignorance.

False accusation.

Hypocrisy.

Desperation for acceptance.

Hiding my true self.

Shaming someone for who they are.

Refusing to listen.

Causing irreparable hurt.

I was guilty of all those crimes.

I grabbed a hair tie, twisted my ponytail up under a wig head, then grabbed one of my most realistic wigs, the one I'd styled to have a small faux-hawk. It was easy to single out wigs if you were looking hard. The shorter the wig, however, the more likely it was that people wouldn't question it. At one of the first conventions I went to by myself, I got a headache and pulled off my wig. Everyone around me gasped because they thought it was my actual hair. I'll never forget their shock, or how special I felt. Like I had a secret that was for me, only me. One I could share with the world, if I wanted.

I used makeup to hollow out my cheeks and soften my eyes. For the last step, I put in colored contact lenses. It'd been so long, they hurt, but now as I looked in the mirror, blue eyes stared back at me instead of dark brown. I needed to minimize the chance of being recognized. It was dangerous enough to approach Reverend Monsignor Kline without risking that he would recognize me.

After pulling on my Tall Men Shoes, a short-sleeved dress shirt, slacks, and a tie, I looked in the mirror. I looked like a Mormon missionary, *not* a Catholic schoolboy. God damn it.

I rooted through my closet again, grabbing a thin vest. I slid it over my shoulders and looked in the mirror.

Now I looked like the campiest guy to ever camp, doing pirouettes on clouds as Freddie Mercury's ghost rode past on a unicorn and sprinkled me with glitter.

Often, Aleks loved being that flamboyant. But Aleks was gone. And even if he wasn't, if I looked like I was "asking for it" (which was such a disgusting statement), I'm pretty sure Kline wouldn't make a move. There was no guarantee that we'd get him anyway, but we had to try and *damn it!* There wasn't enough *time!*

After going through my clothes one last time, I slipped on a polo shirt, khakis, and a belt. I still used Tall Men Shoes, but one of the tennis sneaker variants. I looked back in the mirror. Preppy kid. Beautiful boy. A little rugged and awkward, just starting a growth spurt. Like a thirteen-year-old.

Like Michael.

I double-checked that my phone was charged. Then I opened my door.

Aunt Anne Marie was on the other side, fist raised to knock on the door. She stared at me, horrified, and took a step back.

No surprise there. We hadn't really talked since the other day when I told her I enjoyed being a sinner, so it wasn't like I had a lot of goodwill to draw on.

"Uh. Hi, Aunt Anne Marie," I squeaked. "Just heading out—"

"I didn't see this," she said as she turned her back. "I'm going to my room. I'm going to wait ten minutes, and when I come back, you'll be normal."

"This is my normal," I said as I stepped around her. "You just haven't seen all of my normal yet."

"Alexis—"

"I gotta go."

"Alexis!"

"I'm sorry. I'll talk more later. I gotta go," I said as I slipped past her. My footsteps seemed to thud even more loudly as I went down the hallway. I could hear her behind me.

"You—you can't go out like that. It's not the Lord's will!"

"Just asked God two minutes ago, he said he's chill," I said without slowing. She gasped.

"Have you been possessed? It was that boy, Dima, wasn't it?

You've been different ever since I let you go to that convention with him. You need to be purged from sin. Alexis, stop!"

Just inside the front door, I stopped. I inhaled slowly and turned around. "Aleks," I said, even though that was a lie. Today, I was no one, but she didn't need to have ammunition for her argument. Today, to her, I would lie. "My name is Aleks."

"I don't understand why you'd—why you'd want to do such a thing . . ."

"Being bigender is not a choice," I said. "I've been miserable trying to pretend I was someone I'm not on the days I'm not."

My aunt flinched, visibly upset. "So you want to be a boy?"

Count to five. Deep breaths. If I yelled at her, she wouldn't learn. Getting angry would only close the door, preventing her from listening. And despite all her flaws, despite the horrible things happening under her roof and inside her church, I still wanted to see the good in her. To reach out to the part of her that was open to understanding me. "Sometimes I'm a boy. Other times, I'm Alexis."

"But you're not a boy. You're my beautiful niece."

I gave a tight-lipped smile, like she was trying to tug a scream from me. My mouth tasted like copper. "I'll see you later. There's something I need to do."

"No." She shook her head. "If you go out that door like that, when you come back, your things will be packed. I'll call your mom. You'll be going back."

I opened my mouth to speak but then closed it. So this is what people felt when their families disowned them. Without a word, I continued out the door and down the steps.

Why did it hurt so much? Being around someone who hated people like me wasn't healthy. The environment was toxic from day one, but I hoped. I'd hoped so damn hard. And

I guess I didn't think she actually would kick me out. After a couple weeks, shouldn't she have realized she still liked me? That I was the same soul even if sometimes I was a boy and sometimes I was a girl?

I felt unbearably sad, but I didn't have time to cry.

On the bright side, the tears that threatened to fall made my contacts moist and comfortable without sliding down my cheeks.

I could do this. I knew I could do this and focus on what was happening and what I needed to do, and *not* why she hated me.

And did that even matter if I woke up today feeling like no one?

My ribs could cave in over my breaking heart, the hurt rushing downhill like an avalanche, but there wasn't enough time to grieve. There wasn't enough time for anything except fixing this mess.

I kept my head low as I shuffled along, constantly glancing at my phone for directions to the address Deacon Jameson had given me. After cutting through the woods near the church and going past the lake, I finally arrived at a small duplex. I knocked on the door and waited.

There was a small scuffle before the door swung open. I stared at the guy before me in a George Michael T-shirt and loose sweatpants. In the background, a Gregorian chant cover of "Join Me" by H.I.M. played.

"Deacon Jameson?" I practically gawked. He was barely recognizable. Every other time I'd seen him, he'd been dressed properly in his cassock or a black suit, hair meticulously combed, freshly shaven.

"You're early, Aleks," he said wearily. That gave me pause. Did he recognize me immediately because I didn't look like someone else, or was it because he knew I was coming?

"No. I'm not," I said gently. "Did you oversleep?"

"I . . ." He glanced at his watch. "Oh. I guess I did." He gestured for me to come in as he walked through. "You know how to make coffee?"

"On it," I said. I moved to the kitchenette and rummaged. There was clutter everywhere, dirty dishes stacked in the sink with a few tiny fruit flies. Empty bottles of beer everywhere. I found a battered coffee maker and started to fill the grounds in. By the time I poured in water then hit the power button, I'd noticed that "Join Me" was on repeat. I wondered how a song could sound so beautiful when it talked about dying for love, Romeo and Juliet style.

I stepped back—then immediately turned my head away. He hadn't fully closed the door as he changed, like he was spaced out, or maybe too hungover. And something stirred in me because I could see exactly what Dima saw in the deacon. He must have worked out and dieted like mad and had the best genetics on the planet for a body like that.

When he came back out, wearing black pants and black clerical shirt, tab collar in hand, I said, "Didn't know you wore anything that wasn't all . . . uh. Priestly?"

"You mean the shirt?" he asked as he attached the priest's collar.

"Not just *any* a shirt," I countered as I walked back to the sink. "George Michael was such a pioneer for LGBTQ+ rights—"

"I don't need a history lesson. I know who he is."

Ouch. "Uh, right. Okay." I turned on the sink faucet and squirted dish soap onto a sponge. "We should talk about music sometime," I said, offering my olive branch even though I was rambling. "I mean, not now because, well. Everything. But I was going to tell you I really like the Gregorian chant covers.

They're good. Dima said you'd make ones from songs he liked. I heard you're a great singer and musician. Something about guitar and lute because you're extra?"

While I chattered, Deacon Jameson crossed to the coffee maker, and pulled out two mugs. Clearly, he wasn't in the mood for small talk. Considering everything, I didn't blame him.

"You remember the plan?" he asked, filling one mug and handing it to me.

"I've got it," I said, trying to sound more confident than I felt. I couldn't screw this up. I owed Deacon Jameson. If I wanted to honor Raziel's ideals of helping others, I couldn't exclude him. Not now. "You sure you're up for this?"

"No," he said honestly. "I don't think I'm sure of anything anymore."

I felt for him. He was hurting, badly, and it was at least partly because of me. I straightened my collar a little. "How much time do we have?"

He glanced at his watch as he sipped coffee from his own mug. "Any time now."

"Right. Okay." I paused. "You know you've been looping this song since I got here, right?"

"Oh," he said distractedly, moving across the apartment and turning off his MP3 player. "Shouldn't have this on anyway."

"When this is all over, let's listen together. You know, all of us. You, me, Sister Bernadette, Dima. We can be nice and let him have a woodblock to play."

"Sure," he said in a way that suggested he wasn't interested. Although it stung, I accepted it. He wasn't my friend. He didn't owe me that.

I walked toward his couch, turning my back to sit on it when I caught him staring at me. I paused, mid-sit. "Is this where Michael . . . ?" I stood upright quickly, brushing off the back of my khakis. My heart pounded way too fast and my binder suddenly felt too snug.

"I prayed for him," he said quietly. "It didn't help. Drank until I passed out. That didn't help either."

I cradled my coffee mug. One sip: it was bitter. So bitter. I brought it back to the sink and poured it out. "Sorry. I should have said I'm not really a coffee person," I lied.

"Dima hates my coffee, too," Deacon Jameson said. I faced him. He was smiling, but the smile was so, so sad. "He always was on me to get a new coffee maker. A French press or something. I told him I needed to be humble. He said coffee was nothing to be humble about and that he'd buy me one for my birthday with his money from work. I told him to save it up for school, but Dima does whatever he wants to do. It's admirable. One can only aspire to have that much confidence."

"You really love him," I murmured.

"I have for a long time."

I hesitated. "Did Reverend Monsignor Kline—"

"No. Never," Deacon Jameson said hurriedly. "Dima always looked too old, too butch, even when he was younger. Also, Dima isn't good at keeping secrets."

I thought back to Dima mentioning that Deacon Jameson was close with Kline. "Did Dima know about you . . .?" I let the question hang.

Deacon Jameson shook his head. "Sometimes I wonder if that would—change how he views me. Us. You hear about cycles of abuse. . . I worry that's what I stumbled into with him."

The vulnerability in his voice caught me off guard. I wasn't sure it was my place to reassure him, but I felt like I had to say *something*. "He initiated the romance with you, right?"

"I wonder about that," he said truthfully. He stared into his coffee. "There was this time a few months ago when Dima put a bunch of M&Ms in his coffee, thinking that'd make it taste better. His expression with the first sip—I'll never forget it. He said something like, 'It tastes very *interesting*.' I tried to make fun of him then he said, 'That's Russian enthusiasm!' before dumping the rest of the pack in my coffee. It took all of my willpower not to kiss him right there."

"But you didn't."

"No. Nothing happened before he was eighteen. Before then, though, did I groom him?"

"You're what? Five years older?" I asked. I thought about Mom's rule: divide your age by half and add seven. I was terrible at doing mental math and really relied on a pencil . . . "That's not the worst age gap. It's not great, but it could be worse." Deacon Jameson was cringing. I tried to rebound quickly. "And the fact you waited—I think that says something."

Deacon Jameson snorted. "I think it also says something that Dima went to the camp so soon afterward." His body stiffened, head swiveling toward the door. "He's here."

"How do you—"

The lock rattled as a key was inserted. I watched the deadbolt turn.

"Show time," I muttered to Deacon Jameson.

"I'm not sure I can—"

I cut him off as I pulled him close, kissing him. His body was rigid, arms limp by his sides. Frozen. And I was absolutely positive that his intentions with Dima really were honorable and filled with love.

I quickly moved his hands up to my shoulders, squeezing them before I gripped hard, putting him into position. And for a moment, I was back in time. I allowed myself to think that it was Lee and me, in the hallway at a convention, going wild. And I wondered what Sister Bernadette would think if she saw us executing the plan we'd mutually agreed on. I wondered what Dima would think. Would he be furious? Heartbroken? Disgusted? Or impressed that we did whatever we could to right the wrongs of Saint Martha's?

The door swung in. He was here. And just like we planned, Deacon Jameson shoved me off of him, hard. I staggered back, pretending I was dazed. Immediately, Deacon Jameson crossed the room. "Monsignor—"

"Unbelievable," Reverend Monsignor Kline said. "The boy's not yet in the ground and you're on to the next one."

Deacon Jameson froze. Then, like he was struggling to remember his lines, he said, "I never did anything to Michael. You did."

Kline stepped forward and sniffed. "You've been drinking. Again." He wasn't taking the bait at all. I sucked in my stomach, biting my lower lip as I gazed in his direction. "Where'd you find this one?"

"Does it matter?"

"Depends. Is he a good Catholic boy?"

Deacon Jameson glanced at me. His eyelashes barely bobbed in a blink, indicating the plan was still a go although he was fumbling over everything. I wasn't sure if that was because he was nervous or hungover. "Reminds me of Michael."

"And I thought you only liked butch Russian boys," Kline said. Deacon Jameson turned his head, like he'd been slapped.

Shit. It wasn't working. Kline was redirecting everything to Deacon Jameson, and he was losing composure. We were failing.

I stepped toward them. "Should I go?" I asked, deepening my voice.

"No," Kline said. "How old are you?"

I glanced at Deacon Jameson. There it was, another blink. The go-ahead. I lowered my head, peeking up at Reverend Monsignor Kline. "Fourteen," I said, still trying to keep my voice low.

"Would you like a glass of wine?" he asked. "Joey's always got a full bar."

Holy shit. It took everything for me not to look back at Deacon Jameson. Kline was now recorded on my app offering alcohol to a minor. He was going to fall for this.

"Monsignor, you can't just offer him wine."

"Wine goes with Communion—"

"That's not Communion," Deacon Jameson spluttered. "You're trying to get him drunk so he'll give you oral sex. Just like you did with me."

"Is that what this is about? Envy's one of the seven deadly sins," Kline said cruelly. "Wasn't last week enough?"

Last week?

He'd said he was still a victim, but I hadn't realized—last *week*? I sucked in a breath, biting the inside of my cheek so hard I could taste blood.

I looked at Deacon Jameson. He was wilting. I was losing him. If we strayed any further from the script, this wouldn't work.

"You know what else is a sin?" Deacon Jameson said. "Lust and murder."

"Oh, Joey," Kline said. He took a step toward the deacon. Deacon Jameson backed up so fast, he hit the wall.

"What you did to Michael—" Deacon Jameson began.

"Is completely your fault. You broke your vows of silence."

"I wasn't the only one!"

"Did you raise your voice at me?"

"I'm not letting you touch him," Deacon Jameson said unsteadily, glancing at me. I could see it in his eyes: He couldn't do this anymore. He was giving up. "Look, just . . . do whatever you want to me, okay? Just not him. No other kid. *Please.*"

"Did you know how ugly you've become now that you're older? How difficult it is to give someone like you Communion? And here I thought that maybe there was redemption, that you'd be saved." His voice lowered threateningly. "You'll never become a priest without me. You don't even deserve what you have. That boy will be giving me Communion, and you'll watch, and you'll say nothing." Kline's hand snaked forward, closing over my crotch and packer. I gasped and pulled back.

"Get your hand off my dick!" I snarled, sweating under my wig.

Reverend Monsignor Kline stared at me. "What are you wearing under that?"

My chest started to pound. Shit! He could feel the harness. I didn't expect him to grope me, at least not right away, but now . . . he knew. He felt it. He knew it wasn't attached to my body.

"You need to leave. Now," Deacon Jameson said, voice rising in pitch. "I'm going straight to the police."

"Just like you told Father Moore the other night?" Kline stepped toward me, eyes narrowed. "When I have you strip, what will I find?"

Behind him, Deacon Jameson was blinking his eyes rapidly. Abort mission. Immediately. I wanted to move, to run, to flee, but I was frozen in place, the Tall Men Shoes so heavy I couldn't lift my feet.

Kline stepped even closer. He loomed over me. "Where's the recording device, Alexis?"

Shit!

Without thinking, I kneed him in the groin. I swerved to get past him, toward the door, when his arms wrapped around me, hands groping what they could. "You've been a very bad girl. No room for those," he said in a hushed whisper. "Only difference between you and Michael is that you'll never be found." His hand shoved in my back pocket, grabbing my phone. I clawed his body, catching fibers of his clothes. Not enough. Taking a deep breath, I bunched a hand in his hair and yanked. His fist met my cheek and my head snapped to the side as I staggered back, a fistful of hair in my hand.

"You bitch," he snarled.

I scrambled toward the door again, Kline wrenching my arm back until suddenly he lurched forward, hitting the floor. Deacon Jameson had tackled him from behind, pinning him down. "Run!" he gasped.

I stood, paralyzed with fear.

"You need to fucking *run*!"

I grabbed my fallen phone and took off out the door. My legs were heavy from the Tall Men Shoes but I didn't stop running, tears streaking down my cheeks as I heard Deacon Jameson scream from pain. I couldn't turn back. If I did, it'd all be for nothing. I owed Deacon Jameson. I needed to finish my mission.

So I kept running, crashing recklessly into the woods.

24 NO ONE

It felt like I ran for hours. My body was drenched, binder stuck to my chest like glue, sweat sliding around the packer on my skin. When I was positive the apartment was out of sight, I stopped to catch my breath and pulled out my phone. My heart stopped. The screen was black. I hit the power button and home key—nothing.

No. Nonononono. The recording . . .

I choked, tears slipping down my cheeks. I'd screwed up. If I hadn't frozen, we would've had him.

I turned in a circle. I had no clue where I was. The woods. Probably near the swamp. I didn't have a map or a compass or anything and now I didn't have a phone with a GPS. I wasn't even sure if I had evidence against Kline except for the handful of hair that I shoved in my pocket along with my phone. But what would that prove? That I'd physically assaulted Kline?

I started to walk, hoping I'd see something familiar soon. My chest hurt. My feet blistered with the extra weight of the hidden heighteners. Mosquitos clung to my sweaty, wet skin. I could take off my shoes to walk faster, but there'd be sharp rocks, sticks, poison oak, maybe snakes.

Was Deacon Jameson safe? I'd heard him scream in pain. Should I have gone back for him? Would he end up behind bars, framed for a crime he didn't commit?

Was he even alive?

And Sister Bernadette. Where was she? Was she safe? Would she check in on Deacon Jameson and me? Would she be in direct danger, too, seeing something she wasn't meant to?

I walked faster. I had to. I wasn't sure if I was disappearing deeper into the wilderness or if I was approaching safety.

With each step, I became dizzier. Was it morning or night? Five minutes could have been three hours. Six hours could have been nine seconds. Where would the woods take me? Would there be another side, or would I get stuck here and die?

I wasn't sure. And there was no way to find out. Until the voice came back, tiny and weak and so, so quiet:

Keep moving.

So I did.

I crunched through dead leaves, hard side stitches sending pain straight up my body. My back was at the point of aching so badly it was becoming numb. I started to trip from fatigue and the hidden platforms in my shoes.

I was getting tired. So tired. Everything seemed so much darker. Was I going the wrong direction? Wet droplets hit my face. Rain or tears? I couldn't tell. I pressed on. I had to keep going.

In the distance, I saw a dim, flickering glow. It beckoned me. Like a fly, I was drawn to the light. Just a little bit farther. I had to try.

"Come on, Aleks," I said to myself, reaching for boy-me's essence. The spirit of him shivered, seemed reluctant, but stayed by my side. "We're going to get through this, Alexis," I said as girl-me fluttered inside me, cautious but urging me on. My throat was dry. It was hard to breathe. Water. I needed water. I needed to stop sweating. But there was no time. If we stopped now, we might never get going again. We had to keep moving. All parts of me: female, male, nothing, both.

The dim light became brighter, the trees more sparse as I stepped out next to a road. I exhaled deeply. Down the road to my right, I recognized the outline of the school. That meant not far beyond that would be the church and the rectory.

I stumbled with each step, straining as both parts of me whispered, **Be like Raziel. Do it for Raziel.**

But Raziel fixed little problems. Raziel never had to run away from a corrupt and murderous member of the clergy.

There was so much weight on my back. My feet sank.

> **Don't forget what you came from.**
> **Don't forget why you came here.**
> **Do it for Raziel.**
> **Do it for everyone.**
> **Don't quit on me now.**

Squeezing my eyes shut, I nodded, mentally signing a contract.

I would keep going for Sister Bernadette. I would keep going for Dima.

I would keep going for Michael.

I would keep going for Deacon Jameson, unsure if there was a god but if so praying for his safety.

I would keep going for the victims.

And what would I get in exchange?

Nothing.

Because this wasn't about me. This was for people who, truthfully, I barely knew. And people I would never meet. This was for *them*.

"Alexis!" a voice shouted. It didn't sound like the one in my head, but I couldn't be certain. I strained to go that direction, but I was too exhausted. My knees gave out. I hit pavement, panting. My vision was slowly going black. Not now. Not now. I had to hang in there. I had to cling to consciousness. I had to be lucid so that I could give a police statement. I would *not* let Kline take that from me.

"Aleks!" I swore I heard someone scream as I pressed my hands to the sidewalk, trying to push myself up. My elbows buckled. My chin hit the pavement, hard. I was too weak.

I felt pressure under my arms as I was hoisted to my feet. I blinked a few times, forcing my vision to clear. On one side, Sister Bernadette. On the other, my aunt.

Ahead of me, Uncle Bryan.

"Oh my God, where did you go? We were so worried about you—"

By the time he got within a few feet of me, I was ready.

Gritting my teeth, I looked my uncle dead in the eye. "I need to go to the police station to report an assault."

"Of course," Uncle Bryan gasped. "I'll drive you—"

"You won't drive me anywhere," I said. "Sister Bernadette will. Aunt Anne Marie, you'll need to make a decision. Come or stay."

She frowned. "I—I don't understand."

I inhaled slowly. "Please forgive me because I'm going to

hurt you pretty badly." I looked from Aunt Anne Marie to Uncle Bryan. "I heard the confessions. Through the vent in my bedroom."

My aunt gasped, stepping away from me so quickly Sister Bernadette had to wrap both arms around me to keep me from falling. Uncle Bryan spluttered. "You have no right—"

"*You* had no right to absolve Kline from sin," I said firmly. "Or to help him cover up his crimes."

"You know nothing about canon law."

"I know that people like you are making it worse."

"If you overheard, you knew I didn't approve of his actions," Uncle Bryan said.

"You still forgave him. That's on *you*."

"Alexis—this is complicated. More complicated than you can imagine. What's said between priests stays between priests."

"What about Deacon Jameson, then?" I challenged. "Didn't he confess to you that he was going to the police the night before Michael was murdered? And didn't you turn right around and tell Kline what he was planning to do? You broke a vow right there, didn't you? Even before you helped Kline dump Michael's body in the swamp."

My uncle paled. My aunt turned on him. "Is this—is this true?"

He couldn't answer.

I steadied myself against Sister Bernadette. "This is what's going to happen. I'm going to get a ride from Sister Bernadette to the police. You are going to jail."

"You can't do this to me," he said hoarsely. "Please. I'm your uncle."

"Except I can do it. And I will."

"Alexis, come home and let's talk about this. I'll try to explain. *Please*. Reverend Monsignor Kline did so much for me. He said God chose me and—"

"Shut up." I glanced at Sister Bernadette. "Let's go, Bernie."

"Alexis," Uncle Bryan said. "Don't do this. This is a mistake. God will not forgive you for this."

"Nah," I said, looking over my shoulder. "I think God and I are actually on the same page about this one."

Sister Bernadette smiled at me as she guided me toward the car, cheeks wet from tears. "It's the first time you've called me that."

"What?"

"Bernie."

"If you don't want me to—"

"I like it," Sister Bernadette said, carefully opening the passenger-side door. Gingerly, she helped me get in and buckled my seatbelt with such tenderness I couldn't keep from brushing my fingers under the side of her veil to twist a lock of her curly hair. She took my hand, gently removing it from her hair. "Don't," she said.

"I'm sorry."

"I'm sorry, too. Look, I—"

The backseat car door opened. Aunt Anne Marie climbed in, slamming the door behind her. I looked over my shoulder.

"God didn't give me cancer for my husband to do *this*," she said, tears in her eyes.

"So, am I still a sinner?" I asked her.

"We're all sinners," she said. "Some bigger sinners than others."

I nodded, not trusting my words. Bernie said, "Then we better—"

There was banging on the window. My uncle. Bernie rolled down the window about an inch.

"I know where Deacon Jameson is," he said hoarsely. "Don't turn me in, and I'll tell you where Kline's taken him."

My eyes shot wide. A silence filled the car. I knew Deacon Jameson was in danger, but Uncle Bryan's wording implied he'd been taken from his house—kidnapped, maybe worse. If we could get to him before it was too late to help him . . .

I glanced at Sister Bernadette. She nodded at me like she was reading my mind, then turned back to the window. "Get in. Take us right to him. If you play me . . ."

She couldn't finish. I didn't blame her. My heart was throbbing as my uncle got in the backseat. He reached for my aunt's hand, but she slapped it away.

"Where is he?" Sister Bernadette said.

"At the school," Uncle Bryan said. "Where it all started."

Where Reverend Monsignor Kline first made his move.

25 NO ONE

My uncle had a key to the front doors of the school. Standing beside him in the lobby, I peered down a dark corridor. There was a sound void, like in those pretentious movies set in outer space. Only problem was that this wasn't a movie. This was real life.

Bernie had stayed in the car with my aunt, waiting on dispatch with 911. I didn't blame her for not coming in. She and Deacon Jameson were close friends, so tight I'd thought they were in love with each other. Knowing what we might find in here . . . I couldn't imagine.

With a deep breath, I started walking the hall, keeping an eye on my uncle at all times. Although we tried to be quiet, our footsteps practically boomed, echoing off the walls, announcing our arrival. My heart hammered in my ears. My uncle's footsteps slowed. He pointed at a door. "I can't go in there," he whispered.

I wanted to yell at him, but I didn't. He was a coward, but that was no surprise at this point, and there wasn't enough time to argue.

I tested the doorknob. It twisted easily. My chest tightened up further. I glanced at my uncle. He didn't look at me.

He didn't need to. I understood that expression and knew what was happening. He'd brought me to the end of the line. Behind that door, Kline would be expecting me.

My uncle leaned close to my ear. "If you go in, you may not get out."

"Then I guess I'll see you in hell."

The door swung open to reveal a large office that looked more like a library. I groped for a light switch but couldn't find one. Along the floor, candles were lit, creating a walkway. I followed their path and came to a second door. It was hard to breathe with my aching body, and the air felt unusually thick. I and pulled open the second door, hand covering my mouth. Smoke spilled out of the room.

Fire.

A whole set of bookcases was going up in flames. Squinting, I could make out the shadowy outline of a person slumped against the far wall. I sprinted over, hand still over my mouth and nose. It was Deacon Jameson, unconscious. Knocked out, or drugged, maybe. His face was cut and bruised. Still breathing, but shallowly. Spilled across his lap and the floor were Communion wafers and wine.

Kline, that motherfucker.

I pulled off my shirt, staying just in my binder as I tied the fabric loosely around his nose and mouth like a mask. His eyes didn't open. We didn't have much time.

Gritting my teeth, I grabbed him under the armpits and started pulling. Deacon Jameson wasn't that much larger than me, and sliding him across the floor wasn't as hard as I expected.

The fumes were thicker. It was harder to see. I pulled harder at Deacon Jameson, coughing. I tried not to inhale but it was impossible not to instinctively gasp for breath. As I dragged

Deacon Jameson, his eyes fluttered open, though he still didn't look fully conscious. At least he was alive. For now.

We were almost at the door. Ten steps, nine steps, eight. We were close, we were going to make it. Seven steps, six steps, five—

A shadowy outline stepped onto the threshold.

Four steps, three steps, two steps—

Above us, hand on the doorknob, Kline smiled.

One step—

The door started to close.

With all my strength, I twisted my body, sliding Deacon Jameson out the door, slamming him into Kline. Kline stumbled back, and suddenly, Deacon Jameson was crawling on his own, dragging his lower body toward the second door.

Kline flung himself at me. Thrown off balance, I staggered to my knees, and his shoe connected with my face. I hit the ground hard. With blood in my mouth, I looked up at the monster.

"You've been a very bad girl, Alexis," Kline said. "Shame you were lurking on church property and locked yourself in after setting an accidental fire. Any last words?"

"Yeah." I lifted my face to look him in the eye. "Go fuck yourself."

He kicked me one last time before he closed the door. I heard a lock turn.

Dragging myself back up onto my knees, I pounded against the wood with my fists, coughing. The fumes became heavier. Stronger. My fingernails dug into the wood. Tears streaked down my cheeks.

Exhausted from running through the woods, the lack of sleep, the stress, and now the toxins, my body slowly became limp.

I closed my eyes. Would Deacon Jameson make it out alive, crawling, with just the tiniest head start on Kline? I could never atone for Michael's death, but maybe saving Deacon Jameson's life would count for something.

My body slid to the floor. I turned my head to the side, closing my eyes, shallowly inhaling, delaying the inevitable. My mind drifted to Bernie. Her radiant smile. Her curly black hair that sometimes strayed from her veil. I wished I'd kissed her.

Mom and Dad—they'd be devastated. I wished I'd talked with them more, Skyped more, called more. I didn't think . . . maybe that was the problem to begin with. I hoped they'd forgive me, although they wouldn't forgive themselves.

Finally I thought of Lee. He was the last person I wanted to think of when I was on borrowed time, but he haunted me.

People talked about forgiveness. The peace they felt when letting go.

I thought about his face. His kiss. The way he put his hand on my hipbone. The way he talked about me. The screencaps of his group chats.

My stomach churned from nausea at the thought of forgiving him. He didn't deserve it.

So I wouldn't.

And, for the first time since it all happened, maybe the first time in years, I was truly at peace.

We did good, Alexis and Aleks said in my head.

"Yeah, we did," I murmured, as everything evaporated into black.

26 US

Alexis. Aleks.

For the first time in my life, I couldn't feel a separation between them. I was sure that would change eventually. Sooner or later, I'd wake up as one or the other. And perhaps some days I would switch in between the two. And maybe it'd suck a little less than it had before.

But for now, they clung to each other so tightly it felt impossible to sever them. A third gender? Broad nonbinary? I didn't know anything except that it was us.

They were me. We were me.

Apparently, I'd fallen unconscious before firefighters burst through the door. They pulled me out on a stretcher, got on an oxygen mask, and brought me to the hospital, then monitored me for three days until I regained consciousness. Once I did, blinking in a bright hospital room, Mom and Dad swarmed me from both sides of the bed, crying and covering my forehead and cheeks with kisses. Aunt Anne Marie hovered in the doorway, equally teary.

Bernie sat near the bed, veil in her lap bunched in her hands, curly hair loose. I'd never seen her bareheaded before.

Seeing me conscious made her smile. She kissed her

crucifix after murmuring a prayer so soft I couldn't hear it over the sound of my parents bawling.

Another day passed. I couldn't speak, my throat too raw from fumes, but I was able to keep my hand steady enough to write an account of recent events for the detectives, with a lawyer nearby. The lawyer was Dad's idea. "Just in case," Dad said. I went along with it, even though I wasn't worried about myself. I was willing to accept any punishment, any consequences for my own poor choices, without complaint. Just as long as the other problems were taken care of.

Miraculously, the police tech department was able to get into my phone and retrieve the recording. They'd gone over my body with a fine-tooth comb, collecting evidence, thanking me for the strands of hair in my pocket.

"You might have to go to court," one of the detectives said. "Your recording might not be admissible, so your testimony is paramount."

Weakly, I nodded.

With their patience and my penmanship, giving my statement to the police was a lot simpler than I thought it'd be. On TV and in movies, people always seem to struggle. Maybe it was easier because I knew if I talked, it'd be over for me. Maybe for the clergy, it was too much of a struggle—the web of guilt and obligation, the sunk cost of years of silence.

The detectives told me I was brave, and that my uncle and Reverend Monsignor Kline would go away for a long time. That canon law couldn't save them this time. A suit was in progress against both of them, one the lawyer said they'd take on pro-bono so Michael's family could pay for his funeral.

Once the detectives and the lawyer had left, Dad leaned over me. "Therapy," he said. "I don't care how long it takes to find a good therapist for you, but you're going to therapy."

I scribbled, *What if I can't speak?*

Dad rubbed the top of my head. "I can hear you just fine, kiddo."

Over the next couple of days, I watched Mom and Aunt Anne Marie sit next to each other on one side of the room, holding hands and crying and saying "I'm sorry" again and again and again. After years of pent-up tension, they had a lot to talk about. Their adult lives. Their marriages. Me.

Bernie spent a lot of time in my room too, holding my hand, wiping my forehead when I sweated and giving me sips of Gatorade when I was confident I could keep it down. She rubbed my back when I vomited in a bag and gave me mouthwash, waiting patiently as I gargled and spit it out, barely able to get out a "thanks."

At one point I woke from a nap to find Bernie sitting next to the bed, with nobody else in the room. "Hey," I croaked. My voice was slowly remembering how to work.

"Hey." Her fingers slid through my hair to the back of my head. Her forehead touched mine. Her breath was warm on my face, her lips soft when she finally leaned in, giving me the kiss I'd wanted so badly.

"Um . . ."

At the sound of a throat clearing, we broke contact, me gripping the hospital bed sheets fiercely until I realized it was only Dima standing in the doorframe. He had another plushie in hand. One that looked exactly like my Raziel costume. Custom.

"Dima!"

He burst into the room, sitting on the bed, leaning over me to smother me in a tight embrace. Words poured out in half-sobs. "I'm so sorry I was stupid and went to the camp and never texted you back after the con—was so wrapped in myself I didn't know any of this was going on—I had no clue about Joey and Kline—and if Joey had died, I don't know what—he's told me everything now and—you were incredible. Thank you, thank you, thank you."

I didn't have it in me to say he was crushing me, but apparently Bernie noticed. She moved behind him, gently tugging. "She's still weak."

"Sorry!" he said, stepping back and wiping his eyes. "Um, I have something for you."

"The plushie?" I asked softly. Raising my voice seemed too difficult.

"Oh, well, yeah"—he handed it to me hastily—"but I got that for you a while ago. Wanted to thank you for going with me to the con. But for everything else . . ." He unhooked the crucifix from his neck. "This is for you."

I hesitated. "I'm not Catholic—"

"Then don't wear it," Dima said. "But I want you to have it. It means a lot to me."

"I can't take something that means so much—"

"I want you to have it," he insisted. "It's the only way I can try to say thank you for saving his life."

I studied his face, his features that looked so much like mine, finally getting it. He knew I wasn't going to be converting. This wasn't about expectation. This was a gesture of gratitude and trust. "You're welcome." I slid it into my pocket. It didn't burn a hole through the fabric, so I guess if he existed, God wasn't sending me right to hell. Maybe this decision was the right one, really.

There was a tap at the door. Deacon Jameson stepped in,

wearing street clothes and supporting himself on crutches. "I thought I heard Dmitry squawking from down the hall," he said with forced lightness. "Pretty sure no one would be able to sleep through that."

"I wasn't that loud," Dima said. He managed to sound more convincingly cheerful than Deacon Jameson, even as he jumped to his feet and helped Deacon Jameson walk over to my bedside.

Deacon Jameson sat on a chair, propping his crutches against the bed. "Can, uh, can I talk to you? Alone?"

Bernie took Dima by the arm. "We'll get snacks. And check in on your parents. I think they're getting you discharge papers."

Deacon Jameson waited until Bernie and Dima stepped out, Bernie shutting the door behind her. Then he exhaled. "I don't know where to begin."

"Then let me start," I said hoarsely. "I'm sorry, Deacon Jameson. For not trusting you. And for everything you've been through."

"Joey," he said. "Just—it's Joey."

I looked at him. At his clothes, his collarless shirt. "Does this mean what I think it does?"

"That I want to be on a first name basis with my boyfriend's new best friend?"

I blinked a few times. *"Boyfriend?"*

A little smile came to his face. "It's not going to be easy for me. I've wanted to be a priest since I was a kid. But no one says I can't be a full-fledged, permanent deacon instead. A layperson, not bound by the same vows but still connected to the church."

"After all this?" I asked, stunned. "You still want to be involved with the church?"

"You really don't get it, do you?" He stretched a little, fighting a grimace from pain. "Bernie and I have a special relationship with God. I think everyone does. It's not our place to judge. With Dima—I thought at first he must be a trial from God, or maybe a temptation from the Devil, testing me to see if I could stay on a righteous path of celibacy. But when we kissed . . . I'd never felt closer to God than in that moment. That sort of connection is holy."

"And since that kiss?"

"There might have been a few other kisses, these last few days," Deacon Jameson admitted. "All holy in my opinion. So I'm withdrawing from seminary. But not from God. It's the right decision."

"I'm glad then," I said. "Truly."

"You saved my life. You risked *your* life to bring justice to all of Kline's victims."

"It was the least I could do. It's my fault that Michael—"

"No, it's not. It never was," he said quickly. "And I'm so sorry I lashed out at you. I hope you can forgive me."

"There's nothing to forgive, because I wronged you," I said.

"I already forgave you. You're so much braver than I ever was."

"I don't know about brave. You're talking to a person who ran away from their whole life without a word. A person who ran away from half their identity."

"Look," he said with a sigh. "I've spent more than a decade feeling trapped. I kept secrets that were eating me alive, and the silence hurt more people than just me. Michael . . ." His voice hitched. It was too soon. He shook his head, trying to push the pain from his mind. Something I knew very well. "But I have to believe that God can forgive me, and I have to fight to forgive myself. I don't know what you've been through, but I'm guessing you can relate."

I swallowed. "Yeah, that all sounds pretty familiar."

He held out his hand. "Maybe we can give the friend thing a try. If you want."

I smiled as I took it and gave it a hard shake. "That sounds really good."

"I'm glad." He got up. "I'm not going to hold you up from your parents and your discharge, but if you were serious, I'd love to talk to you about music sometime."

"You remembered that?"

"My memory's pretty good. I told you I notice everything."

"You're on," I said. "But just so you know, you might have to update your taste."

"How dare you talk about Saint George Michael like that!" he said, throwing his hands over his heart in Dima's trademark move. I choked out a laugh.

After he left, I settled against the thin hospital bed pillow, waiting. Wondering. Knowing that no matter what happened next, I'd take it head on.

After all, what would Raziel say? Because that was the voice I wanted to hear in my head now.

Alexis was beautiful. Alexis was brave.

Aleks was not responsible for his own assault.

I was worthy of love and respect. All the time. In any gender.

And so, although I didn't want to, I grabbed my new phone and turned it on. I had one last thing to do, and if I'd promised Bernie I'd learn to love myself, I needed to start now.

FROM: Yagoda, A.
TO: Robin, Lee
SUBJECT: (No Subject)

Lee,

You said you wanted closure, so take what you want from this. I'm not writing for you. I'm writing for me. So, here goes:

You hurt me, Lee.

You went behind my back, saying disgusting things about me, not to mention the trans community. You invalidated me as nonbinary, especially me as bigender. Maybe you thought you were being funny, maybe you wanted to cause a stir, I have no clue what you were thinking. And honestly? I don't want to know.

You apologized. You claimed to accept wrongdoing. But those emails weren't the kind that friends write. I'm sorry that IRL sucks, that college hasn't gone the way you wanted, but that's not on me.

I don't want to discount your feelings, but Lee, that wasn't love. That was obsession. I won't be your addiction. And I won't be a catalyst for abuse.

Because you didn't just call me a slur. You didn't just demean me. Right after that, you did something even worse.

At the panel, remember me kissing everyone? All eighty people in the room?

I remember it so clearly, I could throw up. And the person who suggested it? That was you, Lee.

You orchestrated my assault.

I left because of you.

And I can't, I won't forgive that.

This is the last correspondence I will send you. Don't contact me again. I will block every email, every phone number, every message request.

I hope you learn from this. I hope you get help. And mostly I hope you'll learn to respect people like me. I'm just as human as everyone else. I deserve love, real love, not that possessive obsession you have with me, and I deserve respect—as male, as female, as both, as neither. I'm going to start going to therapy again soon. You should consider it for yourself. It might help you figure out how to treat people better.

I've been self-loathing for so long. I need to cut the strings holding me back. Some memories will stay with me always. But I will deal with these memories and I will make new memories. The new people in my life will respect all parts of me.

I'm going to learn how to share myself with people again, people who've earned my trust. But not you. You're done. You're gone. I don't belong to you. I belong to me.

I hope you understand. I hope you learn so you don't hurt anyone else again the way you hurt me.

I need to take care of me. I need to learn how to love me. All parts of me. I give consent for me to love me—
                                        —and I need to let you go.

Ale/ks/xis, aka Raziel

—

"Yes I said yes I will yes."
—James Joyce, *Ulysses*

AUTHOR'S NOTE

I wanted to write a book about the ongoing problems in the Catholic Church *without* attacking Catholics for their faith. I didn't want to tarnish something that's sacred for many people. At the same time, as a child safety advocate, I knew I needed to write something. I believe that if a person knows about a crime and does nothing, they are as culpable as the perpetrator.

In the course of researching and writing this novel, I turned to seven expert readers, both former and current practicing Catholics, including one who had studied to become a nun, for more guidance. Many of my closest friends and family are Catholic, and I wanted it to be clear that this book isn't an attack on them. However I strongly believe there are major problems with the principles surrounding canon law and absolving people of sin. I absolutely will not apologize for criticizing a system that fails to hold abusers accountable for their heinous acts and, in many cases, fosters more abuse.

Of course, abuse of power exists in many settings, which is why incorporating cosplay misconduct into the plot felt like a natural step for me. The decision to feature a bigender protagonist was difficult, as it was very personal to me. I remember asking my agent if it was even okay to do—would people be interested in reading about someone who identifies like me?

And I felt the same fear that Aleks/Alexis experiences: what if I'm the only one?

Ultimately, as the title hints, *Somebody Told Me* exists because silence isn't the answer. As humans, we can't tolerate that silence any longer.

ACKNOWLEDGMENTS

First and foremost, thanks to my family for supporting me through the dark times. It's been turbulent, and I appreciate all of the support to help me function.

My amazing editor, Amy Fitzgerald. You gave me a rare opportunity that many marginalized writers, especially with those with many facets of intersectionality, never get the chance to experience. Thank you for your patience and understanding with my learning style and mental health issues and letting me sneak in some obscure literary references. Extended thanks to the team at Lerner/Carolrhoda as well.

My amazing agent, Travis Pennington—aka the "real" MVP. I know I drive you up the wall with my "Quick Question" emails that are more like 5000-page stream-of-consciousness rambles where I often forget to ask the question, and somehow you still put up with me. In all seriousness, thank you for not giving up on me when most people would have and for the incredibly inspiring peptalk you gave me about failure.

My husband, my partner, David Williamson. You know when to hold me, and when to poke me enough to make me laugh even though I hate being tickled. I love you with every fiber of my being.

Kale Night—the Eiri to my Tohma, the Viktor to my Chris (or Yurio depending on the time of day!), professional Chupacabra, and alliteration addict—I wouldn't be a writer or alive if it wasn't for you. I love you almost enough to forgive you for THAT PICTURE. *Almost.*

Kate Clarke, aka Ban-chan, Kazuki, Yuuri, Phichit, Haru, Lavi, and all of the wonderful people we've been over the years. Look where we are now, from us meeting on Livejournal, to discovering that we not only lived in the same state but had the same mutuals, to the toast at my wedding, and let us never forget "The Great Rum Bucket Incident of 2016." You were an invaluable expert reader, and you weren't afraid to tell me things that most don't want to hear. I love you. P.S. It's your post.

Rachel Mosteller, for creating *Synthetica* with me in the first place and granting me the permission to let outsiders into our four-year-straight RP. I still have the blue jay feather you found outside and mailed in a card to "Jay" from "Ian." Thank you.

Becca Dupont and Benjamin Loren, thank you for *Attack Girl Tokyo*. I hope I was able to do justice to your series.

Alice Reeds, you were my first real friend in YA and the very first person to read *Somebody Told Me* (in one sitting). Thank you for *everything*.

There are so many additional people to thank that I know I'm going to miss SO MANY by accident (so sorry). But I'd like to credit the following amazing people for their moral support and sensitivity reads: Jennifer and Robin Fordham, Olivia Hennis, M. Andrew Peterson, Amber T. Morrell, Kimberly Ito, Laurie Elizabeth Flynn, Vaidah Katz, Kate Brauning, Kiersi Burkhart, Stephen Morgan, Gabe Cohen, and a million other people.

And of course, the most important thank you of all, my readers. Some of you have been with me since *Jerkbait* (thank you for your patience!), and some of you are reading my work for the first time. Without you, this wouldn't be possible. Thank you.

P.S. I just lost the game. ;)

TOPICS FOR DISCUSSION

1. Why does Aleks/Alexis want to move in with their uncle and aunt, and why do they decide to present only as female while living there?

2. What does the voice in Aleks/Alexis's head represent? How does the voice change by the end of the novel?

3. How is the main character different when she is Alexis than when he is Aleks? In what ways can you tell that Aleks/Alexis is still the same person at their core, whichever gender they are?

4. Aleks/Alexis believes they are doing a good deed by eavesdropping on confessions and trying to help them. How does their alter-ego of "Raziel" represent both their most positive and their most negative impulses?

5. From Lee's emails, what can you guess about his relationship with Aleks/Alexis? What signs of manipulative and controlling behavior does he show?

6. How does Sister Bernadette reconcile her personal values with her devotion to the Catholic Church? What do you think of her rationale?

7. Why does Aleks/Alexis panic at the convention they attend with Dima? How does their reaction affect Dima?

8. What makes Uncle Bryan complicit in the child abuse happening in his parish?

9. Why is Aleks/Alexis so quick to believe that Deacon Jameson is the sexual predator whose confession they overheard? Why does Deacon Jameson feel guilty about his romantic relationship? What are the key differences between Deacon Jameson's relationship with Dima and Monsignor Kline's abuse of Michael?

10. What counterpoints does Sister Bernadette provide to Aleks/Alexis's internalized feelings of shame and inadequacy?

11. Why did Monsignor Kline get away with his abuse for so long? Why was Deacon Jameson not able to do more to stop him?

12. At the end of the novel, how has Aleks/Alexis come to terms with their different genders and the different sides of their personality? In what ways are they beginning to heal from the traumas they experienced?

ABOUT THE AUTHOR

Mia Siegert is an author and costume designer from New Jersey. Their costumes have appeared on Netflix's *Unbreakable Kimmy Schmidt*, the CW's *Crazy Ex-Girlfriend*, and several stage productions of *CATS*. They are also the author of the YA novel *Jerkbait*.

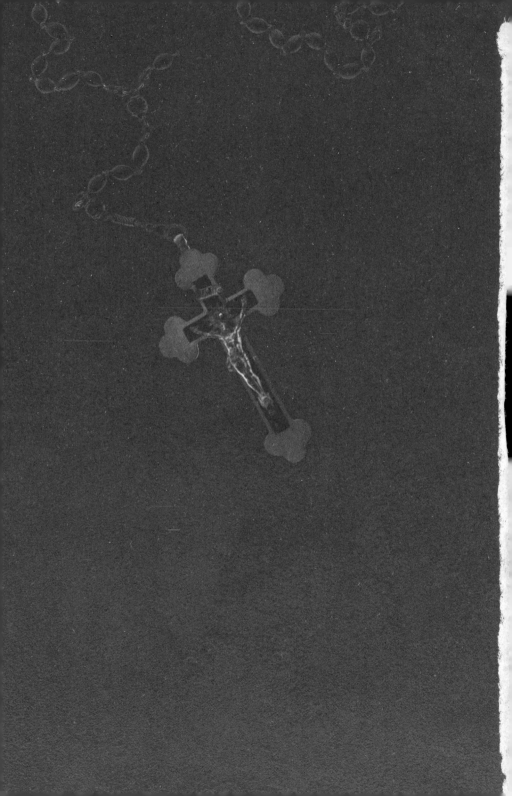